SKY-BLUE SAILOR

by

Bill Hawkins

Printed in Victoria, Canada

Note for Librarians: a cataloguing record for this book that includes Dewey Classification and US Library of Congress numbers is available from the National Library of Canada. The complete cataloguing record can be obtained from the National Library's online database at:
www.nlc-bnc.ca/amicus/index-e.html
ISBN 1-4120-2392-0

TRAFFORD

This book was published on-demand in cooperation with Trafford Publishing.
On-demand publishing is a unique process and service of making a book available for retail sale to the public taking advantage of on-demand manufacturing and Internet marketing. On-demand publishing includes promotions, retail sales, manufacturing, order fulfilment, accounting and collecting royalties on behalf of the author.

Suite 6E, 2333 Government St., Victoria, B.C. V8T 4P4, CANADA
Phone 250-383-6864 Toll-free 1-888-232-4444 (Canada & US)
Fax 250-383-6804 E-mail sales@trafford.com Web site www.trafford.com
TRAFFORD PUBLISHING IS A DIVISION OF TRAFFORD HOLDINGS LTD.
Trafford Catalogue #04-0220 www.trafford.com/robots/04-0220.html

10   9   8   7   6   5   4   3   2

DEDICATION

This novel is dedicated to the memory of my late wife, Valerie, for forty precious years of love and happiness.

Also, to all those who endured – and sometimes enjoyed – their two years' involuntary National Service in H.M. Forces.

ACKNOWLEDGEMENT

My gratitude is due to Larraine Hallman, my rock, for her supportive companionship and ideas, many of which are included in this novel.

And to Margaret (Maggie) Fleming, who tirelessly proofread the story to correct my many grammatical and punctuation errors. All remaining faults are mine.

PROLOGUE

During the period between WW2 and 1960 all young men, with few exceptions, were required to serve two years compulsory service in H.M. Forces on reaching the age of eighteen years. This 'National Service', as it became known, was a means by which the Government sought to maintain a reserve of trained personnel, available for any future conflict.

Unfortunately, those in the Regular Forces thought otherwise and treated these conscripts with contemptuous disdain, as a nuisance; useful only as unskilled (and unwanted) labour.

National Servicemen were given a few months of harsh, often brutal, basic training that, in those days, was thought to be the only method of turning a civilian rabble into trained soldiers. With the remaining twenty-odd months of service still ahead of them, few received further worthwhile training or useful employment. Most idled their time at menial tasks such as cleaners, office boys, and lackeys to NCOs, or officers.

In the Army they did do <u>some</u> soldiering. In the Navy those that served at sea did <u>some</u> sailor-like activities, others were barrack cleaners. In the RAF most became Admin. Orderlies and considered as the lowest of the low.

Except in the Royal Marines, where National Servicemen did serve usefully alongside 'regulars' and become 'trained soldiers', conscripts in all three services were considered by NCO's and officers as a waste of time and money; not in long enough to train for any decent job.

Often, National Service disrupted the conscript's further education, his budding career, or his early ambitions. Not infrequently, it ruined relationships. Nevertheless, many enjoyed the experience, the travel, the comradeship and, in some cases, the idleness. Most felt it had been beneficial and were often heard to say (afterwards)......... 'Wouldn't have missed it for the world!'

Great Britain, for the time being, gained a nucleus of semi-trained, semi-disciplined men; not "trained soldiers" by any means. It also acquired a generation of young men who had learned self-discipline, self-respect, respect for others, and how to work as a team. It forged life-long friendships and, in many cases, changed them from being "mummy's boy" into being a man. Unfortunately, it also taught them to recognise failings in their fellow man. To detest the cowardly bullies who hid behind the protection of stripes, rank and position. To lose respect for the majority of the so-called "officer class", the "Leaders" they would not follow to the main-gate let alone into battle; the highly educated, well spoken 'Ruperts' who thought of themselves as superior beings and treated 'other ranks' (and especially conscripts) as low life.

Strange, is it not, that with few exceptions, the only persons who speak well of officers are - other officers. Strange also, that in civilian life so many conscripts became successful men of substance and wealth, by their own unaided and unsupported ability and effort.

This is the fictional story of one such conscripted National Service man.

SKY-BLUE SAILOR

Chapter One

I awoke like a stricken submarine, gradually rising from the depths of unconsciousness, slowly surfacing to wallow lifeless on the crumpled sheets. For several seconds I lay blind and immobile until I forced one sticky eyelid to open, like a conning-tower hatch, allowing my mental commander to emerge from the darkness and switch on my brain. The off-white ceiling glowered down at me. I levered my other eyelid open, letting the eyeball pal up with its opposite number to focus on the plastic lamp- shade hanging like the sword of Damocles above me. Carefully I turned my head to the side and memory put a smile on my face. She was still there; her tousled sandy-coloured hair and a bare shoulder showing above the blankets that she had fisted up under her chin. The duffle-coat that I had thrown over us during the night for additional insulation when the heat of passion had drifted away, covered her like a lamb's fleece as she lay with her back towards me, her breathing like the purring of a contented cat.

I moved my hand under the covers and placed it lightly on her back, then let it slide gently and smoothly down over her silky skin, following the curves of her waist, relishing the exciting sensation and stopping on her naked hip. She grunted softly, and turned over sleepily to face me, sliding her arm across my chest and a warm leg over my thigh, so that the soft gossamer-like hair between her legs nestled against me. Instant arousal. Her hand moved down from my neck, over my chest and stomach, and gripped me, pleasurably tight.

'Ooooh, what's that?' she whispered huskily as she looked up, her gorgeous blue eyes bleary with sleep, and hugging me even tighter. She was so beautiful, even first thing in the morning without make-up.

'Something I don't want, and need you to get rid of for me,' I said jokingly, I didn't really mean it; I was still shattered.

We had gone to bed at ten o'clock the night before and made love for three solid hours. It was fantastic and she was insatiable. By the time we eventually slept I was totally drained and exhausted.

1

For the last three months we had enjoyed each other several times a day. Not a bad record for newly-weds who would normally have got over the initial euphoria and novelty of married life in that time.

With a deep sigh she snuggled into my armpit, and was soon purring away again. I looked back up at the rippled surface of the ceiling, seeing a cob-web stretched like a frosted thread across the corner near the window that framed the bright sunlight of an autumn morning peeping between half-drawn curtains. There was no sign of the resident spider. The round, brass alarm-clock with its bicycle-bell hat, ticking noisily on the bed-side table, told me it was almost nine o'clock. My brain told me it was Saturday. No work, thank God. I laid my head back down onto the pillow, chin in the air pointing at the cob-web, and closed my eyes, feeling Laura's gentle breathing delightfully tickling my chest, as I thought back over recent years.

I had gone to sea in the Merchant Navy at the ripe old age of fourteen, having added a year to my age when my school was fortuitously bombed during World War Two and all pupil's records were destroyed. Ten years later, while home on leave, I had met Laura and within six months we were married; although what she saw in me I had no idea. Mr. Average, that's me. Five feet eleven inches tall, slim build, brown hair and half-way between being handsome and ugly. Up until then the sea had been my career. I had a Second Mate's Certificate of Competency in my pocket and my goal was to become a Master Mariner; eventually commanding my own ship. Meeting Laura had changed all that. I didn't want to leave her and she didn't want me to go away so, by mutual agreement, it was decided I would come ashore and 'swallow the anchor'; as the saying goes. My one concern was the problem of National Service which, in the early 1950's, was something all young men (well, most) had to undergo for two years. I certainly didn't want to go into H.M. Forces, not even for two weeks, so just before leaving my last ship I called at the Shipping Federation offices in Southampton where the "Officer's Appointments" officer assured me that, because I was over twenty-one years old and had served at sea for more than five years, I would not be eligible for conscription. This was wonderful news and I came ashore happily with that knowledge.

After our wedding, and a short honeymoon in Devon, I began a search for worthwhile employment. I rather fancied the Police Force but hadn't quite made up my mind. To tide us over until the right job came along I took whatever was available. At first I drove a lorry for a wholesale bakery, delivering bread and cakes to retail shops before they opened for business. This meant starting at four in the morning and caused havoc with my new-found sex life. I had to get up for work when my body was still screaming for rest and recuperation. It lasted for less than a month.

Then I answered an advert for door-to-door salesmen, on commission only basis with very high earning potential; or so they told me at a short training course. All I had to do was to sell three spindrier machines each week to earn a hundred pounds. Fantastic. Big money. Laura and I planned how we would spend every penny. For three weeks I pounded the pavements, knocked on thousands of doors, secured a dozen or so appointments to return with my sales blurb 'when the husband gets home'; was propositioned twice by frustrated and lonely ladies, and sold one machine to an old couple with arthritis. I had earned thirty-five pounds in three weeks. I left.

My next, and current job, was labourer to a roof-tiler. Bloody hard graft carrying slates and tiles, precariously balanced on my head, up endless wooden ladders trying to maintain a steady supply to my mate who could rattle them onto a roof, ten to the dozen. Occasionally - no, quite often actually - I would drop some and get heartily cursed, by my mate and by members of the passing public who didn't expect - or appreciate - being bombarded with flying tiles; seagulls were bad enough. The job was really hard. My neck, thigh and calf muscles hurt like hell and by the time I arrived home I was no use to man or beast, let alone Laura. Fortunately, after a week or so, my muscles adapted and husband-like pleasures became more than just exhausted sleep. Nevertheless, it was a bit of a come-down after being a navigating officer at sea, but beggars can't be choosers. It kept the wolf from the door and was - I told myself every half an hour - only temporary until I found something else.

The rattle of the letter-box in the front door woke me from my reminiscences. I heard the dull thud of 'mail' dropping onto the bare lino floor-covering and the postman's curse as his fingers were snapped-at by the strongly sprung flap. I was pretty certain it wouldn't be a million pound cheque so decided to ignore it and go back to sleep, but curiosity got the better of me. After all, mail through our door was quite rare.

3

I slipped out of bed and nakedly tip-toed out into the bland hallway. The solitary envelope lying forlornly on the coir-hair mat was buff coloured with the letters OHMS on it. 'Ha,' I thought, 'it's an invitation to the wedding of my tax-man's parents,' as I hurriedly returned to the warm bed, giggling childishly at my own attempt at humour.

'What's that?' yawned Laura, emerging from under the bed clothes, rubbing the sleepy dust from her eyes and uncovering a bare breast that scattered the butterflies in my stomach.

I teased open the corner of the envelope flap and tore along the top with my forefinger and, pulling out the official looking sheet of paper, spread it open on my bent knees.

'What on earth is it; what's the matter?' she asked sitting up, her face and voice full of worried concern. 'You've gone all white!'

Shocked and stunned, I handed her the letter. I couldn't bring myself to speak.

'Oh, my God,' she cried in utter disbelief. Then more quietly, 'there must be some mistake.'

I took the letter back from her with trembling hands. There was no mistaking the instruction. "YOU ARE TO ATTEND AT THE JOINT-SERVICE RECRUITING OFFICE IN PORTSMOUTH FOR PRE-ENTRY INTERVIEW AND MEDICAL EXAMINATION IN ACCORDANCE WITH THE REQUIREMENTS OF THE NATIONAL SERVICE CONSCRIPTION REGULATIONS".

It gave a time and date only two weeks ahead.

My whole idyllic world crumbled in those few dreadful moments. I didn't want to go into the Services and I dreaded the thought of leaving my wonderful new bride. We turned to face each other, anxiety creasing our foreheads.

'Don't worry darling I'll sort it out,' I said reassuringly, putting my arms around her. 'They've got it all wrong.' But we both knew in our hearts that the only people to have got it wrong were the Shipping Federation. We hugged, and then both burst into tears.

An hour later, head down and very depressed, I cycled my Raleigh 'all-steel' through the city streets of Portsmouth, hoping against hope that the Recruiting Centre would be open on a Saturday as I weaved and wobbled like a drunk, lacking concentration and attracting the attention of a stern-faced policeman chewing the chin-strap of his helmet.

The old, twin-bayed, Victorian building, sagging wearily under the tread of decades of uncaring ammunition-boots, was open. Its grey, unkempt exterior enlivened only by colourful recruiting posters enticing gullible youngsters to forgo their freedom and serve their country. One, picturing a fearful looking soldier armed to the teeth with a variety of weapons, bore the inscription YOUR COUNTRY NEEDS YOU under which some wag had written, in words clearly visible even though an unsuccessful attempt at removal had been made, SO DOES THE WIFE

Inside, a large brightly lit office, obviously made by joining two of the original rooms together, contained a dejected man of about my own age sitting with head in hands on a long cushion-covered bench seat. Was his problem the same as mine I wondered? The only other occupant, a smart military figure with three chevrons and a crown on his tunic sleeve and a huge walrus moustache covering most of his face, stood protectively in front of a hold-all bag on the floor that contained his 'civvies' and a blue and white woollen scarf, ready for a sharp get-away to the afternoon football match. I decided he was my better option.

He listened, apparently interested, to my tale of woe. He had probably heard the same story a hundred times. Then took my OHMS letter from me and gave it a cursory glance. A hole appeared in the bush of hair on his upper lip. 'Hit tells you what you have got to do lad,' he shouted barrack-room style, as if I were on the other side of the street. 'So do it.'
I always thought that Recruiting people were meant to be specially chosen for their 'niceness'...... Wrong!

'We can't be blamed because your bloody shipping people don't know their arse from their elbow, can we?' he whispered in high decibels, dismissing me, his country's newest recruit.

I felt awful as I dragged my feet away from that dreadful caricature of a man. I couldn't possibly ride my 'all-steel' in such a state so, pushing it with one hand on the handle-bar and one on the saddle, I walked home passing, once again, the chin-strap chewing copper who probably wondered if the bike had been nicked.

5

I dreaded having to tell Laura of my failed mission so was pleasantly surprised to find that she had stoically resigned herself to the inevitable, and greeted my return in a positive manner. I felt so relieved. I hated the thought of going in the army but my greatest concern was for her, and her feelings. Now she was proving me to be the weakling as we sat close together drinking tea, calmly discussing how we would cope for the next two years.

At the appointed date and time I offered myself at the Recruiting Centre and submitted my body and soul to the Country's Armed Forces. My greeter was a taciturn Corporal who had last smiled on the day his Grandfather landed on the beaches of Gallipoli. There was no sign of the bellowing NCO of my first visit.

I joined a group of a dozen or so others, waiting patiently to be treated as human beings. We would have a long wait. They were all about eighteen years old and stared at me as if asking where my Zimmer frame was. Silently we sat in miserable companionship until called away, one at a time in alphabetical order; I was an 'H'. When my turn came, the poker-faced Corporal ushered me in through a door into the presence of two white-smocked medics. I presumed (and hoped) that one was a doctor as he ordered me to drop my trousers and underpants. He was elderly, thin and balding, with a stethoscope draped around his neck like a Lord Mayor's chain-of-office. His red-veined eyes looked into my mouth and ears, his fingers tapped my chest and probed between my legs as I coughed to order. His monosyllabic grunts were noted by the second, younger man, who scribbled noughts and crosses on what suspiciously appeared to be a book of cross-word puzzles.

The 'Doctor' gave me a disinterested glance, similar to the one that he reserved especially for inspecting cadavers, and silently indicated with a nod of his head that I should leave his domain by another door. I wondered if anyone spoke in this 'Hall of Silence' as I scrabbled across the room, trying to hoist my underwear and trousers at the same time.

The second room was like a morgue. There were several tables and chairs, some occupied by the earlier, alphabetically listed people who were hunched over paperwork with heavy frowns. I sat at a vacant table and read the front page of the file in front of me. It told me to complete the enclosed 'Educational Assessment Papers', then hand them to the NCO.

Looking around the room I saw a Corporal sitting in a dim corner, dozing. I flipped through the question papers, quickly adding my answers as I did so. They were so simple, like adding three two-digit numbers together or asking the name of the current Prime Minister.

Within two or three minutes I got up and handed the completed papers to the skulking NCO who passed them through a hole in the wall to an adjoining room without glancing at them, or even opening his eyes. Returning to my seat I awaited my next summons. None of the others had budged, although one had started to slowly scrawl an uncertain answer to a question.

My next move was to a room that had all the appearances of an interrogation chamber. In the middle of the floor, beneath a low wattage electric light bulb hanging in a broken shade from the shadowed ceiling, a single table stood with two chairs, placed one either side. On one sat a man in civvies, apparently studying a wad of papers laid out on the table like a fan. The only other source of light came from an unclean window that framed a view of a brick wall standing a few feet away, on the outside. He motioned me, with a wave of his hand, to sit in the other chair. I sat. From my upside-down viewpoint I could see he was perusing my Educational Assessment Papers, over which his pen-in-hand hovered as though writing from a distance. After several minutes of quiet gloom he looked up at me and surprisingly spoke. 'Army, Navy or Air Force?' he snapped.

'Pardon?' I asked.

He focused blank eyes on me as if I was an idiot. 'Do you want to do your National Service in the Army, Navy or Airforce?' he repeated, pedantically.

I hadn't realised that I had a choice. I had automatically assumed it would be the army. The various consequences of the options I was being offered raced through my head as he stared fixedly through me.

'Navy' I replied, hoping perhaps that it could lead to a possible posting to Portsmouth, my home town. How naïve can one be?

'Um' he muttered gloomily, studying my papers. 'Should be all right with your qualifications.' He thumbed through my "assessments". 'Your educational standard is suitable.'

7

I raised my eyebrows. The standard required in answering the set questions would qualify me for a professorship in an imbecile's college.

'Right, Navy it is' he decided, writing something on my papers.

Ten days later, on my return home after a long hard day clambering up and down ladders, keeping two roofers supplied with tiles on a three-storey roof, Laura greeted me at the door looking fraught and agitated as she handed me another buff-coloured OHMS envelope. Nervously I took it, noting that it hadn't been opened.

'It came this morning,' she said.

'Why didn't you read it?' I queried, 'instead of worrying all day.' She wrinkled her nose, stuck out her bottom lip and shook her frowning head silently as I ripped open the seal, and read.

'Oh, my God,' I exploded angrily as I handed it to her. 'It's unbelievable; they're putting me in the bloody Raff.' She handed it back and watched with distressed eyes as I read it again:

"You are required to report to the R.T.O. on the main concourse of Waterloo Station, London, at 12.00 hours on Wednesday, October 12th for onward transportation to the Royal Air Force Recruit Reception Centre, R.A.F. Station Cardington in Bedfordshire. A railway warrant is enclosed." It went on to list the personal items I should take with me.

Pathetically, and full of self-pity, I turned my face towards Laura who, with typical woman's logic said bravely, 'I like the Raff uniform best, it's nice.'

I had just experienced the first of many involvements with the stupid, mindless thinking of Service "square peg - round hole" mentality.

CHAPTER TWO

On that fateful day in November I sat, more depressed and miserable than ever before, in a crowded, unheated, mid-morning train taking me to the 'Smoke' and an unknown future, having said a tearful and heart-rending farewell to my darling Laura who was facing an equally bleak and lonely future.

I took no notice of my fellow passengers. With glazed, red-rimmed eyes I stared out of the smutty carriage windows, absentmindedly watching the wind-blown streaks of rain water racing across the glass, like down-hill skiers, as the dreary, soggy, rural countryside of Hampshire, then Surrey, rushed impatiently past. I had done this sort of journey many times when joining a new ship at some distant port, but never had I left the love of my life weeping back at home. I felt as lonely as a Bishop in a brothel.

Soon the rain-soaked greenness of the countryside started to fade and be replaced by the wet greyness of the outskirts of London, as rows of unattractive houses and commercial buildings separated to let us pass through.

Clattering over junctions and points, past suburban shopping centres, under bridges and through goods-marshalling yards where gangs of yellow-jacketed line workers stopped at the wave of a signal flag to let us rumble past, the train crept slowly beneath the glass canopy of Waterloo's vast terminal, coming to a screeching stop just short of the crash-bumpers alongside an almost deserted platform that suddenly became crowded as carriage doors were thrown open, allowing hundreds of hurrying passengers to flood out. I waited for the crush to subside. I was in no hurry. The last of the arriving passengers were pushing and shoving their way urgently through the platform-gate, past the robotic ticket-collector. Cleaners began boarding the vacated train with their buckets and brooms, like kiddies arriving on a sandy beach, as I stepped out onto the platform and walked unhindered through the gate, already deserted by its guardian who had, presumably, rushed off to his tea-break, or a call of nature. The huge hanging clock over the concourse said it was only twenty minutes to twelve. I had plenty of time.

9

The RTO was located, appropriately and conveniently, next to the Gents toilets. There seemed to be quite a crowd of lads hovering around outside the office door, all hanging on grimly to their small suitcases that branded them as new conscripts; all looked totally lost. I decided not to wait until twelve o'clock and entered the office where two army types were studying the day's racing forecasts. I handed over my chit that allowed one of them to make a cross on a clip-board list hidden under his newspaper. His mate lifted a languid hand and pointed to his right. 'Go right down the far end of the taxi-rank. Turn right again for a bit, then you'll see a line of Raff three-tonners. Report to the bod there,' he instructed in his cockney accent, before returning to scrutinise the available odds.

Seeing my success, the group outside began to enter as I left. The intricate directions were spot-on and I was soon showing my chit to the RAF Corporal in charge of the convoy. He hardly glanced at it but nevertheless ticked my name on his list. 'First vehicle' he ordered.

The driver of my canvas covered lorry was sat on the running board, a cigarette stuck out from the centre of his pouting lips like the bowsprit of a yacht. I then discovered that <u>some</u> people in the Services actually did smile.

'You're the first one mate,' he welcomed, standing up and taking the coffin-nail from his mouth a few seconds after the dangling ash had fallen down the front of his battle-dress blouse. 'You can sit up front with me if you want.' I poked my head over the lowered tail-board and looked in at the rows of hard wooden bench seats that would be certain to be bone-shakers.

'Thanks very much,' I accepted gratefully and climbed up onto the sprung seat next to the covered engine-casing inside the cab.

I sat there alone for nearly an hour watching the frenetic comings and goings of this busy metropolitan terminus, getting colder and colder by the minute, waiting for the other conscripts to arrive and fill the fleet of trucks. I could see, through the window at the back of the cab behind me, the desolate group that filled the seats of my transport. At first, they sat quietly with their own thoughts, then gradually the ice broke and they began to talk to each other. I could hear the buzz of conversations as they began to make friendships that would probably last until the end of basic training and possibly - if they were lucky -

for many years to come. Eventually the cab door opened and in jumped my jovial driver.

'Right' he smiled, as if eager to get back to the Naafi. 'Let's see if this wanker will start.' It did, and we were off, in a crocodile procession, to Bedfordshire. I recalled my Mum saying that to me when I was a kid and it was time for bed. 'Come on' she would say. 'Up the stairs to Bedfordshire.'

Fortunately for me and the driver (his name was Allen, from Devon) the warmth of the engine soon turned the cab into a nice snug and I felt pity for the frozen bodies sat in the back, huddled together shivering, their faces pinched white and drawn as the icy wind found every gap in the canvas top.

Allen didn't talk much. Most of the time he blew through his two widely spaced front teeth in an irritating and tuneless whistle, seemingly happy being his own boss, on the road. The little he did say, I wished he hadn't. The picture he painted of RAF Cardington and the basic training centre that was to follow was horrendous. A mixture of Belsen and a hard-labour camp, with sleepless nights, bullying and sometimes brutality thrown in for good measure. It terrified me, but I consoled myself with the hopeful thought that he was deliberately trying to throw a scare into me. Nothing could be that bad. I was wrong.

The afternoon was fading fast into a grey winter's evening by the time the convoy of refrigerated carcasses drew up outside the Guardroom at Cardington, and everyone was ordered out. Stiffly, with frozen joints, the cream of Britain's manhood dropped from the tail-boards. Some, just a few, landed on their feet and stayed upright. Most sprawled in ungainly bundles onto the tarmac until they managed to scramble to their numbed feet. I climbed out of the cab, warm and unaided, to join them as they gathered in a shambling crowd in response to a shouted command of 'Fall-in, here.'

White-capped RAF Police Corporals in their white webbing, with a holstered revolver hanging from their belt like present-day Billy the Kids, hovered around, looking us up and down with obvious distaste, like Inspectors at a sewerage farm, but not saying a word.

Allen passed quite close to me and muttered something that sounded like 'Snow-drop bastards,' just loud enough for me to hear. I was soon to learn that Service policemen were generally, and often wrongly, seen as the hated enemy to be avoided at all cost.

They kept us standing there, in the wet and cold, for several minutes until a group of four Corporals approached, uncluttered by white webbing but wearing airforce-blue gaiters, and caps that had the peaks slashed so that the rim touched the bridge of their nose, in imitation of Grenadier Guardsmen. These were our Drill Instructors, the dreaded D.I's that we had heard so much about, who - here at Cardington - were very frustrated as they would only have us in their charge for a couple of days during which there would be no drill instruction to allow them to demonstrate their manic personalities.

One of them stood in front of us and screamed in a loud, shrill voice that lifted his highly polished boots several inches off the ground, something that vaguely sounded like 'STAND STILL.'
We were bewildered. We hadn't moved. We couldn't, our muscles and joints were frozen solid.

'RIGHT TURN' screeched the same demented figure. It sounded like 'Rye tarn' so we shuffled to face that direction. One of the other D.I's shouted in a fractionally less hysterical voice 'Quick march,' and we leaned forward, willing at least one of our legs to follow.

'Heft-height, Heft-height,' he chanted in an effort to encourage our untrained feet to keep in some resemblance of military togetherness. He failed miserably, and gave up after the first dozen shouts as we stumbled and staggered our way up hill to what, we were informed, was the Airmen's Mess for our first hot meal of the day. It was aptly named - a mess. As we entered the large hanger-like building we were handed a knife, fork and spoon (our 'eating irons'), and an enamel mug that had seen better days, by weedy Admin. Orderlies of the permanent staff, mostly National Servicemen themselves, who were getting near the end of their two-year 'sentence'.

As new arrivals, the meal was specially timed for us in consideration that many had been travelling since the early hours. The 'eating irons' were on temporary loan until we received our own issue and they had to be returned, clean, before we left the Mess. There was quite a black-market for lost 'irons' among the permanent staff who would happily replace any missing item at an exorbitant price, or a packet of fags. It was widely known that they were not above pinching from unwary erks to expand their entrepreneurial trade. Our first military lesson was 'never let go of your 'irons'.

Then came the serving of the meal. We each were given a stainless steel tray indented to form several bowls. In single file, we moved along the front of the 'serving counter' behind which stood a row of scruffy, pimply and clearly unwashed 'chefs'. As we passed each one, a splodge of something or other would be plopped by ladle into one of the bowls of the tray until we reached the end of the counter where a large container of strong tea - already milked and heavily sweetened - stood. We were supposed to fill our mugs from the dribbling tap at the base of the container but it was slow running, and caused a tail-back in the queue, so the Mess Corporal removed the lid and ordered us to scoop our mugs full by dipping them in the top. A box was considerately supplied for standing on.

The meal was just about warm and barely edible but, to our starving stomachs, it was deliciously welcome. We were told afterwards, because we didn't know, that it had been stewed-steak, mashed potatoes, swede, carrots and peas.

The meal over, trays and 'irons' washed and rinsed as instructed, in tanks of tepid water marked 'WASH' and 'RINSE' respectively (and also labelled 'A' and 'B' for those who could not read) we were marched (?) off to be shown our billets. These luxurious quarters were iron-roofed Nissen huts, each containing twenty beds, ten either side of a centrally placed iron bogey stove full of cold ashes left behind by the previous occupants. Each iron-sprung bed had a mattress and an uncased pillow on it, and alongside leaned a tired steel locker, standing like a guardian sentry over a man's bed-space. At the far end of the hut, a separate room complete with electric fire, was the home of the Hut-Corporal, a sour-faced Scot with an open hatred for all Englishmen, Welshmen, Irishmen and foreigners, not necessarily in that order. He liked to be thought of as God.

We were told to place our personal belongings in an allocated locker then, in typical Service fashion, detailed off for duties that would occupy the next hour. He gave us all numbers, one to twenty. No.1 to clean the ashes from the stove. No.2 to place the ashes in a bucket. No.3 to take the bucket to the door of the billet and hand it to No.4 who was to empty it on the cinder pathway outside to make it less muddy. Meanwhile No's 5,6,7 and 8 were to go to the coal-dump on the edge of the camp and collect coal. While the first four were cleaning themselves up in the ablutions block (another refrigerated place full of toilets and wash basins, with an abundance of cold water from both hot and cold taps) No's 9 and 10 were to light the bogey stove and be responsible for keeping it going, day and night.   No's 11 to 20 could rest on their beds. It would be their turn tomorrow.

We were called to muster outside of the hut at 6pm sharp, to stand in the cold drizzle until another loud-mouthed D.I. decided that the occupants of all huts were ready to move-off to the Bedding-Store where we again queued, resignedly, to be issued with one mattress cover, three blankets and one pillow case per man; from a hole in a wall from where the issuer's arm shot out like a snake's tongue. Then another wait in the rain until all were finished. Only then were we allowed to return to our huts; by which time our bedding was damp, to say the least. The Hut-Corporal told us we were now finished for the day but warned we would be 'called' at 6 am in the morning. 'And no bleedin' noise,' he added, threateningly.

The bogey stove was stoked-up until the casing began to glow red. Only then could we get our bedding dry enough to use. Within an hour silence reigned, except for someone stifling a sobbing cry and an occasional snoring grunt, or raucous fart. The later being greeted by a chorus of 'Dirty bastard' as the callers ducked beneath their filtering blankets.   I fell asleep with a heart of stone, dreaming of Laura, wondering when I would see her again, and missing her like mad.

A loud hammering on the hut door, followed by a D.I. crashing into the billet banging a dustbin lid with a battered ladle, was our peaceful 6am awakening.

'Come on you lazy bastards,' was his cry. 'You're not home now. Get your hands off cocks and on socks.' I really hated that man and several of us were already making preliminary plans for his early demise.   Reluctantly, most of us climbed out onto the cold floor, shivering in our underwear and, in most cases, socks. Those that hesitated had their bed-clothes ripped off by the sadistic D.I. who then upended the bed, dumping the unfortunate culprit in a sprawling heap across his own bed-space.

'You've got twenty minutes,' he howled, 'to get washed, shaved, dressed and fell-in by your bed that had better be made-up proper.' With that, he stormed out to terrorise the next billet as our Hut-Corporal poked a bleary face out from his room to ensure everyone stayed up.

The grandiloquent 'ablutions block' - like a cow-shed with stainless steel feeding-troughs for use as wash-basins - was a short luxurious stroll over an unsheltered strip of boggy land blasted by seemingly storm-force nor-easterly winds, straight from Siberia. Fortunately, our time limitation required this to be taken at a frantic dash to join the chaotic mass of partially dressed bodies, pathetically scrambling for a place at the trough, to enjoy the sybaritic pleasure of splashing two, maybe three drops of icy water on our face, rubbing our teeth with a toothpaste-covered forefinger before unsuccessfully trying to create a cold-water lather on a bristle-covered chin to ease the pain of a rasping razor, then drying ourselves with towels made from corrugated cardboard.

By making a rapid streak back across the Arctic tundra, most of us were standing in some semblance of orderly attention, alongside our beds and folded blankets, when the moronic D.I. deigned to make his reappearance. Without even a gentlemanly knock on the door, he burst in, to stand glowering at eighteen cowering conscripts dressed in a wide variety of 'civvies' ranging from a camel-hair coat to denims and bomber-jacket. He shook his head in a show of shocked bewilderment that switched to stunned amazement when he spotted the two unattended bed-spaces. His face changed to a florid red and his eyes popped-out of his ugly head, like a surprised frog. He opened his mouth into a rounded 'O' just as the two missing sinners, returning from their more fastidious beautification, walked calmly in through the door. The demented NCO took-off like an apoplectic astro-rocket, jumping up and down like a spoilt child in a tantrum, screaming like a banshee. The two recruits stood transfixed and scared to death, as he thrust his nose to within an inch of theirs, in turn, like a pecking chicken, calling them every name his foul mouth could think of. One of them burst into tears as the despicable man stormed from the hut. I was filled with disgust, but had he obtained his objective?... It would be a long time before either of those two lads transgressed again. They had been brutally disciplined.

Our own Hut-Corporal, a meek man by comparison, emerged from his sanctuary, almost apologetic and sheepish, as if ashamed of his confederate, and told us to make our own way to the Mess for breakfast, but to be back by quarter-to-nine. Joyous at this temporary freedom we trotted off like kids let out of school.

15

Our next treat was another medical. We were herded into a cathedral- like building; empty except for two rows of stools on which we were instructed to sit in alphabetical order (so as not to confuse the officers) opposite a row of canvas-screened cubicles that gave the appearance of a Bedouin village, except that it was bloody cold, and draughty. The first two recruits were told to strip-off completely. No.1 entered the first tent as No.2 sat shivering until No.1 emerged to enter the second tent. No.2 then entered the first tent as No. 3 stripped-off and sat waiting his turn - and so on, like an assembly line.

My turn came about No.40 and I ran the gauntlet of tents, in each of which were two white-overalled medics. The examinations were far more thorough than the initial one I had at Portsmouth, but the medics were equally as unfeeling.

Passing along the separated canvas sections I was prodded and pummelled, weighed and measured, looked into and looked at. Had instruments shoved up my nose, in my ears, up my backside and into my mouth; not the same instruments I hasten to add. I was made to bend over and touch my toes with feet wide apart in front of a twinkling-eyed male medical orderly and coughed for a bland-faced, unsmiling female as she lifted my testicles with a wooden spatula. A dentist, smelling strongly of whiskey, tried to fracture my jaw and another female examined my penis - even under the foreskin - with as much enthusiasm as a eunuch watching a strip-show.

The one highlight of this whole procedure was when a recruit charged out of the cubicle containing the male orderly with the sparkling eyes. He ran naked in a high-stepping crouch, out of the building, giving a frightening long drawn-out scream, clutching the cheeks of his bottom with both hands as heads popped out of the other tents, like campers checking the early morning weather. We never saw him again. Perhaps he is still running.

Emerging from the far end, having given samples of blood, urine and sputum, I ran back to the stool and my pile of clothing, feeling violated and defiled, to quickly dress and cover my embarrassing nakedness.

As the last man was processed, each cubicle opened its front curtain and the medics busied themselves packing their equipment, like morgue attendants after a post-mortem. The male orderly in the toe-touching tent was sitting with legs tightly crossed and a look of ecstasy on his flushed face, while in another, two female nurses were in animated and highly amused discussion; one holding a ruler suggestively as the other held her hands as if in prayer, but with the palms ten inches apart.

From one humiliation to another, we moved - less one runner - to the barber's shop and once more placed in an assembly line to take our turn, three at a time, before a trio of former champion sheep-shearers, one with the apt name of Shaun (should have been shorn), who were evidently on piece-work at two minutes per head. I was pleasantly surprised to find we were allowed to sit in chairs. I fully expected to be thrown on the floor gripped between their straddled knees as they carelessly removed every millimetre of our head-hair along with the tops of any lumps, bumps, pimples or moles that happened to be in the way; keeping a squad of staff erks busy sweeping up the huge piles of once proud tresses and filling sacks that, no doubt, someone was selling on to a mattress-stuffer somewhere. Astonishingly, their contract did not include facial hair so one member of our depilated squad, who suffered the unfortunate name of Carol (given him by confused parents), retained his long, droopy, hippie-style moustache that gave the appearance of an inverted head with bushy eyebrows. This discomfited our perplexed D.I's. It wasn't against the rules.

After a short smoke-break outside of the Naafi - we were too embarrassed to go in and face the female staff - we were shepherded, like the shorn sheep we were, into a lecture room where we sat, studying the bald and bleeding scalp of the man in the seat in front, as we awaited our 'welcoming' speech, to be given by the Camp Commander.

As that august officer entered through a door at the back of the room, our Corporal bellowed 'Atten-Shun'. Some of us leapt rigidly to our feet, a few stiffened to equal rigidity, but remained seated. Others looked back over their shoulders with inquisitive interest. The Corporal sighed, and wrongly saluted as the officer walked to the front of the class and stood - a little nervously I thought - behind a wooden lectern that was deeply notched, and carved with a multitude of initials and dates.

'Pha - Good morning chaps,' he began, blowing through his moustache as the discerning and knowledgeable ones among us noted he wore no distinguished medal ribbons, or flying brevet, above his left breast pocket, indicating he was a desk-job, not a WW2 fighter pilot to be admired. There was no response from his wretched audience.

'Pha - my name is Wing Commander Witherington-Platt,' he paused to allow us to absorb the significance of that. 'Pha - I am the Station Commander here and it is my pleasurable duty to welcome you into the Royal Air Force.' He brushed his upper lip, heavy with the weight of an upswept handle-bar moustache, with the knuckle of his right hand as the fingers of the other hand rapped a tattoo on the lectern lid.

'Pha - I doubt any of you will appreciate your first few weeks of induction and basic training, but I can assure you that afterwards, as trained aircraftsmen, you will enjoy yourselves and obtain great benefits that will stand you in good stead in the years to come as you follow your chosen careers'. He looked around, almost disdainfully, twitching his nose as if the moustache was tickling. 'Pha - that is all...... Carry-on.'

'Atten-Shun' screamed the Corporal, repeating the main word in his vocabulary as the C.O. winced and stepped stiff-legged out of the room to 'retire' to the Officers Mess for mid-day coffee and muffins. He didn't have a clue what went on in his own Station. This time we remained seated; too dispirited to move.

'Well, that was Wing Commander Pha Platt' said the NCO, irreverently imparting this item of educational wisdom. 'He's known as 'Pha' because he's always says that when he talks.' I felt highly honoured to add this apparent gem of information to my Service knowledge as he dismissed us to go to our mid-day lunch (sorry - dinner. Only officers have 'lunch').

The Chef's offering was a variation of yesterday's menu. The food was the same but it was arranged differently on our tin trays. Today, there was an addition that delighted our empty stomachs. At the far end of the serving counter, just before reaching the tea-dripping urn, a tall skeleton of an apron-wrapped server stood like a match-stick with the wood shaved off.

'Afters?' he grunted, ladling a congealed lump of molten concrete into the remaining bowl of each tin tray without waiting for a reply.

'What is it?' asked one brave soul, too naïve to know that you upset a chef at your peril.

'Figgy-bloody-duff, you stupid bleedin' erk,' came the angry response from the chef who had already mentally photographed the offending recruit, for future reference, and possible distribution to every Raff 'cook-house' in the country.

When no one was looking, most portions of this offensive delicacy were dumped out of the Mess window where even the majority of starving birds ignored it; those unfortunate enough to spear a sample were unable to take-off again for the next hour, making an easy prey for the prowling cook-house cat.

That afternoon was the comedy highlight of our short stay at Cardington - not that we enjoyed it. We were not meant to.

The uniform-issuing 'Clothing Store' was a large refrigerated warehouse, inside of which ran a long alleyway along the left-hand wall. To the right of this alleyway, a long serving-counter, similar to the one in the mess-hall, stretched into the cold-hazed distance, like the yellow-brick road in the 'Wizard of Oz'. Behind this counter, stationed at intervals in front of racking and boxes, Stores Assistants stood waiting, like front-line troops in trenches waiting to go 'over the top'. Each Storeman (or in some cases Storewomen from the Waafs) issued one particular item of uniform or equipment.

A decade or so ago, the Assistants would have called out the item being issued......... 'Socks. Blue woollen. Medium. Three pairs...... Trousers. Blue. Medium. Two pair..... Cap. Size 7. One.... Beret. Size 7. One..... etc.' Nowadays the issue was silent. The fun had gone out of sadism.

The comedy started with a huge, empty, canvas kit-bag being thrown from the first 'station'. We were instructed to hold the top open with both hands (how can it be done with one?). Then at each successive location the Assistant would give a stare of professional judgement and issue his/her item according to small, medium or large; except in the case of unsized items that were unceremoniously thrown into the rapidly overflowing kit-bag. There was underwear, socks, shirts, best-blues tunic and trousers, battle-dress blouse and trousers, beret, cap, gas-cape (for use as a rain-coat), greatcoat, housewife, cleaning brushes, belt and braces, pyjamas - the list was endless. Only at the very end, where boots and shoes were issued, was a word spoken.

'Size?'

'Nine and a half, please.'

'Don't do half sizes.'

'Okay, Ten then.'

'No tens left, here's a nine.'
'Thank you.'

Back in the billet we emptied the bags onto our beds, like coal-men making a delivery, while the duty 'stove team' chivvied-up the bogey. With the begrudged help of the Hut-Corporal we sorted our individual 'heap' and tried on the stiffly new, crumpled and damp smelling uniforms.

Working on the life-saving principle that it is better to laugh than cry we spent an hilarious hour swapping and changing among ourselves until most of us looked remotely respectable. Some were not so lucky. Those with extra large heads ended up with caps looking like unstable tiaras. Those with small heads were grateful to have ears, to prevent blindness.

With hardly concealed impatience and irritability, our Hut-Corporal begrudgingly gave out the minimum amount of 'Exchange Chits'. He dare not upset the Store staff.

Clutching their chits like bank-drafts, the recipients ran back to the Clothing Store to face further irritability - and in many cases, disappointment. Even the best of the uniforms were ill-fitting but our Hut-Corporal assured us that they would be 'seen-to' by proper tailors, when we got to our basic training camps.

We spent the evening industriously marking every item with name and 'last three' (of our Service number), either with indelible pen or hammered letter-stamp. Failure to this was a disciplinary offence that would result in being 'put on a charge' and appropriate punishment.

How was it then, I asked myself, that so many marked items went missing, to be replaced by marked items missing from someone else's kit?

Theft was endemic, and created a snow-balling effect.

After another visit to the Mess for 'tea', where we were gratuitously offered - and refused - the left-over figgy duff from dinner, our Hut-Corporal gave a demonstration on the correct way to fold blankets and lay-out ones' kit on the bed, for inspection. It would save us getting into trouble at our next camp, he said. Later that evening, we learned that his unexpected kindness was due to him being told he could go on a few days leave, after we left the next morning. God acts in mysterious ways.

20

The one-man dustbin band entered the hut at precisely 6am the next morning. He must have waited outside the door watching the second-hand sweep up to the twelve. With forty-eight hours service in, most of us were beginning to act and think like 'old-hands', so did not leap out of bed with such alacrity or eagerness as yesterday. After all, we reasoned, no one would 'charge' us, or punish us. We were away today, and they wanted rid of us equally as much as we wanted rid of them. Nevertheless, we were not too tardy. We did not want to invite trouble that might possibly follow us. The apoplectic D.I. bandsman was also less energetic and, after ensuring we all had our feet on the floor, he retreated gracefully, and left us to our own resources.

By the time we returned from our leisurely ablutions and unhurried breakfast, the Hut-Corporal was waiting to inform us we had the morning free but would be embussing immediately after dinner for the basic training camp that, in our case, would be RAF Hednesford; a three or four hour journey away, in Staffordshire, near the town of Cannock. 'And before you start acting like kids off on a school treat, let me warn you,' he said, ominously. 'It ain't going to be no picnic. This place is a holiday-camp compared to Hednesford (he pronounced it Hensford). You mark my words.'

How true he proved to be.

CHAPTER THREE

One of the few beneficial things to come out of WW2 was the invention of suspension springs on military vehicles. Our bus was clearly a pre-war one. By the time it deposited us at the Guardroom of the Recruit Training Depot at RAF Hednesford we were all battered and bruised, as well as being weary, hungry and irritable. None of our problems were of the least interest to the two rain-caped D.I. Corporals waiting to push, prod and curse the fifty-nine of us (the runner from the medical hall was still missing) into a ragged formation under the amused eyes of the white-capped Station Police.

'Pick up your bags and turn that way' ordered a bean-pole D.I. with buck-teeth, as he pointed along the camp road, like a scarecrow acting as a sign-post; hanging his head as if embarrassed to give such an unmilitary command. 'Right, move off.'

'Heft height - Heft Height,' came the inevitable chant from the D.I's who were trying, unsuccessfully, to move us in a remotely military fashion. The fact that we had not been taught to march as yet, was our excuse as we shambled along like a column of wartime refugees fleeing the enemy - although fleeing was not the word that came immediately to mind.

The camp looked as homely as a disused factory, as we trudged past row upon row of pervasive and unpainted wooden huts, terraced like an Alaskan gold-mining settlement, that edged one side of the huge, bleak, undulating, puddle-strewn parade ground that seemed to stretch for miles into the rain-misted distance. A sodden bundle of airforce-blue coloured bunting hung from the top of a solitary flag-pole, like a drunken matelot to a lamp-post.

'Bloody Hell!.... Dodge City', observed the lad behind me, hefting his heavy kit-bag into a more comfortable position across his aching shoulders as the rain poured down unrelentingly.

Reaching a spot that was about as far from the Naafi and mess-hall as is possible without entering the outskirts of Birmingham, the cadaverous D.I. uncertainly shouted 'Halt-er-Stop.' We dropped the lumpy kit-bags down, heedless of puddles, and came to an exhausted stand-still outside of three rusty, corrugated-iron roofed, Nissen huts, one of which had a broken window pane covered with two strips of wood, like an elasto sticking-plaster.

'D Squadron Lines,' the NCO informed us as he opened the door of the centre hut and stood inside, to keep himself and his clip-board dry. 'The following names in next door.' He pointed to his right, almost dropping his pencil. 'Yoozal be D.1.' Looking down at the clip-board he called out twenty names, of which I was one.

'The next lot will be in here,' he said, jerking his thumb over his shoulder and calling out another twenty names. 'Yoozal be D.2.'

He looked up to see if we were still stood, soggy and cold, in the pelting rain. 'The rest of yooz, in there.' He nodded his skull-like head forward and to his left. 'Yoozal be D.3.'

'Right' he said, straightening his head after a long pause to ensure our thorough soaking. 'When I says "move", yoozal get inside your billets, dump yooz gear and get back out again, sharpish, 'cause I got to get yooz over to the mess-hall for tea; so bring yooz irons.' He went to move away from the doorway, then changed his mind. 'And bring yooz gas-capes with yooz. It's rainin'…'

He barely escaped death by trampling when he eventually grunted 'Move.'

'Bloody Nora,' cursed a scouse voice as we rushed in. The hut was a mirror-image of Cardington, but we didn't wait to examine it. Grabbing our eating irons, and throwing gas-capes over already drenched greatcoats, we dashed back outside to be herded the seemingly endless miles to the hanger-like mess-hall where our ruthless NCO made us wait, yet again, as he ponderously divulged more gems of knowledge.

'When yooz gets inside and gets yooz grub' he instructed, 'Yooz sits on (he meant 'at') the tables marked 'D' 'cause yooz are 'D' Flight.'

'Great,' I said to the chap standing next to me. 'We've been named after a bloody table.'

Our Corporal Yoozal had not finished. 'When yooz finished, yooz makes yooz own way back to yooz billet and reports to yooz 'ut-Corporal, now MOVE.'……. We moved.

The end of the queue of hungry airmen was outside of the door, in the rain. We tagged miserably onto the end, noticing two even more miserable looking dogs sitting, soaked and forlorn, on the wet grass, looking at each passing erk with doubtful, pleading eyes, hoping for an occasional gifted morsel that would have been more forthcoming had they waited at the exit door. They would have been a matching pair except that one was a matted-hair cross border-collie, and the other a mangy Jack Russell. All I ever saw them get at this end was a sideways kick from one of the animal loving airmen, who then ended up with a snarling terrier hanging by its teeth from his calf muscle.

Inside, the Hall was standard Air Force issue. The same long serving- counter with the same inevitable open-lidded urn of tea at the end, and the same po-faced server/chefs flopping unidentified dollops of the same cordon-bleu food onto the same tin trays. The only difference between here and Cardington was the size of the place and the vast numbers of erks cramming food into their mouths, before some urgent need of their training schedule required them to be elsewhere.

We gazed around at the swarming pandemonium of airforce-blue with dismay and relief. Dismay that this was to be our future for the next six weeks, and relief that this evening, at least, we were 'at leisure'. Tomorrow was another day.

Back in our hut (that we eventually found after a nomadic tour of the camp), now watered and fed, we chose our beds and made them up with the bedding piled at the foot of each. This was courtesy of the Hut-Corporal, a huge, square-jawed, time-served NCO with WW2 medals on his tunic, who was drifting towards his demob. For all his size he proved to be a soft-voiced gentle giant of a man who, through long experience, never offered or volunteered his help, but it only took a requesting knock on the door of his separated room to gain his unstinting advice, or assistance. He had however, done us one more favour for which we were very grateful. He had lit the hut bogey-stove, and stoked it to a roaring heat. We immediately, and affectionately, nick-named him Desperate Dan.

The rest of the evening, having sorted and stowed our uniforms and kit, we spent getting to know each other. We were a motley crowd, soon to be welded into a strong, comradely team, bonded by shared pain, exhaustion, and a mutual hatred of the detested D.I.'s.

First, and most importantly, there was me. Jim Highman, ex-mariner, nicknamed 'Daddy' by the rest of the Flight owing to my six-year seniority over the eighteen-year olds. Almost everyone in H.M.Forces acquires a nick-name (or sobriquet if you are an officer) that normally has an historic or descriptive background. Some, with common names such as Smith or Jones, are identified by the last three of their Service number, i.e. Smith 123, or Jones 987. Nobody originates these names - they just happen. At sea I was always 'Lofty', despite the fact that I was a mere five-foot eleven inches tall. (I would regain this nickname again after I left Hednesford).

On the beds either side of me were the two Bakers. Tom from Gloucester was 'Baker 119' and Gerald from Stafford was 'Baker 124'.

Also on my side were Richard 'Tiny' Hamilton, a six-foot one-inch giant from Ipswich: Eugenius Bolek, a London-born son of Polish parents who stoically bore his nickname of 'Testy', short for testicles: Thomas 'Gentleman Jim' Burrows, a foul-mouthed Londoner who had a good heart: Bob 'Geordie' Cash, a quiet reserved lad from Tyneside: Maurice 'Fanny' Fanshawe, a fat, greedy pig of a lad from Leeds: Stewart 'Bomber' Harris, a streetwise chap from Liverpool, named after the famous WW2 Air Marshall, and Dennis 'Jock' Dalgleish, from Inverness, who completed my side of the billet.

Opposite was Michael 'Turnip' Adams from Somerset who spoke like a Zummerset turnip, and looked like a mangleworzel. He was to send the D.I's into depressions of helpless despair, and prove to be the greatest surprise of the lot.

Next to him came 'Davies 331' from Swansea and 'Davies 296' from Pembroke, two South Walians whose Christian names we never did learn. Then Bernard 'Lord' Byron, a nondescript lad from Maidstone in Kent: Peregrine 'Professor' Albright, a highly educated and very likeable lad from Winchester who allegedly had turned-down a short-term commission as an officer in the Army in preference to an even shorter two years as a National Serviceman in the RAF: Don 'Weasel' Ferratt from Bristol who's features matched his name: Bill 'Florrie' Ford from London: Cecil 'Happy' Handcock, a real miserable sod from Swindon in Wiltshire; and last - but by no means least - Bill 'Tosser' Grayling, a scrawny chap who suffered acutely from an over-imaginative sexual mind, and equally high libido. He earned his name because of the grunts, sighs and movements, seen and heard from his bed, several nights a week, and having been caught relieving his urges in the Ablutions Block on the second day.

A fine body of men by any standards you may think............ Wrong.

At 6am the next morning, the Hednesford version of the Cardington dust-bin band burst into the billet like a thunderstorm. Our days of leniency were over. We were now in the RAF proper - or so we were told by the clone-like moron of a D.I. who crashed us from our slumbers by ripping off blankets and upending beds - a favourite pastime of the D.I fraternity. It made a good start to his day to see us race to the distant Ablutions Block in the cold, damp, early morning air, for a wash and shave in consistently cold hot-water, then return to dress and make-up beds with our version of 'boxed' blankets... all within the generously allowed twenty minutes.

'Stand by your beds,' was the next screamed order. This was an exercise to allow the pleasure-seeking D.I. to see how far he could throw our incorrectly 'boxed' blankets in one direction and immaculate (and unused) 'filthy' set of mess-tins in the other. Finally, to satiate his desire for humorous satisfaction, a 'manky' pair of boots, a disgusting webbing-belt and/or rusty 'eating-irons' would be liberally distributed throughout the length and breadth of the hut. Reasonably happy with his efforts, he then passed on to the next unfortunate, repeating his performance time and time again, until the billet was a shambles of waist-deep 'unacceptable' equipment.

'Right' he would howl venomously, standing hands on hips, in the doorway, like a latter day Mussolini. 'You have got fifteen minutes to clean this 'orrible mess up. Then I will be back, and if it ain't right you won't get just a short breakfast time...... you will miss it all together.' He grinned triumphantly to himself as he slammed out of the door, leaving us to scramble around among the debris for our own items, and get them back into 'proper' order.

Our Hut-Corporal discreetly remained in his room, probably as disgusted as we were humiliated.

It was half an hour before the twisted D.I. returned and, to rub salt into the wound, he did not even glance at our painstaking efforts. 'Outside NOW' he shouted, adding further insults as to our ability and parentage, as we rushed past him to fall-in outside, on the roadway. 'Quick March' he yelled, two inches behind the ear of the last man. 'You've got ten minutes to get your scran.'

Doing our untrained best we moved off, with him chanting like an asthmatic goldfish. 'Heft, Heft, Heft, Heft height, Heft.' To his manic delight, at least a dozen of us were out of step, and he pounced, furiously assuring everyone of their future.

At the back, 'Turnip' Adams marched unconcerned, left arm swinging forward with his left leg and right arm with right leg, in a vigorous shoulder-twisting sway. The D.I. went berserk.

'Don't swing your arm and leg together you bleedin' moron,' he screeched. 'Turnip' shuffled his feet and resumed as before, only to receive another ear-drum shattering invective.

'Oym doin' moy best soir' said 'Turnip' in a calm Zomerset Zider tone that threw the D.I. into another frenzy.

'Well, your best ain't bleedin' good enough - and don't call me Sir.'

'Okay, Soir' said 'Turnip'.

By this time we had reached the mess-hall and our tormentor left, shaking his head resignedly as we raced to make up our lost time.

Heaven had, thankfully, ceased emptying its contents onto Hednesford camp as 'D' Flight was collected from the mess-hall by a mature and less psychotic D.I. who marched us back to the billet to return our 'irons' and mugs, then out onto the parade ground - now crowded with other squads of airmen in various stages of competence - for our first instruction into the mysteries of military movement. He marched us up and down, left and right, turned left, turned right and turned about. We stepped off, halted and changed step; hopefully improving all the time.

By mid-morning Naafi-break, we were marching reasonably well, and by dinner time we all thought we had the hang of it. All that is, except for 'Turnip'. No matter how much attention he was given - even one-to-one at times, as the rest of us were stood at ease for a welcome breather - he could not co-ordinate his movements correctly. Even our relatively mild D.I. of that first morning became exasperated at his complete failure to get 'Turnip' to put left foot and right arm moving forward together.

By the end of a wearying day, although footsore, we were a little chuffed with ourselves as we marched off the square and back to our hut. No longer were we a total rabble. Except, of course, for the cack-handed (or should I say footed) Turnip, by now discreetly hidden in the middle rank, out of view.

This was the pattern of our daily routine for the next few weeks. Drill, drill, drill. The vast improvement in our ability, to look and march like servicemen, made no difference to the deranged megalomaniac whom we had first met. He was our main instructor, and remained a lunatic psychotic until the very last day of our basic foot-drill training. Nothing we did pleased him. In his mind we were all stupid ignorant erks who, in his words, would never be any better all the time our arses pointed downwards. All of us that is, except 'Turnip' whom he neither helped nor recognised. He just ignored him as beyond redemption.

It was during this period that we 'enjoyed' an individual interview with the Careers Officer. A funny looking Flight Lieutenant with a huge, de rigueur moustache, that grew right up his nose.
When my turn came I marched smartly in and saluted.

'Ha, Highman,' he said as he shuffled through the notes on his desk without looking up at me. 'And what would you wish to do during your two year service?'

I resisted the temptation to say 'be happy', or 'go home', as he indicated I should sit on the less-than-secure wooden-chair, that faced him across the table. 'Well, Sir. I want to go into the Civil Police when my time is up, so ideally, I would like to train as an RAF Policeman. It should help me in that career.'

A fleeting look of distaste flashed over his hirsute features, and he looked up as if seeking guidance from the blank off-white ceiling. 'Mmm, at least you know what you want, Highman. More than some,' he confided. 'Personally, I think you would make a good policeman.' (The prat didn't even know me). 'Mmm, yes. I will put you down as recommended for the Service police.'

He threw a scrawl across the bottom of the paper, staring at it as though trying to decipher what he had written; then placed his pen down on the table, precisely parallel with the edge of his notes, and sniffed. I was dismissed. Interview over. I rose, saluted the top of his head and left the office to rejoin D Flight at square-bashing, wishing I had requested a really cushy job - like Careers Officer.

We also had the promised visit to the Tailor's Shop where the 'tailor' (an obviously failed Gents Outfitter) gave our ill-fitting uniforms a thirty-second glance then slashed at it with a chalk, like a crazed surrealistic artist, before throwing it to one of a coven of seamstresses, sat screaming secrets to each other above the buzzing of their sewing machines, as they vainly tried to follow the tailor's haphazard chalk marks. The alterations invariably made the fitting worse but anyone complaining was ear-marked as a trouble-maker.

The three hours, from one to four on Wednesday afternoons, was the designated 'Sports' period when recruits had the opportunity to take part in a limited choice of 'recreational' sport. In actual fact there was no choice. We were detailed, according to the PTI's whim. If you liked football you got rugby. If you liked rugby you got jumping. If you liked running and jumping you got football. If you hated all sports you were put in a boxing ring with a squashed-nosed, cauliflower-eared, brawler from an elite slum area. We learned a lot about other sports that we had never even considered before. Perhaps that was the idea?
One chap, a weak-wristed champion chess player, ended up in the rugby first fifteen, and a hydrophobic airman failed to excel as Captain of the water polo team, at the local town's public swimming baths.

Saturday and Sunday afternoons were 'free time', but we were not allowed out of camp - not fit to be seen in uniform by the public. There was no camp cinema or other recreational facility at all, except the Naafi canteen where sometimes, those of us who didn't have to send 'allotment' money home, could afford a cup-of-tea out of our twenty-eight shillings per fortnight pay, to sit watching the Naafi girls purposely hip-swaying as they collected empty cups and plates from the tables. Not that I ever knew anyone who had any luck with them. Twelve girls, not all beauties by any stretch of the imagination, among five hundred blokes. Not good odds; for the men anyhow.
Irrespective of weather, or religious denomination, we paraded on the square in best bib and tucker every Sunday morning, medals and swords to be worn. 'D' Flight had neither but sometimes we would stick a dinner knife down our sock, just for spite. The whole Station complement marched into a cavernous hanger, empty except for a D.I.Y. altar and as many chairs- of any description - as could be mustered. We had no band to lead us in, so evenly-spaced D.I's kept the step by their unmelodious, but respectfully reverential, crooning of the recruits marching hymn; Heft-height, heft-height, heft. All at differing decibel levels, according to whether they were positioned alongside officers, permanent staff or common erks.

Officers had their chairs reserved, as did the NCO's and permanent staff. It was a rush, by the several hundred recruits, to see who could get the remaining ten. It was called democracy. The rest of us stood around the cold breeze-block walls while the lucky ones who could not gain entry, were shut-out, to eventually (promptly) drift back to their billets.

Weekends were the only opportunity we had for letter writing and I spent many hours, every Sunday, writing home to Laura. Answering her weekly letter, telling her of RAF life, without mentioning the misery, heart-break and humiliation, trying to convey how deeply I loved her and how much I missed being with her. Most of the lads were doing the same, only to girl-friends and Mums. There were quite a few moist eyes.

Apart from that, our leisure time was spent stretched out on our 'pits' talking, dreaming of civvy life, and loved ones. Everyone, that is, except for 'Tosser' who divided his time between gazing at a girlie magazine (his proudest possession), and visiting the Ablutions, using the excuse that he had the 'trots' from the roast lamb the cooks ruined for Sunday dinner. He thought it tasted funny........ Every week?

It was during the first week or two that I acquired an unwanted, and unwarranted, reputation as a 'hard-man'. It all started when three of us were leaving the mess-hall one dinner-time and came across three lads beating hell out of a fourth. I went to intervene, but my mates held me back, saying it was nothing to do with us. Well, had it been one-on-one I would have agreed but I could not stomach watching three-onto-one. Shrugging off the restraining hands I approached the fight and told the three to leave the other guy alone.

'Sod off and mind your own business. He's a poof,' snarled the leading queer-basher as he poked my shoulder with his finger.

I have never liked being poked so I hit him, hard. He went down like a sack of spuds clutching his mouth and nose. His two pals ran off, being the cowards they were, as he got up unsteadily, blood from his cut lip dripping between his fingers.

'I'll get you for this,' he spluttered, spraying blood everywhere.

'You, and whose army?' I replied, with a bravado I did not feel.

The incident went around the camp like wildfire and I was being cast as 'the hard-fisted ex-merchant navy Mate'. Little did they know that that breed died with the demise of the sailing ships.

The next day, our deranged D.I. said he wanted me to be Hut-Leader. That meant I would march the lads to and fro and ensure they were where they were supposed to be, when they were supposed to be there. The 'perks' were no hut cleaning duties, and no daily chores. I had already learned that you do not argue or disagree with a D.I., so went direct to the Flight Sergeant, who was a reasonable man.

'Why don't you want the job?' he asked, when I explained the purpose of my visit.

I asked if I could answer honestly, and he nodded. 'These lads have to take a lot of shit, Flight Sergeant,' I said, 'and I don't want to be the cause of any more.'

He turned down the corner of his mouth and a smile creased his experienced face. 'Fair enough. Who would you recommend then?'

'Aircraftsman Hamilton' I answered without hesitation. 'He was an army cadet and knows quite a bit about military life; and the lads respect him.'

The senior NCO nodded, as if in agreement, and told me to leave it with him. The next day 'Tiny' Hamilton was promoted to 'Hut-Leader'. He was chuffed, and so were the rest of the Flight.

Later that same day I was cornered, alone, by the moronic D.I. who put his nose within an inch of mine, like an Eskimo's kiss, and sneered 'Who's been running to the Flight Sergeant then?'

'I didn't run Corporal, I walked,' I replied with controlled sarcasm. He pushed his face impossibly closer. The smell of garlic was revolting.

'Don't try to be funny with me Highman,' was his truculent response. 'You might enjoy thumping eighteen year olds but you don't frighten me.'

I looked him straight in the eyes, challengingly. There was no one around. 'I don't enjoy thumping anyone Corporal, unless they are hiding behind their stripes.'

He snorted a lump of snot onto his upper lip and walked away, wiping his mouth with his sleeve. I never mentioned this incident to anyone, but it soon became common knowledge, so he must have said something in the 'head-basher's hut' (the recruits name for the D.I's quarters). He could not have been 'flavour of the month', even among his own kind because, from that day onwards, I was never personally insulted, abused or humiliated by him, or any of the other D.I.'s.

Halfway through our six weeks at the Hednesford Hilton there were some welcome changes. Foot-drill square-bashing became minimal, and we were given .303 rifles, to begin arms drill. There was also a strenuous 'fun-day' on the Assault Course that reduced our numbers to fifty-six with two sprained ankles and a complaint of stomach pains from Davies 331. The staff instructor told him he was malingering, and ordered that he continue the Course, but Davies 331 collapsed and was whipped away to hospital where they diagnosed a bad hernia. The rest of us prayed that the instructor would get a severe bollocking. He deserved one. He could have killed the lad.

Another break in routine was a whole day on the bitterly cold, wind-swept firing range, where our only respite from the weather was a ditch in which we ate our packed-lunch dinner of curled-up sandwiches, as we watched our caring instructors resting, with their feet up, in the small Range-hut.

Diligently supervised, we were each issued with five rounds of live ammunition and, after a short demonstration and safety talk, told to fire at the cardboard cut-out figure of German helmeted targets that would pop up in the butts. Happily we banged away, visualising the targets were wearing Corporal's chevrons, getting bruise cheeks and shoulders for our efforts. One man managed to score an outer on his target. The remainder of us apparently missed altogether, and the 'staff' in the Range-hut complained bitterly when a bullet smashed one of their windows and embedded itself in the concrete wall. This really was unbelievable; the hut was behind the firing line. We wondered what had happened to the other two hundred and seventy eight rounds.

During the second-to-last week of our sojourn, we received a half-day lecture on 'Badges and Ranks of the three Services', and learned about Pilot Officers who were not pilots and Flying Officers who did not fly. Squadron Leaders and Wing Commanders who were Doctors, Dentists, Accountants etc, and had never seen a plane, let alone a Squadron or Wing. Vice-Admirals and Air Vice-Marshals who had nothing to do with sexual behaviourism. Technicians with upside down chevrons on their sleeves (Aussie Corporals) who had no authority outside of their own technical Section. Captains who never went to sea. Sailors wearing three 'Sergeant's chevrons' on their sleeve who had no rank at all. Warrant Officers who you did not salute, but still called 'Sir'. Leading Seamen in the Navy who had lots of power and authority and Leading Aircraftsmen in the RAF who had none at all. There were Privates in the Army who were not at all 'private' and generals who were not general. If an officer commanded a ship in the Navy he was addressed as 'Captain' even if only a Sub-Lieutenant, and in some regiments of the Army a Sergeant was called 'Corporal-of-the-Horse'. So many anomalies. So very confusing. No wonder we saluted everything that moved (and painted it white if it did not).

The final week arrived. We were the Senior Flight. Every day we trained for the ceremony of the 'passing-out' parade. We were as smart as they could make us in six weeks. Except of course for 'Turnip'. They had given up on him, and after the second week he was removed from the recruit training programme and placed on Admin.Orderly duties. He loved it and was a little disappointed when they refused to discharge him. He would 'pass-out' with the rest of us and do his two years. He would be useful in a Pay office or sweeping the mess-hall in some remote Station, they said. However, everyone in 'D' Flight was required to be involved in the 'Pass-out' parade so they gave 'Turnip' the role of carrying the RAF ensign, to be held upright against his left shoulder; that occupied one arm. His other arm was to be kept rigidly still, in line with the right leg seam of his trousers. Problem solved. His legs, on their own, were okay.

We were up early on the day of the Parade. Polishing, pressing, cleaning and brushing. Two things were uppermost in our minds. After the parade was over we would be informed of our next 'posting', and tomorrow - December 22nd - there would be a fleet of coaches outside the Guardroom to take every man Jack (sorry, 'erk') home for Christmas leave. Goodbye and good-riddance to RAF Hednesford.

At ten o'clock we marched onto the Square, ready for the eleven o'clock 'March-Past'. A Senior Technician was finishing his preparation of the record-player, in readiness to play the record of the 'Dambusters' when given the signal to do so by the Parade Officer. The Officer due to take the salute would mount the dais at 10.50 am.

34

At 10.45am, the RAF ensign was 'marched-on' across the square, by 'Turnip' Adams, to its appointed place at the side of the dais. Everyone watched with bated breath. Mouths fell open. Eyes widened in astonishment.

Aircraftsman Michael 'Turnip' Adams marched smartly across the one-hundred yards of parade-ground. The ensign perfectly upright and tightly held against his left shoulder. His right arm, stiff as a poker, not held in line with his trouser seam as he had been instructed, swinging shoulder high in perfect co-ordination. Right arm forward as the right leg went back; as smart as a Guardsman outside of Buckingham Palace. He crashed to a faultless halt on his designated spot and did an immaculate about-turn to face his Flight colleagues. His poker-face split into a wide grin at their gob-smacked amazement. He had won. He had fooled everybody. He had got away from doing four weeks of square-bashing. He had beaten the establishment, hands-down. It was too late for retribution. He was off tomorrow, with the rest of us. He was our HERO.

The Parade that followed was flawlessly executed, and highly praised by the Station Commander who was then whisked away by his obsequious juniors for one, or six, large gins in the Officer's Mess.

All we had to do now was to await our 'postings', which would be sellotaped to the breeze-block wall of the mess-hall in about half-an-hour, and pack our kit ready for the 'off' tomorrow. It was all over.

The weather was cold but dry as we made our way in small groups to the mess-hall, excitedly timing our arrival to coincide with the time the 'postings' were due. The low, oppressive blanket of cloud was ominously heavy, but we hadn't a care in the world. It could snow a blizzard if it wanted.

Inside, the Hall was empty. There was still half-an-hour to go before it opened for dinner. Chefs were clanging and clattering behind the steel shuttered partitions that separated the Hall from the cook-house and serving area. 'D' Flight huddled in small conversational cliques, patiently saying little.

'He's coming,' called the look-out man at the door, and we all stood back to allow the sallow-faced Admin.Officer access to the wall. There was a hushed silence as he slowly, methodically and bloody annoyingly, stuck the lists up with exact symmetrical lengths of tape, before turning back to the door. As soon as he disappeared there was a mad rush.

The first page said that, of the fifty-six men of 'D' Flight, thirty-two were going to RAF Stations in Singapore as Administration Orderlies (the labour force of the RAF). Seven were going to Pay, Accounts and Records Centres. Two were going to Air/Sea Rescue Units for on-the-job training. Four to the RAF Police Training Centre at Netheravon, in Wiltshire, and the remaining eleven to various trade-training units. Everyone pushed and shoved to see the sheets listing who was going where.

'Oh, shit!'….. 'Good oh!'….. 'Bloody 'ell!'…. were just a few of the expressions of joy, or disappointment, heard among other expletives as each reader spotted his name.

I strained my neck to see between the bobbing heads. I saw the four names listed under 'RAF Police' and bitter disappointment welled-up inside me; my name was not one of them. Anxiously, I ran my eye down the list. Christ!, I did not want to be an Admin. Orderly, or go to bloody Singapore.

Then I spotted it, and looked along the line:-

AIRCRAFTSMAN J. HIGHMAN. 2705895. TO RAF MARINE CRAFT UNIT. RAF BODWINTON DEVON. AIR/SEA RESCUE LAUNCH CREW. 4th. JANUARY.

My heart lifted; that was even better than the police. I could have jumped for joy. The name below mine, who was also going to ASR was a lad in D3 hut. I only knew him by sight and he was going to the unit at Dover.

I looked around at the mixture of sad and happy faces. Naturally, I wanted to learn where my D1 mates were going, especially 'Turnip' who had pulled-off the most amazing hoax that would, most likely, become part of RAF lore. I had to congratulate him. He was standing propped-up against the wall, his face as white as an arctic snow-cap, his eyes staring blankly - at nothing. What on earth was wrong?

I turned back to the list on the wall. There it was:-

AIRCRAFTSMAN M. ADAMS. 2704232. TO RAF PAY & RECORDS OFFICE. SWINDON. WILTS. ACCOUNTS CLERK. 6th JANUARY.

Wonderful, that was just what he wanted, and only a few miles away from his home town. So, why did he look so shocked? Then I noticed that everything after his Service number had a line drawn

through it and in its place someone had written, in ink
…………………………………..
TO RAF RECRUIT BASIC TRAINING DEPOT. HEDNESFORD.
STAFFORDSHIRE. TRAINEE DRILL INSTRUCTOR. 4th. JANUARY.

He, who laughs last, laughs longest. The Bastards had won after all.

CHAPTER FOUR

Jimmy's letters were a Godsend to Laura. It was as though they were her life; all she lived for. Each morning found her waiting, eagerly peering out through the side-window curtains, for the elderly, blue-uniformed, peaked-capped postman to shuffle along the pavement of the cold, windswept street; hoping the huge bulging sack slung across his shoulder would contain a letter for her. Five out of every six weekdays, for the last two months, she had been disappointed, and for the remainder of each of those long days she would be miserable and depressed.

She longed for Jim with all of her heart. She missed the feel of him beside her in bed. Missed him touching her, and the long passionate love-making. Missed the feeling of fulfilment and pleasure he gave her, and the sound of his contented sighs. Missed the cuddles afterwards, as they fell into exhausted sleep, and the feeling of his presence alongside her when she woke in the morning. She was so lost and lonely without him.

Her Mum tried hard to cheer her up. She had been through it herself when Dad was away in the Navy for two years at a time, between the wars. Jim had only been away for a couple of months, but Mum understood; it was Laura's first time.

Luckily, Laura had found herself a job. It wasn't much, just serving in a grocery shop, but it occupied her time and her mind, and kept the wolf from the door by eking out the small allowance Jim managed to send home out of his meagre pay. Unfortunately, the job also gave her another 'wolf' to contend with; Tom, her boss, a forty-year old who took every opportunity - when his wife wasn't around - to brush against her and 'accidentally' touch her bum. At first she felt offended and embarrassed, and almost left once, but then realised (or at least naively thought she did), it was all harmless fun; providing it went no further. He was good to her in many other ways, quite sweet really, and she had to admit to feeling complimented by his attention. An occasional extra pound in her wage packet (supposedly after a good sales week) was very welcome, and he promised her a good Christmas bonus - providing his wife didn't get to know.

39

He never tried anything really naughty, so where was the harm? He seemed happy having her around, but she knew she would have to be careful in the summer, not to encourage him by wearing short dresses or mini-skirts.

The red-letter days, usually on a Tuesday, were wonderful. Jim's letters were so full of love and yearning, and so very sexy. He would say, in detail, what he would like to be doing to her - and where, and when, and how, (Good job the letters weren't censored like they used to be during the war, she thought). These were the bits she would read before rushing off to work, like a giggly school-girl on her first date. Tom would greet her with a lecherous grin and say 'Had a letter today have we?' when she arrived at the shop, all flushed and excited.

All day the pages would burn a hole in her apron pocket, her anticipation mounting by the hour as she wished the hands on the clock to speed up.

Back at home, in the evening after work, she would read his letter again, skipping the loving bits at first to read about what he was doing, and how he was getting on. He never mentioned the bad, unpleasant parts of his life, but reading between the lines she knew he was going through some sort of purgatory, and it made her so sad. She wanted to be with him, to be able to hold him and to comfort him. She desperately wanted to read the sexy bits she had skipped earlier; where he says how much he loves her, and wants her. She could hardly wait to get tea-time with Mum over and finished, so that she could go to her own room and lay on the bed with his letter. To read his words over and over again, knowing they would make her hot and frustrated.

Jim had been Laura's first, and only, lover. He had introduced her to the pleasures of love-making and given her an appetite for sex. She missed him, and the love-making, so much. He had made her into a woman and now she needed to be that woman. To love and be loved. How was she going to get through the next few days until he comes home for Christmas leave? How was she going to get through the next two years?

She wished with all her heart that she had the money to go out and buy nice clothes and saucy underwear to excite him - not that he needed any stimulus; he always said he would fancy her even if she wore sack-cloth, but the thought of deliberately dressing, and undressing, to excite him even more, was very arousing.

She pushed the bolster-pillow long-ways in the bed, between her legs as a substitute for him, cuddling into it and trying hard, usually unsuccessfully, to fall asleep.

Waking in the morning was like being dragged back to cold reality after a beautiful dream. The surrogate pillow, still trapped between her thighs, was just a piece of flock-filled linen, a pillow; not her Jim. There was no head on the pillow next to hers. No broad shoulder to cuddle into. She turned over onto her back. The stippled ceiling of the one room bed-sit in her Mother's house reflected her mood; bland and depressing. She pulled the sheet and blankets up over her shoulders and under her chin, sliding both hands under the covers, down over her chest and onto her stomach, wishing they were Jim's hands caressing her naked aching body. Closing her eyes she imagined his fingers between her legs, gently rubbing and pressing, getting quicker and more passionately urgent. The mounting arousal made her stomach flutter, his fingers probing deeper as her back arched and a massive climax surged through her whole body like a prolonged electric shock, leaving her trembling and exhausted, like a wet rag. A lonely, unhappy wet rag.

A knock on the bed-sit door, just a few feet from her face, made her jump guiltily, and she heard her Mum's voice call through the inch of panelled wood. 'Breakfast is ready, love.'

CHAPTER FIVE

At Hednesford, the next morning dawned without a sunrise, it just became lighter. Heavy black clouds scudded low across the grey sky, tumbling like the fluffy seed-balls of a dandelion weed blown before the cold, winter wind. Leafless trees, resembling scarred wooden pillars supporting an oak-beamed roof of an ancient pub, bowed their ancient bones, reeling like drunken boxers before an onslaught. Flurries of sleet stung the faces of D Flight as we trudged crab-wise through the slush, heads buried deep down in the enveloping collars of our greatcoats, sheltering behind our shoulder-slung kit-bags. With streaming, dripping noses, bent backs and frozen hands grasping kit-bags and suitcase, we slouched silently along the endless path, skirting the windswept parade ground. The weather might be foul but we were happy. We were going on leave.

Goodbyes had been said, and promises to keep in touch had been made, back in the hut. Ahead of us, opposite the Guardroom with its clutch of 'Snowdrops' miserably contemplating their Christmas duty in this God-forsaken hole, a row of contracted coaches were lined-up with their luggage compartment flaps hanging open at their sides like hungry chicks, engines ticking over, drivers reading newspapers and chatting idly among themselves, waiting to take several hundred erks to destinations as wide apart as Inverness and Plymouth.

Anxiously, I searched for mine, staggering along the line. Sod's Law dictated they would not be in numerical order. Mine was second to last.

No.5, said the board in the driver's window in an almost indecipherable hand-written scrawl. 'OXFORD - READING - SOUTHAMPTON - PORTSMOUTH - CHICHESTER, it read. The driver was hunched over the steering-wheel, fag hanging from his lower lip, reading 'Sporting Life'.

'Put my gear underneath?' I enquired indication the under-slung luggage space.

Lazily, he lifted and turned his balding head. His raised eye-brows giving an unspoken answer as he spared me a sour, fleeting glance, before turning his attention to the current starting prices. Clearly, he was not offering his help so I pushed my bag and case into the empty hold hoping that by the time we reached Portsmouth it would be almost empty again. Gratefully relieved of the burden I climbed into the coach giving the driver a sarcastic 'Thank you,' which he totally ignored.

There were only a few aircraftsmen already on board so I chose one of the many vacant window-seats and spread myself out, with one knee up on the cushion beside me to discourage anyone from sitting there.

By 11am, our scheduled departure time, the driver became animated and agitated as he stood up. His long, lean, hatchet-face scowling. His ferret-like eyes straining from his bowed head as he leaned forward to look out of the open door. Obviously, he was still expecting more passengers and luckily, so far, I still had a whole seat to myself. I wiped my coat-sleeve across the steamed-up window beside me and peered out through the smeared glass to see another bunch of bedraggled, kit-laden erks approaching. Mentally, I cursed them to get a move on. Not only did I want to get moving, I also wanted the bloody door closed to keep out the arctic chill.

The group splintered as they stumbled along the line of coaches, getting smaller until only half-a-dozen or so remained. Only three stopped to push their gear into our luggage hold and I glowered down on their bereted heads, willing them to get a move on.

I stared aggressively at each individual as he walked up the aisle between the seats, daring him to even think about sitting with me. My hostile scowl worked and they all passed by, towards the back.

Testily, the driver rose from his seat, reverently folding his *Sporting Life* paper and placing it in the door pocket before stepping out into the bleak morning to viciously slam the side flaps of the luggage hold closed. Grumbling, he returned to his seat and wriggled his backside comfortable as he lit another cigarette and wound down his window to toss the dead match away, letting in one last wintry blast of bitter Staffordshire air. Then, with a grunt and a grinding of gears he pulled away, narrowly avoiding a scrape with the adjacent coach. Obviously it was not his vehicle.

I sprawled across the two seats, relaxing luxuriously down into the rough, damp newness of my greatcoat until only the top of my head gave evidence of human occupation. Slowly, I relaxed and dozed off to a lullaby of jolts, bangs and jerks as the driver forced a passage south, through the cities, towns and traffic, with a display of skill only acquired from a life-time of experience, on a dumper-truck.

It was nearly seven hours later when we drew up at the coach terminal outside Portsmouth Dockyard gates, with a crunching skid and screech of brakes that woke the security conscious Dockyard Police who momentarily panicked at the thought of ram-raiders on H.M. property.

Eventually, the swaying coach became steady enough for me to stand and shuffle wearily out of the door. My stiff aching muscles screamed in protest as I pulled open the luggage up-and-over side-door to claim my baggage. The driver graciously declining to give any assistance, other than to climb irritably out of his seat to close the exit door with a friendly parting offer of 'I'll shut the door, shall I?'

I watched and waited in the cold, dark drizzle as he crashed the gears into a tyre-burning start for the last leg of his journey. Gratefully, I waved him goodbye with a Churchillian salute as he clipped a tired looking bus-stop standing harmlessly on the corner.

I must have just missed the local bus and had to wait twenty-five shivering minutes before one came along displaying the eagerly awaited WHITE HOUSE, MILTON, on its oblong back-lit destination board. I knew I was back in civilised Portsmouth on account of the Conductor helping me aboard and stowing my bags under the spiralling stairway.

'Christmas leave, Son?' he asked, as he cranked a ticket from the silver machine strapped around his neck and resting upon a big beer-belly.

I nodded back. I could not trust my frozen lips to work properly.

'I was in the Andrew m'self,' he said pleasantly, grabbing hold of a stanchion to steady himself as we moved off. 'Twenty years, man and boy' he added thoughtfully, as if to himself, as he clawed his way to his next customer.

By the time we reached my stop I was comparatively warm, thawed-out by excitement, all a-tremble with butterflies, shaking in anticipation of seeing and touching my Laura after so many long weeks away from her.

I didn't even notice the foulness of the bitter darkness as I turned the corner into our street. She saw me coming. She had been looking out of the glistening window for the last half-an-hour.

I was still two doors away when she burst out of the front door and ran to me, knocking the kit-bag off my shoulder as her arms went around my neck. Dropping the case, I grabbed her around the waist. All we needed was a romantic orchestra playing in the back-ground to make it a Hollywood film set. There were probably a dozen people peeking from behind curtains as we embraced, oblivious to them or the weather, until I realised that Laura was only wearing a flimsy dress, hopefully for my benefit. She must have been freezing. Reluctantly, I let her go and picked-up my kit-bag. She went to lift the case, but I shooed her away - it was too heavy.

'Get indoors quick' I said breathlessly, and followed her in.

I had hardly got through the door, into the hallway, before it closed with a slam behind me, and I was twisted around to have her arms wrapped tightly around my neck. She kissed me hungrily, breathing sweet nothing in my ear. It is very difficult to remove a stiff, wet greatcoat while glued to a pair of luscious lips, but I managed it, and she wrapped her legs around my waist, clinging like a Koala bear-cub to its Mother, as I carried her into the living-room, my hands cradling her bum. Shaking with pent-up passion I lowered her onto the settee, her dress unashamedly riding up her thighs in total disarray. She opened her legs, invitingly, and taking hold of the peak of my cap, threw it off my head into the far corner of the room. Her eyes opened wide, and for a second or two her mouth dropped open; then she burst into hysterical laughter.

My passion ebbed as I looked at her quizzically....'What?'

Spluttering, hand over mouth, she pointed to my head. 'What have they done to you?'

I took a good look at myself in the mirror hanging above the fireplace. It was the first time I had seen myself with someone else's eyes. In camp we were all the same. No one took any notice. I sneaked another look at my shaven, scab-covered head and turned to face her, worried at first because of what I must look like to her. Then we both exploded into uncontrolled giggling, laughing away the embarrassment.

She ran her hands over my bald skull like a fortune teller reading the bumps, muttering 'Oh, my poor darling.' Then passion kicked in again and I hungrily undressed her as she struggled with the unaccustomed metal buttons of Service clothing. There was a last giggle from her as she pulled-off my trousers to reveal the Service issue, Mark 4, passion-killing underpants which, fortunately, soon joined the rest of our clothing, neatly strewn all over the floor. I was sex starved after six weeks celibacy, and she was her usual insatiable self; a perfect combination.

Christmas passed in a blur of love-making, eating, drinking, and more love-making. We took a few hours of respite to be with her mother for Christmas dinner - a delicious feast, especially after the chef-ruined pig-swill of Hednesford - but we were both eager to return to our love nest. We had so little time to make up for the lost weeks. My Laura was fantastic and, to be truthful, really amazed me with her wanton, whore-like behaviour. I did not know she could be that way. Even our wild first months of marriage was never like this, but I certainly was not complaining. She was entitled to be as sex-starved as me. Nevertheless, it was unbelievable, and by the time my leave was over I was an exhausted, but very happy, physical wreck of a man.

The wonder of it all made our parting at the railway station even more miserable and poignant. My heart was like lead as I waved goodbye to her lovely figure, standing alone on the platform. Only another twenty-two months to go was no real consolation.

The ten-hour train journey to Cornwall seemed an eternity. As tired as I was, I could not sleep. My mind was in turmoil thinking about Laura, how I would miss her, and wondering what the immediate future held in store for me. Having to change trains at Southampton and Exeter did not help matters, and by the time I arrived in the West Country I was weary, fed-up, hungry, and as dry as a bone. Laura had made me sandwiches for the journey but I had assumed - wrongly - that I would be able to get a drink somewhere.

The train hissed slowly into the dismal West Country station and jerked to a halt, throwing me across the empty carriage, still holding my kit-bag at arms length above my head; caught in the act of taking it down from the over-head racking. Cursing the railway, the RAF, Cornwall, and especially that prat in the Shipping Federation, I stepped out onto the deserted platform thinking to myself, 'Who, in their right mind, would be doing this at eight o'clock on a miserable January evening?' My travel orders said I was to report to a waiting RAF vehicle, for onward transportation to the Marine Craft Unit at RAF Bodwinton.

'No one yer now, m'dear,' said the ticket-collector, sat bent-backed on a stool in his little caboose studying a cross-word puzzle that he had not even started. 'Was a lorry 'ere until 'alf past seven, but eem gone now.'

'How far is it to Bodwinton?' I asked, hopelessly contemplating what would probably be an unpleasant night ahead.

He chewed his pencil as though considering my request. 'Oy dunno' he muttered dropping his veined eyes back onto his puzzle, 'Twenny or thirty mile, I guess.' He was silent for a few minutes as I gazed around in despair, looking for inspiration.

'Lorry be back in the marnin',' he told his cross-word puzzle, then remembered I was there and raised his head. 'You can get yer 'ead down in the Waitin' Room if 'e want,' he offered, pointing a bent fore-finger along the platform. 'It's up thar.' I was just about to thank him for his kindness when he added, 'When the nine ten's gone I'll make us a cup-o-tea.'

It was quite a small station, and after my train had pulled-out it was as quiet as a grave, except for an occasional irate hoot of a car horn from somewhere beyond its avenue of walls, and the anonymous rasping squeaks and squeals that can be associated with any building being buffeted by the wind. Dim haloes of light shone down on the barren platforms from widely spaced fixed lamps, adding to the denseness of the surrounding penumbra. A single hanging lamp, dangling loose from a high standard at the exposed end of the platform, swung like a pendulum in the winter breeze, casting eerie shafts of light and shadow across the silver streaks of rain-track that disappeared into the gloom.

Resigned to my fate, I humped the kit-bag up onto my stiff shoulder and stumbled along the cold row of closed shops and shuttered offices; an uninhabited world. Just me and the desolate old man still sat alone under a low-wattage bulb in his sentry-like box, like a monastic leper.

The dull glow of a barely illuminated sign over a pair of doors, reminded me that I was bursting for a pee. I dropped my bag down heavily onto the cold concrete and entered the semi-darkness of the 'Gents'. The acrid stench of urine made me retch. Two of the three light-bulbs in the ceiling had been smashed. The floor was swimming in the over-flow from the urinal and it did not need a Sherlock Holmes to see the cause was the drain-hole, blocked with fag-ends discarded by smokers who had dared not breath-in the obnoxious fumes. Holding my breath, and with a handkerchief to my nose, I dashed across the wet floor to the trough, fumbling with stiff fly-buttons. I needed to relieve as much pressure from my strained bladder as possible while holding my breath, before the need to continue breathing overcame the revulsion of that bloody awful smell. God alone knows what the cubicles were like. Luckily, I was able to almost finish before being forced to abandon-ship and rush outside to adjust my dress in full view of the absent public. 'Jesus; when was the last time they were cleaned?' I asked myself, grateful that I had left my kit-bag outside on the platform and that my needs had been nothing more serious. Inquisitively, I opened the adjoining door marked LADIES, then quickly shut it. It smelled worse than the GENTS!

The relatively clean, cold smutty air, that filled my lungs and cleansed my nostrils, made me feel like a drowning man thankfully surfacing, as I dragged myself and bag to the Waiting Room that, I had no doubt, would be equally as smelly and dirty; and probably just as cold. I pushed open the frosted-glass door of my bed-room for the night and was very pleasantly surprised. It was clean, and smelt quite fresh. Even more welcoming was the heat from the brown-painted cast-iron radiators on two of the walls. 'This will do me' I thought as I stretched myself out on the hard wooden seat, not a mile away from one of the radiators. All I needed now was a hot drink and something to eat. I knew the former would be arriving soon because a train had just passed through after the briefest of stops, and the big round clock on the wall opposite me said it was ten minutes past nine. The glorious warmth soon thawed me out but the pangs of hunger were beginning to bite as I unbuttoned my greatcoat.

'Train's gone,' announced the old chap, poking his head through the door, as if I were a waiting passenger that had missed it, 'so I'll be brewin' up in a sec'.' Again, I started to thank him but he interrupted. 'Fancy fish un chips?' he asked, 'There's a Chippy opposite and oiy'l be a getting some for myself'.

Saliva gushed out of my mouth like blood after some careless dentistry.

'Yes, please' I answered inadequately, as he disappeared like a cuckoo on a Swiss clock...... Why hadn't I thought of that?

He was back within ten minutes, carrying two tin mugs of steaming tea, strongly sweetened on the assumption that I took sugar. He sat beside me, placing the mugs on the floor, and withdrew two soft, lumpy, newspaper- wrapped packages from the side pockets of his railway overcoat; every movement followed by my starving eyes and dribbling mouth.

49

'I've salt and vinegar'd 'em,' he reported, handing me one of the warm packets. 'That's one and a tanner you owe me'.

They were the most delicious fish and chips I had ever tasted - or will ever taste. Not a single crumb escaped my searching fingers as we sat in companionable silence, savouring every mouthful, until finally crunching and screwing the empty, greasy paper into a tight wad.

'That was fantastic' I said appreciatively, handing him what was almost the last of my dwindling fortune, and swigging down a mouthful of the equally delectable tea. 'Thanks a million'.

'Sor right, mate' he answered, pocketing the coins and staring into his mug as if seeing something strange and mysterious in its empty bottom. 'I was in the war,' he recalled dreamily.

I mentioned that I too served at sea as a young Merchant Navy Cadet during the latter part of the war, but it didn't seem to evoke any interest.

'Got sunk myself once, off Crete' he said accepting a cigarette from the packet I offered. 'And mined off Malta'. His eyes were loaded with memory, his wrinkled face suddenly illuminated by the glow of the Woodbine as he drew heavily on it. 'I'll be a goin' 'ome as soon as the ten thirty's gone,' he confided, as though deliberately changing the subject. 'Then you can get some kip. The 'Gents' is just up the platform a bit, if you wan' it.' I told him of my earlier visit and the filth there.

'Ain't 'ad a cleaner for a week' he apologised. 'She got the flu. And by the way, I got to turn off the 'eatin' when I goes. I'd like to leave it on for 'e but the mornin' bloke will report me if I does.' He rose from the hard inflexible seat and edged towards the door. 'I'll leave a note for Albie in the mornin' to let 'im know you're 'ere,' he said over his shoulder. 'If 'is Missus haven't kicked 'im out the wrong side of the bed 'e might make 'e a cuppa when he comes in.'

He closed the door behind him and I got up to flick-off the light-switch on the wall, hoping the darkened room would dissuade any visitors from coming in, and leave me in peace. I didn't realise at the time that the station closed for the night.

The kit-bag was too big and bulky to use as a pillow, so I took out my crumpled best-blue tunic and trousers, luckily packed near the top, and rolled them up for a headrest. Not ideal, but better than nothing. My hip bone complained against the unyielding wooden bench as I laid on my side, knees up in the foetal position, but it was something I would have to endure. I can never sleep on my back.

It was uncomfortable, but warm, and I was watered and fed. My heavy eyes sagged and the 'HA-BISTO' advert on the wall blurred into a mist as I fell asleep.

A long drawn-out 'Shhhh' of exhausted steam woke me as a train rumbled into the Station and ground to a squealing halt. I wedged one sticky eyelid open. The Bisto boy still looked down on me as the huge wall-clock tocked its sweeping minute hand onto the Roman figure four. I focused harder. It was twenty-past seven.

Still only semi-conscious, I rolled over onto my back. My hip-joint came back to life, screaming in agonising protest. I rubbed it hard, straightening stiff knees along the seat. Then, wrapping my greatcoat around me like a cocoon, I sat up shivering, and stretched out an enquiring hand hoping to feel the lovely warm radiator. The room was an ice-box, and my mouth felt like the inside of a stoker's jock-strap. Stiffly, I stood up; stamping my feet on the floor, and flapping my arms around like a playful dolphin's flippers, in an effort to re-start my frozen blood circulation. At that moment, the door opened to admit a small, bird-like man with an over-sized head, on which was perched a pill-box hat emblazoned with a railway badge. I was more interested in the steaming mug of tea he was offering. His pointed chin waggled 'Mornin',' as I grabbed the tea in case he changed his mind.

'I've put the 'eatin' on, so should be warmin' up soon.' His wizened face regarded me with curiosity. 'Don't know why Charlie switched un off last night. Could've left un on for 'ee. Miserable old sod. Thinks the war still on.'

I mumbled my gratitude as my hands and lips thawed out on the chipped enamel, feeling the hot liquid gurgle down inside me - NECTAR.

Albie was either a very busy man this time of the morning or unsociable because, without pause, he turned around and went back out onto the platform grunting 'Can't stop. Lots to do.'

By 8.30, according to the railway's clock, I was standing, unshaven and scruffy, outside of the Station entrance in the cold, windswept street - empty except for two or three scurrying figures - waiting for the scheduled transport.

At 9.15, dead on time by RAF standards, and three quarters of an hour late by everyone else's clock, a thirty-hundredweight, open-backed, drop-side truck came around the corner. The dull grey-blue of its paint-work and RAF roundels on the front mud-guards was a welcome sight. A bespectacled face with a nose like a wedge of cheese peered out from its wound-down window.

'You for Bodwinton?' the face asked, pronouncing it Bodinton.

I nodded and grimaced. I wasn't feeling very amiable.

'Get in, it's warmer here,' he invited; leaning across the passenger seat and clicking open the door. 'Toss that in the back' he instructed, indicating my kit-bag. I climbed into the cab as he opened his own door and got out.

'Got to collect some stores' he said, disappearing into the Station. 'Won't be long.'

Fifteen minutes later, with the cab rapidly losing its heat, he returned carrying a small parcel. Obviously his mug of tea had gone down well.   'Engine spares' he announced, his breath blowing like a steaming kettle in the cold morning air as he climbed in, squirming his bottom into a once-bright yellow tasselled cushion, and switching on the ignition.

'Where you from?' he asked, more for something to say that any interest.

'Portsmouth,' I answered casually.

'Na. What Station I mean.'

'Oh, sorry. Hednesford.'

He turned his head to me in surprise. 'What, the Recruit depot?'

I nodded, and he seemed a bit shocked when I said I was a National Serviceman.

'Bit old ain't you?' he commented ungallantly, ramming his gear stick forward, crashing it into gear.

Other than to answer 'S'alright' to my question 'What's Bodwinton like?' we drove in silence through the A and B class roads of rural Cornwall. I was eager to learn about my new Station, but the taciturn man behind the wheel showed no interest in me as a person, or my natural curiosity. I glanced sideways at him from the corner of my eye. His big bony head was almost skeletal, as though all the fat had been sucked from beneath the pale skin, and black circles hung like hammocks beneath his eyes, like drip-trays. Every few seconds his

52

forefinger would poke his glasses higher up onto the bridge of his aquiline nose in a nervous habit, accompanied by a deep sniff. His battle-dress was standard issue, but the stains and creases on it were not. Neither was the grey woollen scarf he wore in place of collar and tie. The D.I's and Service police at Hednesford would have had a field-day with him - or a coronary. I was not surprised to learn, later that day, that Leading Aircraftsman Archie Perkins was known, with typical inverse Service humour, as 'Poser'.

Almost an hour later we turned left, following a finger-pointing signpost inscribed BODWINTON. 1 MILE, onto a single-track road, lined with a mixture of high hedgerows and flat-stoned walling that was so narrow we almost touched both sides. An occasional naked tree bowed slender branches down-wind to indicate that a strong breeze was still blowing as we crawled along, like a slow barge on a tarmac-covered canal.

A large sign, bearing the name BODWINTON over a strange foreign looking word that I presumed to be its Cornish language equivalent, stood mud-spattered at the side of the road, and almost immediately we began to pass isolated houses, some lying back away from the road and others standing on its verge, as though waiting for a bus. Then into the village itself where its one street of ancient terraced houses, one pub, three shops and a church, parted to allow us through. No sooner were we in, we were out again.

'Is that it?' I ventured bravely, hoping to see at least an affirming nod. 'How far is it now to the Station?'

He didn't waste his breath. He had no need to. We turned a shallow bend to see a striped red and white wooden barrier, waist-high across the road. A small brick building, at the barrier's hinged end, carried a sign on its outward facing wall informing anyone who wasn't sure that this was 'No.14. Marine Craft Unit. Royal Air Force Bodwinton'

We crunched to a shuddering halt and waited a full minute, nosing the barrier, before my driver impatiently gave a blast on his horn. A hatless Corporal in battle-dress emerged blinking in the rain, to raise the barrier. The red and black brassard on his left upper arm was the only indication he was RAF police.

'In a hurry Poser?' he grunted, as we drove past.

'Prat,' answered my companion, when well out of earshot.

'Shouldn't I have reported to the Guardroom?' I asked with some concern as we continued along the road. That was normal procedure.

'What for?' he answered. 'That prick doesn't even know what day it is.'

I let it pass, deciding to go wherever he took me.

Less than one hundred yards along the pitted road, carpeted with rotten leaves from the gaunt trees that lined its route, a row of drab, dilapidated huts, each exhibiting its Section name on weather-worn doors, lay behind unmown lawns and unkempt flower beds.

'This'll do you,' said my driver, pointing out the hut marked STATION ADMIN OFFICE as he braked to a sliding halt on the dead leaves.

'Cheers' I acknowledged gloomily, glad that the journey was over, and pulling my kit-bag down onto the mucky ground as he wordlessly drove away with his usual gear-grinding expertise.

The front entrance of the hut opened onto a small, square space, hung with framed photographs of what I guessed to be aerial shots of the Station. A door to my right was labelled STATION ADMIN OFFICER. FLT.LT.APPLEBY. The one to my front marked STATION ADMIN OFFICE. W.O.WEBB. Most importantly, the one on my left was the one with the welcoming word TOILET. I certainly wanted that.

Having successfully relieved myself of excess weight, I knocked on the Admin Office door. No response. I knocked harder. Still nothing, so I cautiously turned the brass handle and pushed the door open. A Senior Aircraftsman sat behind a varnished desk littered with papers and files on top of which lay an open girlie magazine.

'What ya waitin' fer - a bleedin' invitation?' he greeted unsmilingly in a broad cockney accent, tearing his eyes from the picture of a naked model doing her version of the inverted splits. I told him who I was, and something must have clicked in his brain.

'Oh, yea. I've got somethin' 'ere on you' he said, lifting the open magazine by its bottom edge to face me upside down, while his other hand rummaged through the clutter on the desk top. The picture struck a cord. I recalled seeing a woman acrobat in that sort of inverted pose as her male partner leap-frogged over and between her legs. That had been on a theatre stage, and she had been dressed in a leotard.

'Ha,' he grunted successfully, sliding a file from the bottom of the heap, carefully replacing it with his magazine. He opened it officiously, and after scanning the contents decided I would benefit from knowing what it contained.

'Aircraftsman James Highman. No.2705895. Age 25. Married. Wife's name Laura. Former occupation, Second Officer in the Merchant Navy.' His eyes, now interested, looked up at me. 'Bit old ain't yer?'

'Yes, I was born old' I replied sarcastically, but if he heard he chose to ignore it.

'Assignment,' he continued. 'Billet 18. To join HSL.3840. Flt.Lt. Harrison. DFC.'

'What's HSL?' I asked stupidly, and instantly regretted. I should have waited to ask someone more friendly.

''igh Speed Launch,' he said pityingly. 'You're Air-Sea Rescue now, in case you didn't know.'

Eager to return to his magazine, he pointed towards the entry door with his finger in a curving motion to his left. 'Outside, turn left. Your billet's about five up on the right. No.18,' he confirmed.

Humping the lumpy kit-bag, yet again, across my shoulders I trudged up the slushy leaf-strewn road, noting the buildings as I passed. WORKSHOP...... NCO's MESS......AIRMEN's MESS..... CLOTHING STORE..... ENGINE STORE..... BOAT STORE, etc.

Then the tarmac road came to an end. From thereon, well-worn cinder paths fanned out like probes nudging the wooded back-ground. One, leading off to the left, went through a canopy of trees seemingly shivering in their winter birthday-suits, and I caught a glimpse of a river or creek sparkling in the breeze through their bare branches. Another, shooting sharply to the right, led up to a breeze-block, single-storey building sign-posted OFFICERS MESS. The two paths in the centre forked towards a gaggle of Nissen Huts (the RAF must have millions of them) that stood in a huddle, like a run-down P.O.W. camp, deserted except for smoke streaming down-wind from the cowl-topped chimney flues sticking up from their moss-covered corrugated roofs.

The first pair were marked S.N.C.O's and N.C.O's, and looked marginally better than the next two that were No's 17 and 18 and bore the name-boards HSL 3848 Crew and HSL3840 Crew, respectively.

I dumped my bag down outside the door of No.18 and straightened up, listening. There wasn't a human sound, or sign of life. It was like standing in the middle of a virgin forest. Only the whining of the wind through the ceiling of tall, denuded trees and the distant tapping of wood against wood   disturbed the peaceful silence. It was as exciting as a peat-bog.

I reached for the brass door knob, shining only from frequent use, and turned it as I gently pushed with my shoulder. Nothing moved. I tried to twist the knob further but it was turned as far as it would go. Irritably, I shoved harder and with a click it flew open and I fell into the hut, doing an Irish fox-trot on one hopping foot.

'What the....?' Shouted one startled voice from the dim interior, and a bare, unshaded light was switched on. The yell came from a dishevelled head that peered, one-eyed, over the top of a blanket on the nearest bed. Beyond, heads began to surface and look in my direction. Some angrily, some inquisitively, all sleepily.

'Sorry,' I called quietly, as if trying not to wake anybody, then tip-toed back to the door for my bag.

'Who are you?' asked the same voice, now propped up on one elbow with eyes glaring like the daggers of death.

'New crewman,' I whispered. I didn't think for one moment that a formal introduction would be welcomed.

The tousled head crashed back onto the pillow and I was invited to shut the sexually active door, as the other heads submerged back under their blankets. A hidden hand touched a hidden light-switch and I was left in a grey-darkness with the only daylight coming from the ill-fitting window shutters. No way could I blunder around the billet without causing a disturbance and incurring everyone's wrath so, leaving my bag, I slipped out, carefully closing the protesting door behind me, and made a chilly return to the Admin Office. This time I went straight in without knocking. The same, skinny, cockney SAC was sat behind the desk, but he wasn't reading his girlie magazine; neither was he slouched over his desk. He was sat bolt upright, face flushed and eyes bulging. My first thought was that he was suffering a fit, but as I opened the door wider, the reason became apparent. Standing in front of the SAC's desk stood a tall, moustachioed, immaculately uniformed figure, with a brilliantly polished crown and wreath on the cuff of its sleeve. It was breathing fire as its head snapped around to transfix me. I had never come face to face with a

Warrant Officer in all of my long seven-week career in the RAF. Certainly not one holding a girlie magazine between his figures like something the cat had brought home.

A gap appeared beneath the flawlessly trimmed handlebars that seemed to act as a cradle for the flared nostrils.

'Who are you, and what do you want?' he hissed in my direction, with barely controlled anger.

I snapped to attention, and looked him straight in the eye. I had faced death before, and life-threatening hazards such as Liverpool-Irish Bosuns and RAF Drill Instructors. He didn't frighten me.

'A.C.Highman, Sir,' I trembled. 'Posted in today.'

He bent over the desk and snatched a file from beneath the petrified SAC's hands. I could see it was mine. I waited for the wrath of God to descend on me as he quickly scanned it. When he turned his attention back to me, I was amazed to see the transformation of his face. His eyes were softer, and no longer glaring. His voice almost friendly as he stretched his mouth into a smile.

'Ha, the Merchant Navy chap. Welcome aboard lad,' he said amiably, surprisingly using the nautical greeting. 'Nice to have a man posted to us, instead of useless sex-starved wankers.' His eyes swivelled venomously to the SAC who had obviously been the recipient of the SWO's wrath.

'Come into my office' he ordered, and I dutifully followed.

Once inside the diminutive, fastidiously tidy office, he motioned for me to sit on the only other chair, a none-too-safe folding wood one, not made for comfort and clearly designed to dissuade prolonged visits. Removing his cap, he threw it expertly onto the hook of a tall hat-stand, his thinning hair looking bedraggled in contrast to his otherwise total perfection. He rubbed his forehead, elbows on table, running straight fingers along the permanent crease caused by years of cap wearing.

'How do prats like him become SAC's?' he asked his pristine blotter, presumably not expecting an answer.

After a few minutes of private contemplation he remembered my presence and asked if I had been to my billet. I told him I had and that they had all been asleep. Then, belatedly, I worried if I had dropped them in the cart; but he went on to explain that both boats had been 'out' all night and only berthed in the early hours.

'Pop up to the Mess and get your dinner' he said, checking his wrist-watch, 'then come back here at two and I will run-through things with you'.

CHAPTER SIX

A baleful glare from the cockney SAC met me as I re-entered the Admin office at exactly two o'clock. His desk was cleared of the morning's clutter and he had straightened his tie. I returned his stare with equanimity. He outranked me but I was older - and I was learning fast. 'The SWO told me to come back at two,' I said. His resentful eyes were full of anger.

'What's 'e, yer long lost bleedin' Uncle or sumfin?' he snarled, his face flushed. He was still fuming from a major bollocking. 'We don't like arse-hole creepers here.'

That got under my skin. I took a step towards him, as if examining a slimy maggot. He leaned back in his chair, away from me.

'You threatening me?' I said in my best Humphrey Bogart voice. ''cause if you are, I'll show you what I do with jumped-up twats like you.' He began to shake his head, just as the door opened. The SWO looked at me and then switched his gaze to the SAC, then back to me. Correctly assessing the situation and wisely not making a comment.

'In here, Highman' he ordered, stepping back and entering his own office.

Despite the fact that he must have been a very busy man - and let's face it, SWO's were the people who ran any Station - he gave me the next hour or so of his valuable time. I held the most junior rank in the RAF and his was the highest non-commissioned, yet he soon put me at ease, as I once again perched insecurely on the rickety chair.

'Bodwinton,' - he pronounced it Bodinton as well - 'is a satellite Station of the main unit based at Plymouth,' he began. 'We've got two boats, to cover the Western Approaches to the English Channel and the Bristol Channel. Each takes a turn at being duty boat, but there's rarely any excitement - not like the old days,' he added wistfully. 'Most of the jobs are to act as crash cover for flying exercises, or when aircraft carrying V.I.P's over-fly the area. All that means is a boat, or sometimes both, go to a designated position and wait there, rolling their guts out, in case anyone has to 'ditch'. Every month one boat goes to Plymouth for a long week-end; weather permitting of course 'cause it's over a hundred miles and they've got to go around Land's End. HSL's aren't heavy weather boats as you will soon find out. This trip is so that the boat and crew can be inspected to keep everything up to scratch, and allows engineers to do any heavy repairs or maintenance that the boat's mechanic hasn't - or can't - do himself; but everyone, from the O.C. down, knows that the most important reason is to allow the crew to have a long week-end break.' He paused, and took a cardboard packet of *Passing Cloud* cigarettes from the desk drawer, carefully selecting one as thought they had varying flavours. He lit it from a match and inhaled deeply, then blew out a stream of smoke like steam from an exhausted railway locomotive coming to a halt that hovered around his head like an angelic cloud. He didn't offer me one. I suppose that would have been a breach of discipline.

'There's sod-all to do in the village,' he continued. 'Only one pub and that gets crowded with more than four customers, but the beer's good. There's nothing else for the likes of you young lads to do, and the couple of young 'Judies' are guarded like the crown jewels by their parents, and the local lads. The nearest town with entertainment is over ten miles away, and there's no transport except one bus a day at ten in the morning, coming back at six, so you can see the monthly "weekends" are very valuable. There's nothing at all to do on camp. Nothing except eat, drink, sleep and do your duty stag. That's why discipline is kept to a necessary minimum. It's not a bull-shit unit so keep your nose clean, behave yourself and you will enjoy your time here. You'll find the launch crews are good lads, and your skipper is one of the best. His name is Flight Lieutenant Harrison and all he will expect from you is that you do your job to the best of your ability - and that had better be good.' He stopped to grind his fag-end into a glass ash-tray. 'Your crew will be getting a shake at four o'clock, for tea, so I suggest you have a walk around the Station in the meanwhile and get to know where everything is. Nobody will mind if you poke your nose in and have a chat. Everyone's bored to tears and only too pleased to meet a new face - even those idle sods in the Guardroom,' he said with a laugh. 'Oh, by the way' he added by way of dismissal. 'You only salute officers the first time you meet them each day, and only then if you, and they, are wearing caps or berets. Right, off you go.'

The next hour was an eye opener for the likes of me coming straight from basic training. Finding where everything was took about three and a half minutes.

Following the SWO's advice, I opened some of the hut doors to introduce myself. Ten minutes in the clothing-store, with an LAC who was as queer as a nine-bob note, was more than enough, but in the Engine-Store I met a Corporal from Southampton who was a mine of information on everything and anything <u>not</u> to do with the RAF. He told me that there were coaches contracted to H.M.Forces that left Plymouth Dockyard main-gate at 4pm every Friday and called at Bournemouth, Southampton and Portsmouth, getting to Pompey at about 11pm and leaving again, for the return journey, at 5pm on a Sunday. They carried all Servicemen, mainly matelots and Marines, but there were usually several Raff 'bods' from the MCU so, sometimes, transport could be arranged to and from the Dockyard gates. If not, the taxis were pretty good and would allow four or five to cram - in, to share the cost. Providing no 'bobbies' were looking, of course. He didn't know when my boat's week-end at Plymouth was due.

I entered the Holy of Holy's, the Guardroom, with some trepidation. The last people to allow slack discipline and dress were the 'snow-drops'. The outer door was open. A desk and an unoccupied chair filled its emptiness. Papers hung from clips hooked onto nails driven into the breeze-block walls. A coloured picture of a Harley-Davidson motor bike, in a broken wooden frame, stood drunkenly on the window sill, and a black telephone stood importantly on the desk.

'Anybody in?' I called, making myself jump at the sound of my own voice, like an intruder burgling a house.

After a few shuffles and bumps, the inner door was opened by a clutch of podgy fingers followed by a short, round-faced erk wearing a collar-less shirt beneath his unbuttoned battle-dress jacket.

'Come in' he invited, stepping back without asking who, or what, I was. I went into a room furnished with two iron beds, one of which was covered by a mattress, crumpled blankets and an indented pillow on which rested an open paper-back titled *How to get your girl*. The other bed groaned under the weight of a heavy body laying full length, booted ankles crossed, battle-dress blouse wide open, reading a Western novel *Blazing Saddles* that he dropped onto his ample stomach to enable him to inspect me along his broad, broken nose.

'You're the new bod that Poser brought in this morning,' he told me with impressive acumen.

'Yes, Corporal,' I answered, noticing the two chevrons peeling off his sleeve. 'A.C.Highman.'

His sniffed at this unexpected and unusual formality, and swung his legs off the bed onto the floor, slowly standing (or more aptly uncoiling), growing taller until he towered above me from an altitude of about six feet three inches.

'Mmmm,' he muttered, going into the outer office and returning with a clip of paper. 'Oh, yea. HSL 3840. In hut 18.' It was a statement, not a question, so I stayed silently looking up at him, with a growing crick in my neck. 'You been up there yet?' he asked. I presumed he meant the billet.

'Yes, Corporal, but they are all asleep.'

He nodded understandingly, and then turned to the erk who had by this time returned to his instructional book. 'Put the kettle on, Golly,' he said. The erk rose reluctantly, without answering.

'That's Golly, my duty Admin Orderly,' explained the Corporal, regaining his seat on the bed, and relieving my neck. 'We call him that 'cause his surname is Blackman,' he sniggered at his own humour. 'And I suppose they call you Lofty?' Much to my surprise he held out his hand. 'I'm Corporal Browning' he said, indicating the RAF Police brassard on his upper sleeve. 'They call me Gravy, 'cause of the cooking stuff,' he explained unnecessarily. We shook hands, and he motioned with an open palm that I should sit on Golly's bed. He was a 'regular', but very friendly with, unusually, no prejudice towards National Service men. My preconceived ideas of RAF Policemen went out of the window as we chatted away, including Golly in our conversation, as we sat like a group of gossiping housewives over a cup of tea.

He seemed genuinely interested in my time at sea, and of my original wish to go into the Service police.

'Be grateful you didn't,' he said grimly. 'We're nothing but bloody gate-keepers half the time. Not every Station is as good as this. Most are all bull-shit and blanco. I wanted to re-muster into ASR,' he mused, 'but the Provost Marshal won't entertain it. Miserable bastard.'

At four o'clock, I made my way back to Hut 18 in the darkening gloom of the early evening, and shouldered the sticky door open. My new crew-mates had been called and were sitting on the ends of their beds, arranged so as to be as close to the red-hot stove as possible, with blankets draped around them like dozy Mexican tramps. We began the ritual of introductions.

They seemed pleased to see me, if only because I would ease their work-load on the boat. They had been short-handed for quite a few weeks, since one of their numbers had been posted elsewhere, via a hospital. 'Up to his neck in syphilis', as one graphically explained.

Being all 'regulars' they weren't too pleased, at first, to learn I was a conscript, but brightened up considerably when told I was a qualified professional seaman. One by one, they dressed themselves in the ASR 'Rig-of-the-day' consisting of battle-dress trousers and blouse over woollen roll-top jerseys that were originally white but now varying shades of cream and grey. In the Navy, these jerseys were known as 'submarine sweaters' but in the RAF they were called 'Live and dies' for the obvious reason that the lads lived and died in them. Most of the lads had only one jersey so, when not being worn, it wasn't folded away in a locker. It was stood upright, unaided, in a corner, its whiteness and purity matched only by that of their long woollen sea-boot socks.

My five crew mates were: SAC. Eric 'Toby' Jugg, the boat's junior engine mechanic who was a thin-haired, slim Midlander with an ugly broad Birmingham accent: LAC. Peter 'Doc' Broome, the medical orderly; a small, pimply, skinny, well-educated lad from Hertfordshire: LAC. Alan 'Sparks' Wrighton, the radio operator, with his Brillo-pad hair style, Roman nose and Mickey Mouse ears, from Kent; everything about him was ugly except his wonderful, happy personality: LAC. Dave 'Donkey' Rigg, a serious faced Geordie deck-hand from Sunderland; He was the only married man in the billet, except for me, and had all the troubles in the world on his slight shoulders, mostly due to having an extremely beautiful wife who liked the good life, and who he was rarely able to get home to; hence his concern. Last, but not least, LAC. Ronnie 'Romeo' France, the singing Welsh deck-hand from Carmarthen. He was the boat's gigolo whose good looks, and lovely lilting voice, melted the heart of any female, be she virginal, motherly, worldly wise, or another man's wife. He had no scruples. He was a magnet to any woman, much to the disgust of his ignored mates, and the anger of other suitors. He was reputed to have attended a bereavement club on some pretext or other, and slept with one of the recently widowed members that same night; after making dates with three of the others. He was the sort of man that other men immediately hated, but soon came to like. He had a wonderful personality, providing you weren't the one being cuckolded.

'Forty', as our boat was affectionately named, was the duty-boat that night. All that meant was that the lads could not leave the Station (so what's new) in case there was a 'crash-call'. I had visions of her being a nautical bumper-car attending an aircraft deliberately 'ditched' into the sea by a demented 'kamikaze' pilot. If there was a 'shout' they would be called for by Tannoy, but for tonight only, it would not include me. I wasn't on the books, yet.

So it was that we sat grouped close to the glowing 'bogey-stove' all evening - no fancy Naafi club here - playing cards, writing letters (that included me) or just nattering. Toby gave me a verbal introduction to the three remaining members of Forty's crew, in his horrible round-vowelled accent that I won't even attempt to mimic.

Our skipper, he said, was Flight Lieutenant Harrison. DFC., whom the SWO had already told me about. He was a middle-aged ex-fighter pilot, decorated in the Battle of Britain of WW2, and now medically exempt from flying duties, owing to wounds received.

'He's a good bloke,' said Toby. 'Very fair.'

Like all the Station's officers, he 'lived-out' in the village, except when duty-dog. Then he had to sleep on a camp-bed, in the Officer's Mess.

The coxswain was Flight Sergeant Rooney, called Flight to his face and Mickey behind his back. He had been in ASR since the very early days of the war and knew every inch of the boat, and every 'wangle' that an erk could dream up. There were rumours that he too had been decorated for something or other but never wore a ribbon on his tunic, or spoke about it. Anyone having the temerity to enquire would be ignored. He was quite a fatherly type, according to Toby, but did not suffer fools gladly. His billet was with the other NCO's in the 'Palace' - an up-market Nissen hut made luxurious from their own pocket, and the reluctant efforts of 'defaulters'.

Our Chief Engineer was Corporal 'Jock' Thorpe who lived (thank God) in the Junior NCO's hut. A slight-built man in his mid-thirties, Jock was quick tempered, but never physically violent. His thick guttural Glaswegian brogue sounded like gibberish to all but another Scot. Even the skipper and Flight hardly ever spoke to him, unless absolutely necessary, for fear they would not understand his answer.

The warm fug of the hut was sleep inducing, and as I hadn't had much sleep the night before, I decided to 'crash-my-swede' early, content in the knowledge that I had written a long loving letter to Laura, and was free to sleep undisturbed until breakfast time...... heaven.

A gentle hand, shaking my arm, brought me back to the land of the living. I unstuck one eyelid to see Doc standing over me.
'Wake up Lofty - time for scoff.'
'Cheers' I said, holding my bent arm up over my eyes to see my wrist-watch. 'Blimey' I thought, 'Where am I, the Ritz?' It was eight o'clock!!
Another blurred face hovered over me. 'Pull yer finger out, Lofty' it said, 'We've got to be aboard by nine.'

The morning was a dull grey roof hanging low and heavily over our heads. Frost sprinkled the bushes and pathway, like salt, as we hurriedly dashed to the Mess for a healthy fried breakfast flopped onto our plates with trained elegance by an unshaven server with a big boil under his chin. No doubt he had a medical 'chit' in his pocket exempting him from shaving.
A Sergeant, wearing a striped butcher's apron, appeared behind the serving counter and looked enquiringly across at our little group. Toby returned his gaze and raised a hand, as if casting a vote, but the NCO dodged back out of sight to save answering the expected barrage of complaints. The serving erk sniffed a drip back up his nose and wiped a sleeve across his mouth, carefully avoiding the painful boil pulsating like a red warning light.
At three minutes to nine, we left the hut and ambled down the rime-covered cinder path, through the stark archway of leafless trees rustling in the bitter winter breeze. Five men, huddled in thick woollen Live and dies of varying hues of white, up around their ears and chin. Hunched-back, with hands pushed deep into trouser pockets, shuffling along in heavy sea-boots; and one.....me, feeling out of place in a collar and tie, and leather shoes.
At the bottom of the path, to the left, a short wood and concrete jetty stuck out, like an obscene finger, from the water's edge into the gently babbling creek. A pair of mute swans glided effortlessly along the hull of one of the two HSL's, moored one either side of the jetty. To my

professional eyes they appeared short, beamy and very powerful (the boats, not the swans), like restless Rottweilers straining to be let off the leash. Paint-work gleamed watery in the morning frosted dew, and RAF roundels stared from the bows like the devil-scaring eyes on a pagan native fishing craft.

At precisely 9am, to the very second, the first sea-booted foot of our group stepped onto the gun'le of 3840 and cocked a leg over the wire guard-rail. One by one, like weary Dockyard 'maties' clocking-in for work, we boarded the apparently deserted deck, standing uncertainly like a gathering of expectant fathers outside a maternity ward.

A door at the rear of the superstructure crashed open, making us all jump, and a peak-capped figure in a snow-white jersey stepped out.

'Move then, you idle shower,' it commanded, 'It's nearly dinner-time.'

'Mornin' Flight,' grunted his lethargic crew as they dispersed to their daily chores, leaving me standing like an abandoned super-market trolley. The chevroned arm with its polished crown beckoned me.

'Come inside lad. You must be Highman.'

Inside the cramped wheel-house it was comparatively warm, as I wedged myself into a corner opposite him.

'Skipper will be down shortly,' the red-cheeked NCO said with a twitch of his bristly moustache, clipped short, military style. 'He will want to see you, but in the meantime I am Flight Sergeant Rooney, and I am the coxswain of this tub.' There was more than a hint of pride as he said that. 'I hear you were in the Merchant Navy lad. Is that right?'

'Yes, Flight' I answered, unwilling to say too much for fear of bragging - or, worse still, being lumbered. News travels fast.

He waved a hand around the wheel-house. 'Know anything about this lot?'

I looked around, noting the familiar steering wheel, engine controls, compass, RDF, etc. Just like a miniature model of a large ship's bridge, except that it was cramped. 'A bit, Flight,' I replied uncommittedly, and then added as an excuse, 'I was a big ship man.'

He humped, and twitched his moustache again, as if considering his next question, but he did not get the chance to ask.

'Good morning, Flight,' greeted the newcomer, crouching through the door and somehow finding room to join us. He was wearing the ubiquitous white sweater but his cloth-peak cap and two rings on the epaulettes of his battle-dress blouse proclaimed him an officer. I did my best to stand to attention in the confined space but my bereted head hit the over-head compass repeater, and my hip collided with a sharp-edged locker.

'Morning, Skipper' returned the Coxswain without moving a muscle in recognition of the officer's status. I still had a lot to learn about shipboard routine in the Service. 'All the lads are on board, and this is A.C.Highman,' he reported, nodding towards me.

The officer swivelled friendly eyes towards me from his bowed head, and I saw the faded, diagonally striped ribbon of his DFC, that led a row of campaign ribbons, beneath the pilot's brevet wings over his left breast pocket.

'Welcome aboard, Highman,' he said kindly. 'I have read your file and it is nice to have another professional seaman in the crew. With me and the Flight Sergeant I mean.'

He turned to leave. 'I will leave you in the Coxswain's capable hands' he added 'but we must have a talk sometime.'

'Well, he seems to like you,' observed the Flight Sergeant in what I took to be an approving voice. 'I.........'. He never finished what he was going to say because a scruffy, oil-streaked face appeared in the doorway, shouting what sounded like 'Radyenyerarflut.'

'Thanks Jock,' smiled the coxswain, seeing my bewilderment. 'That was our engineer, Corporal Thorpe, reporting the engines are ready, when I am fit,' he explained. 'Don't worry, I didn't understand a word either but it is a routine report that we are used to.' He fiddled with a switch on the bulkhead. 'Will you go aft and keep an eye on the lines while the engines kick-over?' he ordered in a requesting manner. 'We run the engines everyday for ten minutes or so.'

Still unaccustomed to the boat's fixtures and fittings, I left the wheel-house and stepped carefully aft onto the stern where I acquainted myself with the mooring ropes, and means of securing them. I was leaning over the side, checking the lead of the back-spring, when a loud explosion lifted me off my feet, nearly throwing me overboard with shock. For a second or two I was stunned, thinking the boat had blown up; then realised one of the engines had been started. Dense black smoke erupted from the exhaust at water level, causing a loud popping and splashing, as the jet-effect made the hull surge forward against the restraints of the mooring lines. I was ready when the second engine burst into life and the whole valley of the creek reverberated with the roaring boom that sent flocks of birds shooting skyward in agitated frenzy from their post-prandial roosts, while wild-fowl flapped across the surface like winged Charlie Chaplin's. The two swans swam angrily to the opposite bank, wings partially opened, like reluctant chocolate boxes, then turned back to await their customary treats.

Tranquillity returned as the engines were switched off after a successful warm-up, and I was despatched to the Clothing-Store to draw my 'Live and die' white sweater, sea-boots, socks, duffel-coat and oilskins from a protesting store-man who was unwilling to part with anything from his personal store that would entail paper-work of any description. I left fully equipped, leaving him seething over a year-old copy of *Gardener's Weekly*.

Back on board, now dressed for the part, I was placed with Donkey and Romeo to 'learn-the-ropes', and by the end of the day knew enough to undertake my duties effectively and efficiently (or so I told myself) including the best place to sleep at sea in heavy weather; where to hide one's flask to prevent it being emptied by other thirsty throats; when not to use the temperamental pump-toilet at sea, to avoid one's waste being regurgitated into one's dropped trousers; and many other practical and very useful things. Seamanship and boatmanship were touched on - very vaguely.

Life became pretty blissful. Every day we trooped down to the boat, trying hard not to be early - or late, for cleaning and maintenance. Every alternate twenty-four hours we were duty crash-boat, but never called-out. The crew of 3848 were studiously ignored as being friendly, but inferior. The fact that their boat was faster than ours was not even to be considered. We had the better boat and crew, of course. Our skipper talked to theirs, and our coxswain spoke to theirs, but among the hierarchy of the lower-deck a rivalry, not always friendly, existed. Bloodshed was never involved, or contemplated. Not with malice anyhow.

Each week we went to sea for half a day, to give the engines a work-out and, more importantly, to break the monotony. Once or twice a month we would be deployed on ditching duty out in the Channel, usually about half way between the Cornish coast and France, during

68

air exercises, or when V.I.P's were flying. This entailed sailing out to a designated 'on-station' area until recalled when the flying was finished, or the V.I.P's went home to tea.

At first, the pure exhilaration of the two 650 hp Thorneycroft engines roaring us along at forty-knots, was thrilling and awe inspiring, especially when sea-breezes created small waves that had the pounding, hard-chine hull throw spray wide to either side of our speeding bow. Unfortunately, the novelty soon wore off and sea-time became an uncomfortable, wearying and sometimes painful chore. Especially in bad weather when we would be rattled around inside the hull, like peas in a pod. HSL's are, as the name implies, built for speed; not endurance. As the weather deteriorated so our speed would be reduced, to prevent hull damage. If a gale blew, we could barely maintain steerage way. At such times, and when the boat was stopped 'on-station', she would roll from side to side like a babies rocking-cot, right over onto her beam ends in an arc of over 100 degrees while pitching at the same time, up and down like a nodding donkey oil-well pump. One minute pointing her stem at the heavens and the next driving deep into an on-rushing sea. As if this wasn't enough, she would perform a violent cork-screwing movement that had even the strongest-stomached crewman staring into a paper-bag for hours on end. They were not heavy-weather boats by any stretch of the imagination. Unless there was an 'Irish storm' (flat calm) it was impossible to remain stationary, so the skipper would have us patrolling up and down in the 'on-station' vicinity. At least this gave a variation of the stomach-churning motions.

In between these fun-times, our greatest enemy, apart from 3848, was boredom. We ate, we slept, we talked, we played cards, we read, and occasionally when money permitted, we walked into the village for half a pint of Cornish Best. Nobody welcomed us, except the Landlord. It was as if we didn't exist in the eyes of the locals, who looked on us with total disinterest.

We all had a 'Service calendar' hung above our beds, and every day was religiously crossed-off; one more nearer to the end of our 'time'. In my case, this was the completion of National Service, a mere two years. A flea-bite compared with the long service lads who set minor mile-stones of annual leave, promotion dates or a change of posting.

Without exception, everyone's dream was the eagerly awaited bi-monthly, long weekend, trip to Plymouth, when most of the Southerners among us could get home for a few hours, while the others would rave-it-up in the hot-spots of Plymouth town to actually see, and sometimes touch, real women!

Our turn was fast approaching, and uniforms were being dragged out of damp, smelly kit-bags, to be given a thorough overhaul. I had written regularly, twice a week, to Laura and her replies would be read over and over again. I could hardly wait to see her, and hold her, again, and to oblige my unmarried mates by 'giving her one for me, Lofty.'

Only bad weather would prevent us from making the short run to Plymouth, and that would have to be really horrendously bad. Our skipper was as keen and eager as any of us. His home was in Somerset.

CHAPTER SEVEN

The great day came. Glorious Friday. It was cold, wet, and overcast but there was no wind - fantastic. Our prayers had been answered. The birds did their normal air-burst routine when the engines sprang to life with their usual thunderous, throaty roar, then returned to their tree-top perches - or water-side nests - to sit watching disapprovingly in the early morning half-light, as we slipped away from the jetty, trailing a cloak of oil and exhaust fumes. It was a few minutes before six-thirty in the morning. We were on our way to Plymouth.

Everyone was closely shaved, and those with hairy upper-lips had them neatly trimmed. Hair had been cut to an acceptable length on those who had hair of an acceptable length to start with (mine still mimicked a snooker-ball, but at least the wounds were healed, and the scabs had dropped-off).

Down below, in the cramped confines of the foc's'le, best-blue uniforms, cleaned and pressed, hung in lines, like a dry-cleaner's shop, ready and waiting to make us look like 'real' airmen.

By eleven o'clock, our eager stem cut through the grey-green, placid waters of Plymouth Sound. Our rumbling engines pushing us to the very limit of the harbour speed restriction - well, maybe a fraction above - as the Skipper took an early sniff of Somerset fresh air, polluted a little (so he said) from its journey across Devon.

Our parent unit welcomed us with a reception committee of two bedraggled erks, waiting on the otherwise deserted quay-side to take our lines, who, once they had dropped the rope's eyes over the bollards, disappeared like genies between the solid, smoke-stained, red-brick buildings, before they could be spotted by labour-seeking NCO's.

'Thank you, lads,' our coxswain called after them, sarcastically, through the open wheel-house window, as he notched the brilliantly polished engine throttles into neutral.

Our perfunctory inspection by an understanding Base Commander was over and done with by one thirty, and by three o'clock, after a hurried meal, the three of us that were going home were standing waiting for the transport arranged by the Base Warrant Officer, to take us into town, leaving 3840 in the tender care of our multi-lingual

Scottish Corporal and the two base engineers who would have more problems understanding him than with the two Thornycrofts.

Sat in the Portsmouth coach, outside of Plymouth Dockyard's Main Gate - the other two had boarded different coaches - was an education. A hooter, like the wartime air-raid warning siren, rent the air with its haunting wail at exactly 4pm, beating the opening of the huge wooden gates by milli-seconds. From between the slowly widening gap squeezed a dribble of eager, desperate, dockyard 'maties'. The dribble became a stream, the stream became a flood. Thousands of them. Walking, running, barging, pushing, and cursing. Many pedalling furiously on push-bikes, dodging around like the ball in a pin-ball table. All other traffic and movement came to a halt. Point-duty policemen were ignored and gave up their efforts. Pedestrians cowered in doorways for fear of being crushed. Dogs ran away, tail between legs. This was the infamous daily 'out-muster', repeated at other naval bases in Portsmouth, Chatham and Rosyth. The end of the working day, when a quarter of a million men emptied out from a few square miles of Government property to scatter to their homes, in the bat of an eyelid. A massive rugby scrum, as unstoppable as a runaway train, and probably the hardest work most of them had done all day. Within minutes, this human tidal bore had swept past the line of coaches and into the City, causing mayhem and chaos, wisely avoided by the local citizenry defensively barricaded behind their front-doors.

As the flood eased, so it was replaced by an army (no, Navy) of sailors and marines off on week-end leave, each carrying his small attache case full of 'goodies' for wives and children. All walking rapidly, like light-infantry soldiers - they are not allowed to run - towards the City buses and row of coaches that were soon packed full.

By ten past four we were on our way. The cold interior of the coach quickly turned to a thick, smelly fug as fifty-odd servicemen settled down, as only servicemen can, to endure the long journey home. Four seat-less matelots made themselves comfortable, stretched out on the aisle floor, and desultory conversations soon died away to be replaced by a chorus of grunts, snores and unconcerned farting. Jesus, do all sailors live on cabbage?

It was ten-past-ten when the coach shuddered to a halt on Portsmouth Hard outside of another twin-set of Dockyard gates, now shut tight like the doors of a frequently vandalised church. Just ten minutes late, not bad for a driver without incentive. Who ever heard of a serviceman giving a tip?

The cold, fresh air smelt wonderful after the stench of the last six hours of confinement as I crossed the road and boarded the Corporation bus waiting to begin its penultimate round-trip of the day to White House, Milton. From its smeared window I gazed out across the harbour, to where the lights of Gosport were twinkling their reflection on the cold black water. It was good to be home.

The White House pub appeared almost deserted as I jumped down from the bus. Only one or two lights glimmered dimly through the glazed windows that carried adverts for Brickwoods beer, and blank-faced doors shut out the unlikely prospect of late customers. Still, it was almost closing-time, and who in their right mind would want to be out in this bitter weather? I didn't care. I was nearly home.

Shivers of excitement coursed through me as I trudged the last few steps with my head crouched low into the rampart of my greatcoat collar.

Turning the corner of my street I saw her silhouetted in the front-room window, holding the curtains aside. She waved, and I broke into a run.

We didn't sleep much that night, or the next. Apart from anything else we had a lot to talk about, and Sunday came around far too soon. When it was time to go, I didn't want her to see me off from the pick-up point. I knew it would be too emotional, but she insisted. We stood hugging and kissing on the pavement, under the lecherous eyes of the half-a-dozen matelots already seated on the coach, until the very last minute when the driver called 'You coming, son?'. He didn't know how near the truth he was, as I stumbled up the two steps with my small haversack hanging low on my stomach to cover my embarrassment.

I sat in the window seat looking down at her lonely, desolate loveliness, and mine was just one of the seven hands that eagerly waved her goodbye, as we drew away. At least that had put a smile on her face.

Tears of utter misery soon changed to tears of laughter under the irrepressible high-spirits of my naval companions who's lusty, but harmless humour, totally lacked malice.

'Bloody Hell. Was that your Missus?' asked one.

'No wonder you look shagged out, mate,' said another knowingly, as I nodded.

'Bet you'll be glad to get back to your camp for a rest,' commented a third.

'Better than any of the 'splits' we got at Guzz,' observed a middle-aged Leading Seaman, shaking his head ruefully, and referring to the Service women at Plymouth. 'Does she wear "women's webbing"?'

'Yes,' I answered with a grin, knowing the expression was 'navalese' for stockings and suspender belt. 'All the time.'

'Does she wear those new type hipster knickers?' asked a young rating, sat opposite me with eyes sparkling lustfully.

'Shut your filthy rotten mouth,' ordered the Leading Seaman sharply, as the others darted warning looks at the young sailor who blushed, knowing he had taken the joke too far.

The friendly banter continued in the matey intimacy of servicemen sharing the same discomforts and hardships, until the coach slewed to a halt outside Southampton Central Station where a dozen or so more bodies climbed sadly and wearily aboard. The bond was broken.

Plymouth, at eleven o'clock on a cold and miserable night, is not a welcoming sight for drowsy, lethargic service personnel returning from an all too short a leave period with their loved ones; or in some cases, with someone else's loved one.

Sweating over the hamburger steaks and frying onions sizzling on the hot-plates of their late-night stall, a pair of heavily perspiring entrepreneurial caterers, one with a teddy-bear on the bib of his apron and the other with I LOVE MUM tattooed on his hairy forearm, were maniacally serving the endless mass of sailors and marines pouring off the procession of coaches, buses and taxi's, arriving outside the closed gates of the Naval Base. Many of the navy men rushed through the small side-gate, running the gauntlet of the Dockyard police, eager to get back aboard their ship before the 23.59 hrs dead-line. Others, not so restricted by time, stood smacking their lips around the hamburger stall and its two neighbouring kiosks selling tea and coffee, and fish and chips.

Several pairs of naval shore-patrolmen discreetly watched the returning liberty-men from the shadows of shop doorways, turning Nelsonian blind-eyes to several drunken sailors being helped back on board by caring shipmates. Not so lucky was the one caught stupidly urinating in the same darkened doorway that concealed a brace of Patrol-men. He was quickly bundled into a van with caged windows, wisely parked in a side road.

Standing openly on the street corner, a lone constable of the civil police, himself a former navy man, smiled reminiscently under the misty light of a street lamp, flexing his knees sympathetically.

Among the tide of navy-blue and khaki uniforms, those of us in sky-blue stood out, like yellow-gowned Buddhist monks in a synagogue, as we clambered aboard the truck sent to take us back to the MCU, a nice warm bed in the transit hut, and a mug of hot tea scrounged from the Duty Watch. At times like this I was glad I hadn't been 'selected' for the Navy.

The morning started with the familiar explosive roar of HSL engines, perfectly timed as a breakfast call, and I felt sorry for my naval friends of last night, most of whom would have been blasted from their hammocks many hours ago by Tannoy broadcasts, and twittering bosun's 'calls'. Were they, at that very moment, scrubbing and holy-stoning decks in their frozen bare feet?   Join the Navy and see the world. Join the Raff and ask .... why?

A good hearty breakfast, followed by a leisurely stroll along the concrete jetty - where hunch-backed Herring-gulls, in their winter plumage, stood head-to-wind watching the smaller common-gulls swooping about like children, and skimming the sea-surface snatching at anything remotely edible, - brought us to where Forty was gently straining at her mooring lines, engines purring, and nudging her fenders in the light swell coming in from the exposed Sound. A huge black-backed gull, perched regally on a bollard, stretched its neck, threw its head right back with hooked-beak wide open, and gave a raucous, screeching, caw-caw-caw for no apparent reason, reminiscent of a Hednesford D.I.

'Good-morning, holiday makers,' called the coxswain with heavy sarcasm, his hatless head poking out from the wheel-house window like a mole from its hole. 'Enjoying the sunshine?'
Unwittingly, we looked up at the grey blanket of swollen cloud.

'Morning Flight,' we answered in dejected unison, but he had already disappeared.

The skipper, in his virginal white jersey, came out on deck as we climbed aboard over the guard-rail. 'Good leave, lads?' he asked.

'Yes, thank you, Sir,' we chorused, energetically making our way to the nearest place to sit down.

He smiled knowingly at our enthusiasm. 'Right then, we will shove off in ten minutes.'

'Radyenyerflut,' came the melodic Serbo-croat greeting from the open engine-room hatch.

Out past the desolate break-water - cheerless guardian of the Sound and reputed home of the biggest Moray eels this side of a spear-fisherman's dream record book - our bow rose over the smooth surface as the throttles went forward and the props dug deep to thrust us ahead at an economical speed of thirty knots. We could do forty in good weather with the throttles hard up to the stops. At this rate we'd be home in less than four hours; too late for dinner, too early for tea.

Approaching our home berth in the river, we were amazed to see members of 48's crew waiting to take our lines as we chuntered slowly alongside. This was unprecedented. Why this honour? We soon found out. They couldn't wait to tell us they were sailing tomorrow for 'special-duties' in the Irish Sea....... 'And we might be going on to Scotland after that,' they crowed boastfully, thoroughly enjoying our crestfallen faces.

'Why them and not us?' we asked ourselves. 'They get the cream and we are left here to rot.' Our morale plummeted to rock bottom. Even Flight looked miserable. We would have loved the chance of doing something different, somewhere different. The skipper did his best to cheer us up. 'Never mind, perhaps it will be our turn next,' he said. Some hopes. The last 'special' had been a year ago according to Donkey.

The invective from our articulate, eloquent engineer was particularly obscene..... at least it sounded that way.

'48's' good fortune was the talk of the camp and the good-humoured banter from the shore-staff did nothing to ease our disappointment. Comments such as 'Better boat....better crew....better everything,' went unheeded, except that more than one person was crossed-off our Christmas card list. They meant no harm. Neither did we as we thought about slashing their bicycle tyres. But we were determined not to be bitter or resentful, so none of us were on the jetty next morning to see them off as they motored out, grinning like Cheshire cats by all accounts.

We did not wish them misfortune but our devout prayers were answered when, three hours later, they crawled back in with a big ragged hole in their bow. They had hit a floating object, (Salisbury Cathedral we suggested). It was such a great pity they couldn't see the funny side of it - we did.

'Flight Lieutenant Harrison to the Wing Commander's office please,' announced the Tannoy some ten minutes later, and we crossed fingers, wrists, arms and even legs, waiting for his return. We could see it was good news as he came hurrying back along the path, smiling all over his face.

'Chop, chop, lads,' he called breathlessly. 'We've got to take their place.' He nodded toward the "boat with a hole" and climbed aboard. 'Get them moving, Flight Sergeant. We have only got an hour to transfer all the extra stores from '48'.' He stepped back onto the jetty calling to me over his shoulder as he rushed off back to the C.O's office, 'Highman, make sure we get all the charts and things from them,' he ordered.

It was a hectic, chaotic panic, and with the reluctant help of the other crew we didn't meet the dead-line. That was their small victory. It was seventy-five minutes later when we slipped away from our berth with only four hours of daylight left to get to Milford Haven, a little over one hundred miles away, almost due North, where we were to refuel and stop the night.

It was a good trip and our spirits were high. The sea was slight and, at thirty knots, we covered the distance in good time, passing between St. Anne's Head and Angle Point into the Haven with nearly an hour of daylight left.

A dun-coloured RAF fuel bowser was waiting to top-up our tanks as we moored alongside the Town Quay under the interested stares of a small crowd of locals, gathered to watch the arrival of such an unusual visitor. We were not unhappy to see many of them were of the female variety.

Much to Romeo's annoyance, Doc and I were given the chance of an even closer look when we were ordered to go into town (just across the road actually) to get nine portions of fish and chips, two without salt. Walking the hundred yards or so, and queuing in the steamy chippy, we seemed to be the centre of attraction - much to our disgust, of course.

Back on the quay-side the bowser driver was shaking a perplexed head trying to make some sense of our Corporal's instruction to 'Gititowerunteckennoot.'

Considering we had very little money among the six of us erks, we had a great time ashore that evening. After a half-pint each at the pub opposite the quay, we strolled along the main road and found a dance being held in a Church Hall. A four-piece band was struggling gallantly to be heard above the general din of well over a hundred young people, all shouting to be heard above the noise of their own voices. Lads in drain-pipe trousers, thick crepe-soled shoes and D.A. haircuts, twisted and twirled their jive partners whose short, flared skirts revealed more bare thigh than was beneficial to our continued good health. Our entry caused quite a stir. It was as if everyone stopped for a split second, to look in our direction. Even the band missed a beat or two. Servicemen were a bit of a rarity in this small town and we were certainly the only ones in the Hall that evening. The local lads, outnumbered three to one by the girls, gave us wary, protective glances while the lasses stared ogle-eyed, like their Mothers had done during the war when the place was full of men from all three services - and Yanks. The only difference now being, these girls wouldn't wake up in the morning with a pair of new nylon stockings hanging over the bed rail. More like a pair of sweaty woollen socks.

Romeo soon disappeared under something resembling a rugby scrum. Donkey, being a laconic and not too-happily married man, kept away from the girls and became palsy with a group of the local lads whereas the others, even Doc, were quickly snapped up and dragged, very willingly, onto the dance floor by the men-hungry girls. Me, well I was happily married so didn't go quite so willingly. Well........

The dance finished at half-past ten. Donkey and I walked back to the boat with two or three of the local lads, promising we would try to get permission for them to come aboard for a 'look-see' if they came back in the morning.

Like all other HSL's, Forty had no facilities for 'overnight' accommodation. It was a case of sleeping bags wherever room could be found. The skipper and Flight 'pulled-rank' and commandeered the two cot-beds in the sick-bay and Corporal Thorpe had his bag on the floor between them. Toby somehow found space in the warm oil-laden atmosphere between his beloved engines.

Donkey and I, being the first erks back, chose the best 'beds' available in the foc's'le, on the cushion-covered seat-lockers either side of the table. The next two laid on the hard deck under the table and whoever was last had to make-do on the table itself.

Doc and Sparks returned aboard half-an-hour after us, having 'walked' their girls home and being rewarded with a kiss for their effort. Toby got back just on midnight, and woke us all up. He had been given more reward for more effort, or so he told us.

Romeo staggered back, sleepless and shattered, at seven in the morning, just as we were brewing tea, having been 'sneaked-in' to the home of two sisters while the parents were asleep in another room. He had been amply rewarded by both and had a pair of frilly knickers in his pocket as a trophy. He was given a massive 'rocket' from Flight who threatened to put him on a charge if it ever happened again, and then ordered him, as punishment, to clean up the boat while the rest of us went across the cold, deserted quay-side to a warm, delightfully smelling, early morning café where the skipper treated us to a delicious fried breakfast, oozing with unhealthy grease and liberally covered with tomato sauce. No doubt he would claim it against expenses but nevertheless we thanked him most heartily in the hope that he would repeat the gesture - often.

The order to move ourselves came indirectly from the skipper as he rose from the table, scraping his chair back over the lino-covered floor, saying to the Flight 'I'll go and get myself a paper.'

'Up you get then, lads,' said the Flight taking his cue. 'We've got work to do.'

Unenthusiastically, we got to our feet, stuffing little 'doggy-bags' of 'goodies' for Romeo into our pockets. None of us too eager to leave this cosy haven. Watered and fed we could easily have sat there all day chatting among ourselves and with the jovial red-faced owner, and his three other customers who were 'dockies' and should, presumably, have been elsewhere, working.

The cutting chill of the raw outdoors hit us like a blast from the arctic as we emerged from the stuffy, aromatic atmosphere of 'Den's Diner'. Flight strode off briskly and erect as we, the unwilling, followed with heads shrunk into greatcoat collars, like tortoises. Hands rammed deep into pockets, shuffling along like something after the Lord Mayor's Show.

With their customary, unannounced explosive bang, and a cloud of black exhaust fumes, the engines burst into animated life. The thunderous growl reverberated around the harbour like an echo in an empty drum. Resting sea-birds in their thousands erupted, en masse, in an agitated frenzy then, finding themselves unharmed, reeked indignant vengeance on Romeo's freshly swabbed decks.

No orders were given, and none expected, as the lines were cast-off at a nod from the skipper's head, and Forty eased her way, stern first, from the quay-side where the two local lads, expecting a ship-board visit, stood disappointedly waving at Donkey's raised arm as he coiled the mooring lines and secured the fore-deck, ready for sea. Romeo's baggy, sleepless eyes looked in vain as he lifted the huge fenders in-board. There were no sad-eyed sisters to wave him goodbye.

Westward, and then north, past St. David's Head and across the wide expanse of Cardigan Bay, the engine's deep-throated rumbling roar drove us through the slate-coloured sea, on our six hour voyage to Holyhead.

Small waves burst under the hard-chine bow flinging showers of shattered sea to either side like a fine, white moustache. Occasionally, a heavy spray broke over the bow to splash against the wheel-house window, momentarily obscuring my view until spun away by the spinning Kent 'Clear-view' screen, as I did my one-hour 'trick' on the wheel.

Apart from Romeo, sat wedged, knees up, in the corner of the wheel-house, chin drooping down onto his chest, trying hard to catch-up on some much needed sleep, there was neither sight nor sign of anyone. They probably all had their heads down.

I was in my element; charging over the slight sea-swell at twenty-five knots like a millionaire's racing gin-palace. Only there was no gin.

There wasn't even any tea. I looked around the empty horizon. There was nothing out there to see except Forty's bobbing stem-head and the big black-letters of our call-sign emblazoned across the fore-deck for aerial recognition purposes.   This was the life......or it was until Romeo sneezed, woke himself up, broke wind, and grunted 'Want a cuppa?'

Donkey took over the wheel from me at three in the afternoon and we stood talking, mostly about his unhappy marriage. The sky was a uniform grey, like a winter blanket covering the white-capped waves of the mud-coloured Irish Sea. Except for a large oil-tanker way out on our port beam, the hazy horizon was empty.
'I can't trust her, Lofty,' whined Donkey. She's always out somewhere, at dances and parties. And I've heard rumours of other blokes sniffing around.'
I listened, nodding sympathetically and thanking my lucky stars I wasn't in the same position, with Laura. He must be going through Hell.
'Neighbours give me queer looks when I'm home on leave, as if they know what's going on. Trouble is mate, she's so beautiful. She attracts men like flies, and she's a horny bitch too,' he said, his voice dropping to a whisper, his mind far away.
What could I say to this likeable Geordie? What can anyone say? I wanted to be supportive, to share his burden, but what? How?
Romeo's voice, coming from somewhere out on deck, broke the spell. 'South Stack coming up at two o'clock, Flight,' he yelled, referring to the most westerly point of Anglesea appearing on our starboard bow, and using the Service method of direction with the boat's bow being twelve o'clock.
The coxswain stepped out on deck, sleepy eyed from the sick-bay, closely followed by the skipper emerging from his so-called cabin; a compartment the size of a shoe cupboard with just enough room for a chair and a desk.
'I'll take her now Donkey,' said Flight nudging his way behind the wheel. 'You and Lofty go and make a brew. Some toast wouldn't go amiss either.' We both sighed. Toast-making was an art on Forty. Our one and only electric fire would be placed on the foc's'le table and its long flexible lead plugged into the tea-urn socket; after the tea had been 'mashed', of course. One man, the Toaster, would spear a slice of

bread with a fork and hold it within half-an-inch of the red-hot element bars while his assistant, the wedger, held the fire as steady as possible with two pieces of wood to prevent it sliding - or being jolted - off the table; at the same time ensuring that no one tripped over the electric lead. To toast both sides of one slice took about two minutes. To do twenty slices took nearly three quarters of an hour. A labour of love that required a third hand, the spreader, to butter each slice, by which time everyone's tea mug was either empty or cold.

Back in the wheel-house, I found Flight on his own, chewing on an unlit pipe, absentmindedly jogging it up and down between pursed lips, like a toy mallet hitting a nail. The skipper had his head stuck into the radio-room listening intently to the screeching bleeps of Morse Code as Sparks, wearing his electric ears, fiddled with knobs and dials on the wireless set with his left hand while his right hovered over the black-knobbed morse-key, occasionally tapping it with two fingers and thumb.

'What's happening, Flight?' I asked conspiratorially, taking advantage of the skipper's absence. None of us had been told a thing so far, as if it was all very hush-hush.

He took the pipe out of his mouth and looked sideways at me with a wrinkled nose and protruding lower lip. 'Don't know much myself Lad,' he answered with a shrug of his shoulders. 'All I've been told is that we're doing a 'ditching' job somewhere as cover for a VIP flight.' He returned his attention to conning the boat as the skipper came into the wheel-house.

We were approaching the long weather-beaten breakwater and would be alongside in a few minutes so I clambered my way aft to prepare fenders and mooring lines, feeling disappointed. 'Ditching Stations' were not very exciting; in fact they were bloody boring. With all the secrecy and urgency we had been involved in I thought the job would be something a bit more dramatic.

Holyhead was another Milford Haven only bigger, and being a major terminal for ferries to Ireland, it was that much busier. It looked pleasant enough as we nudged our bow gently alongside a seaweed-covered stone quay, that loomed high above us. Doc Broome stood on the gunwale, outside of the guard-rail and stepped nonchalantly onto the slippery iron-rung ladder set into the stonework, climbing up with a heaving line looped over his arm to haul up the fore-deck mooring rope.

A head appeared over the edge of the quay. 'I will take your line boyyo,' called down a lilting Welsh voice, holding a hand out towards me.

I swung my right arm back and threw the heaving line upwards, like a discus thrower. It was a high, awkward cast but the heavy 'turks-head' knot just managed to reach his grasping hand and he hauled the eye of my mooring rope up, hand-over-hand, onto the waiting bollard. I waved my hand and called out 'Cheers mate,' but the head had already vanished.

The silence was deafening when Jock and Toby shut-down the engines, and for several moments there was a hushed stillness, until our battered eardrums began to hear the sounds of normal, everyday activities.

With the boat tied-up and secure, the skipper called us together on the after deck; the only place where there was room for all nine of us.

'Sorry not to have spoken to you before now chaps,' he apologised, 'but I have not had all the facts until now.' He paused and fumbled in his pocket. 'We are here to cover a VIP fly-over sometime soon and then we are off to Bonnie Scotland - the Outer Hebrides to be precise - to a guided weapons firing range for duties that, at this moment in time, I am not aware of, apart from the fact that we have to embark an Air Vice Marshal at Mallaig, and take him with us. While we are here in Holyhead, we will be accommodated in The Valley Hotel which, I understand, is only a few minutes walk away. There is a fuel bowser waiting on top of the quay to refuel us but his pipes are not long enough to reach down so we will have to wait for the tide to rise. That should be about six or seven o'clock this evening. The bowser has also brought foam mattresses for all of us because it is highly likely we will be spending more than a few nights on board, before we return south.' He paused again, withdrew a small penknife from his trouser pocket, opened it and closed it as if checking its mechanism, then returned it to his pocket. 'As you can see,' he indicated the slime-covered quay wall, 'there is a fair rise and fall here so we will be keeping two-man watches all night to tend lines.' He looked around at our attentive faces. 'Any questions?'

'When do we go back south again Skip?' asked Romeo.

The officer shook his head. 'No idea, Lathery. Your guess is as good as mine.'

'Onychanzalif?' rattled the engineer Corporal.

'Almost definitely not I'm afraid Jock,' replied the skipper, correctly decoding the request for leave.

'Ach-weel,' acknowledged the Scotsman, lifting his eyebrows resignedly.

The Valley Hotel was a dirty, grey-brick Victorian building that had seen better days. Its scruffy facade and unclean windows marked it as a stop-over for those who were choiceless, indifferent, or whose circumstances gave them no option. Inside was fractionally more welcoming. The reception desk was guarded at each end by potted rubber plants whose sagging, dusty leaves hung in neglected lassitude. Jaded leather arm-chairs stood vacant on thread-bare carpets, and undisturbed dust layered sills and shelves. Behind the unpolished desk the receptionist, a grey-haired lady as old as the building itself, blinked rheumy eyes that had seen everything in their time as we entered through the grinding swing-doors. In front of the desk an ancient bell-boy, dressed in a tatty uniform - probably rescued from a museum's dustbin - that hung, two sizes too big on his fleshless frame, unfolded himself and stared. His red-rimmed eyes glowing thankfully as he saw our total lack of luggage.

The RAF did us proud. The room I shared with Donkey didn't have room to rock a mouse, let alone swing a cat. The distance from floor to ceiling was more than from wall to wall. One of us had to get into bed to allow the other to open the door of a cupboard that was nothing more than a hole in the wall. The chest of drawers consisted of one single, shallow drawer that, once opened, resisted all attempts to close it. I swear the room was a converted broom closet. Either that, or Victorian people were much smaller than us.

From the window there was a beautiful view out over the harbour, or maybe it was a deserted warehouse, we couldn't tell; the glass was so dirty. Never mind, it was better than the foc's'le floor, and it was free.

The one good thing was the food. It was excellent. Nicely cooked, and plentiful. There wasn't a lot of choice on the menu though because it was ordered from, and delivered by, a neighbouring restaurant. The Valley's kitchen was suffering from an 'operational dysfunction', so we were informed by the geriatric bell-boy as he served our meals, slopping most of them onto the worn carpet, en passant. 'In any case,' he warbled, 'we don't employ a cook.'

Donkey shared the 8pm to midnight 'watch-on-board' with me, taking it in turns to 'doss-down' in the foc's'le. It wasn't an arduous duty, just keeping an eye on the mooring lines and adjusting them as necessary. Nevertheless, we were pleased to return to the hotel. We gained access through the locked door by means of a key, issued by the 'management'. This was made necessary by the fact that the staff locked-up and went to bed at nine o'clock every night.

Getting undressed was like trying to do a Scottish sword-dance on a handkerchief, as we hopped and jostled each other in our well-appointed rabbit hutch. If we had had a brain between us we would have done it one at a time, but it was a giggle, and eventually we contrived to get our heads down, properly.

At nine in the morning, the trembling bell-boy knocked on our room door and entered, without waiting for an invite, bearing a tray laden with two cups of tea - half empty - and two helpings of eggs, bacon, sausages and beans, most of which was still on the plates. By ten we were back on board.

Flight was on deck sorting out the lines. Jock was down below playing with his pistons, or whatever engineers do. The skipper had been whisked away to the near-by RAF Station by car sent specially to collect him, and the other four were still snoring their heads off, in the hotel.

'Won't be doing much today lads,' said Flight, starting to put a new whipping on the end of a heaving line. 'Have a walk into town if you want, but be back by twelve.'

Donkey wasn't very interested; he had letters to write he said, so I decided I would stretch my legs with a walk around the harbour. Professional interest, I guess.

Skipper was returned to us, during the mid-afternoon, in a staff car driven by a really attractive Waaf who declined our pleading invitation to stop awhile.

'Must get straight back,' she said with a mind-reading smile, climbing back into her driving seat and pulling smoothly away as our illustrious officer lowered himself, very carefully, rung by rung, down onto his command. Two of us discreetly stood-by on deck, ready to offer a helping-hand, as he stepped on board and unsteadily weaved his way to his caboose, calling for the coxswain to join him. It was obvious he had been well entertained at the Station.

'Cor! She was a beauty,' observed Sparks, referring to the Waaf driver.

Donkey's doleful eyes focused on him. 'Dunno,' he answered. 'Only looked at her legs.'

'What did I miss?' queried Romeo, peevishly emerging from the foc's'le, his nose twitching like a ferret.

Me, being a happily married man and devoted husband, declined to comment.

'Fifteen two, fifteen four, and the rest won't score,' chanted Toby, moving his back-peg up four holes in front of the leading peg, on the crib board.

'I've got six in my hand, and a lousy two in the box,' I grumbled, throwing my cards down, face up, on the foc's'le table and moving my back-peg. I was still way behind.

Toby swept the cards together in a pile and began to shuffle them as Flight stuck his head in the doorway. 'Not too much noise, lads,' he ordered. 'Skipper's got his head down.' We shared a knowing look.

'Any news, Flight?' asked Toby, dealing the cards.

'Only that we will be leaving sometime in the morning,' was the reply, 'so don't get too pissed tonight.'

How could any of us do that? We didn't have enough money between us to warrant a smile from a bald headed, toothless prossie. We did however, have the courtesy to accept Flight's offer to buy us half-a-pint each before the others shuffled off to the dubious delights of 'The Valley' while Donkey and I 'retired' aboard for our 8 to midnight stint.

CHAPTER EIGHT

She was as still as a statue. Just standing there, as naked as the day she was born, but ten thousand times more sexually attractive. Her gorgeous face halo'ed by sleep-tousled hair, her lips slightly parted in an enigmatic smile. Slowly, my bleary eyes devoured her loveliness, downwards from the luscious, sensual lips to the twin mounds of full, firm breasts, surmounted by swollen nipples and supported (not that they needed support) by her cupped hands, as if offering them for my delectation.

Lower still, across the flatness of her stomach as yet unmarked by child-birth, to the small tuft of silken hair that covered the cleft of her womanhood between the pair of fabulous legs, slightly parted, that stood over me at the bed-side. My Laura, my love, my wife.

'Come back to bed darling,' I pleaded, my throat tight and husky. Jesus, I wanted her.

Her eyes sparkled as she lifted one foot and stretched her leg across me so that her knee pressed into the blanket, straddling me. 'I'm ready when you are my love,' she whispered, as I struggled to get my hands from under the covers, to touch her.

'Lofty, Lofty,' she cried, pressing her body down on me......Hey! wait a minute, something's wrong, my Laura never calls me Lofty!

'Wake up, Lofty.' I heard the voice again, this time it was gravely and masculine; not thick with passion.

I opened my eyes. Oh, Christ! No! The shadowy silhouette hovering over me was certainly not my Laura. Even in the darkness of the room I recognised the 'Brillo pad' hairstyle and Dumbo ears.

'Time to get up for breakfast,' said Sparks as he pulled the curtain aside, creating a shower of dust, and letting in what passed for an early March dawn in Anglesea. 'Not that we're goin' anywhere today,' he added contradictorily. 'It's blowin' a fortnight out there but Flight says to call you anyhow.'

The filth on the outside of the rattling window was streaked with wind-driven rain, like an old ladies varicose veins, framing a grey overcast sky interrupted by black lumps of scudding cloud, racing to nowhere.

'Wassa time?' I slurred, but he had already left the room leaving Donkey still sleeping and snoring blissfully. My arm was heavy as I lifted it over my face, twisting my wrist and trying to focus on the five quid Rolex wrist-watch, bought in Hong Kong a few years ago. Ten past seven; well near enough, give or take fifteen minutes. My ten-ton head dropped back on the pillow.

The door crashed open. 'Come on, you lazy sods,' yelled Sparks, pulling the bed clothes off me, Hednesford style. 'It's ten to eight and breakfast finishes at eight.'

I sat up with a start as the door slammed shut. Donkey was still covered up in his pit.......why me and not him?

'Come on Donkey, or we'll miss brekkers' I grumbled, shaking the lump that was presumably his shoulder, and grabbing my towel. The only response was a muffled fart that seemed to lift his blankets.

He was still huddled up - buried asphyxiatingly deep under the blanket - when I returned from the bathroom, and in no way was I going to pull the insulating covers off him. I made one last shouted effort 'Wake up, Donkey,' as I slammed the door on my way down to the breakfast room with one minute to spare.

An hour later, the four of us fought our way along the deserted quay-side, leaning into the Force Six wind, like Olympic ski-jumpers leaping off the high ramp. A lonely gull squawked angrily, took off vertically, then dropped back onto its take-off point like a big hop, unable to make headway. White-crested wave-lets scudded across the sheltered harbour, to die amid the windswept flotsam of wood, cork, a dead sea-bird, plastic bags and bottles, and other detritus floating in a surface scum of oil, trapped against the granite sea-wall like a maritime rubbish tip.

'Oh, to be at sea on a day like this', sang Sparks, miserably into the roll-neck of his jersey.

'Yea, on the bleedin' Queen Lizzie,' answered Romeo, ramming his beret down over his ears.

Sulkily, Donkey ignored them. He was hungry. His belly rumbling and gurgling as it digested the one pork sausage and slice of bread I had managed to smuggle up to the room for him.

Doc said nothing. Round-shouldered and hunched, he looked like a headless tailor's dummy in a shop window, advertising cold-weather clothing. His beret sat on top of the once-white 'Live and Die' surrounded like a rampart by the upturned collar of his great-coat. There was no sign of face or neck. He must have eye-holes in the top of his beret.

The boat was bumping heavily against the stone quay, crunching and squashing the fenders and ranging several feet backwards and forwards, straining at her mooring lines, as we clambered down the iron rungs of the stone quay, onto her jerking deck.

'Well, if it isn't the Seventh Cavalry', greeted Flight with his normal annoying jollity. 'What are you doing here?'

'We're on bleedin' 'oliday, ain't we,' muttered Donkey with equal sarcasm, pulling his chin out from his jersey.

Flight shook his head in wonderment at his valiant crew. 'Don't bother to go below' he said, 'we aren't going anywhere in this weather but the skipper wants to find a quieter berth, so stand-by fore and aft my hearties.' He pointed his head back into the wheel-house. 'All on board skipper,'

'Thanks Flight,' came the muffled reply from somewhere below. 'Start 'em up Corporal.'

'Radyenyerrskip.'

Our new berth was allocated by the Harbour Master; his choice influenced by St.Bogface the Patron Saint of pathetic Raff deck-hands. Not only was it alongside a sheltered pontoon that was secured to rise up and down with the tide, thereby doing away with the necessity of us having to tend our mooring lines all the time, it was also situated nearer the town, and within smelling distance of a Fish and Chip shop. In fact, the only drawback was that it was slightly farther away from The Valley Hotel. Perhaps, thought the optimists among us, we could persuade the skipper to find us nearer accommodation? Anywhere would be better than The Valley - wouldn't it? Unfortunately the choice was out of the skipper's hands, he told us. It had been arranged by higher authority. 'You can always eat at The Valley and sleep on board,' he said, tongue in cheek. We stayed at the hotel.

The bad weather continued for nearly a week and life was a doddle. With no tending of mooring lines to worry about, our four-hour duty watches changed to 'all-nighters'. The six of us erks were paired-off to do one-night-in-three on board, as ship-keepers. It was a sleeping duty made so comfortable by the new mattresses that, if anyone came aboard, we wouldn't have been any the wiser - providing they didn't start the engines. Had the IRA, or some enterprising boat chandler, paddled us away in the darkness we could have woken up in paradise.... No officer or NCO's. Of course, our officer and NCO's didn't have this worry. They had all-night-in, every night, at the Hotel. It was, they said, a privilege of rank, earned by their service time, brains and education. We six erks were not convinced. The one big draw-back, and our main cause for grumbling, was that we had to walk back to the Hotel for breakfast after a night duty, sometimes in very inclement weather. That we then had the rest of the day off didn't come into the equation. Life was a bind!

This 'time-off' was not such a good thing. There was nowhere to go and nothing to see. Being a poorly paid National Service conscript, and a married man to boot, I was always broke. The others weren't all that much better off. The town itself could be 'discovered' in ten minutes flat, and the local girls lost interest in us once the novelty of our uniforms wore off; and they learned our pockets were empty. So we spent most of our free time stretched out on our 'pits', mentally doing physical exercises to keep ourselves in the peak of condition, or maybe reading, or writing home. I did a good deal of the latter as I was becoming very concerned about Laura. My twice-weekly letters to her, increased to three. I wanted to reassure her of how much I loved and missed her. Since my last short week-end leave, her twice-weekly letters have become irregular, and now reduced to one. The love and passion in her words have disappeared, and they now seem luke-warm. When I asked why, she says she is working long hours, and always tired. I found that hard to accept as a reason. If that is the case she doesn't have to write long letters. A short loving note would be better than nothing. I am becoming increasingly worried. I know something is wrong. I dread opening her letters when they arrive in case it is a 'Dear John'. Has she stopped loving me? Is our marriage on the rocks for some unknown reason? I can't phone her, we don't have a phone. I can't get leave to see her, and even if I could I haven't the money for the fare. My mind is in turmoil. I try hard not to let my mates see that I am worried and depressed but, living in such close proximity as we do, they are all aware that I'm not my usual self. Even Flight has asked if anything is wrong, but of course I said there wasn't.

We spent several more weeks of idleness alongside the pontoon waiting for something to happen, before something did.

Except for the skipper, who was in his own caboose, we were all sat in the foc's'le and wheel-house drinking tea and having a mid-morning break from doing nothing, when we heard a hail from outside.... 'Hello, thirty eight forty, anybody onboard?'

Being in the wheel-house, and nearest the door, I poked my head out and looked up to see an immaculately dressed RAF Corporal standing on the quay-side peering down at us from under the highly polished peak of his cap. 'Yes Corp? What can I do for you?'

The impeccable NCO (who we later learned was personal driver to the local RAF Station's Commanding Officer) regarded the bare-headed erk standing on the launch's deck, wearing tatty trousers and a greyish-white jersey, with disdain.

'Is Flight Lieutenant Harrison on board?' he snapped, arrogantly and without recourse to a common 'please'.

'Who wants him?' I answered innocently. Two could play at being awkward.

'Okay, Highman,' smiled the skipper, emerging on deck having heard the request. 'That's enough.' He tilted his head up to see the obviously peeved NCO. 'I am Harrison. What is it that you want Corporal?'

The Corporal snapped to attention with a smart and totally unnecessary salute that the skipper acknowledged with a nod of his bare head. 'Group Captain requests your attendance at the Station straight away, Sir. I have a car.'

'Blast,' cursed the skipper, under his breath, then called back, 'I will be with you in five minutes,' as he ducked back into his caboose saying, 'Ask him if he wants a cup of tea while he is waiting, Highman.'

It was cold and breezy, and a sleety drizzle was starting to fall. Most unpleasant. Not the weather to be standing about on an exposed quay-side. Without a word to anyone I went below to my hot cup of tea. Vengeance is sweet. I hadn't forgotten the Hednesford D.I.'s.

'What's the panic, Lofty?' asked Flight, who had probably heard all of what had been said.

I looked over the top of my mug, through the rising steam. 'Dunno, Flight. The brass wants the skipper, and sent a driver for him.'

A smile creased the Flight's face almost closing his eyes. He didn't care much for bull-shit types either. 'You're a rotten bastard Lofty. Do you know that?'

It was late afternoon when the skipper returned in the staff car driven by the same scowling, stiff-backed Corporal. He was perfectly sober this time, and wearing a satisfied smile on his face, as he called for Flight to join him in his caboose. Speculation in the foc's'le was rife, ranging from taking Royalty round Liverpool Bay on a jolly, to target-towing for aircraft on firing and bombing exercises.

The smug look on Flight's face, when he returned to the foc's'le, told us nothing. Neither did he. We would be sailing at 7am the next morning and be told our mission soon after, was all he would say, as he went ashore to our Hotel, to arrange for early calls and breakfast in the morning.

Our engines burst into life with their customary explosions and cloud of blue-black exhaust fumes, shattering the early morning tranquillity of the quiet harbour and waking every bird and human within earshot. A strong Sou'easterly breeze whistled through the rigging and fluttered the RAF ensign flying from our gaff. A solitary, duffel-coated rigger from the Harbour Master's staff, no doubt cursing the stupidity of such an early morning departure and the inconsideration of his boss, stood disinterested and unneeded on the pontoon as we slipped our lines and growled slowly out to meet the rolling waves of the inhospitable Irish Sea.

When we were clear of the harbour breakwater, Toby, Romeo and myself were summonsed to the wheel-house to join the skipper and Flight. A glance at the compass told me our course was just West of North that I estimated, would take us to the West of the Isle of Man. Were we going to attack the IRA with our new boat-hook?

'Sorry for the mystery chaps,' began the skipper, leaning cross-armed on the chart locker, 'but I've not been permitted to say anything before, for security reasons.' A lumpy sea caught us on the port quarter and the lurch made him put a hand out to steady himself. 'It's nothing very exciting I'm afraid - unless anything goes wrong. A very senior member of the Royal family is flying over to Belfast this morning, and our job is to provide crash cover between the Isle of Man and the coast of Northern Ireland.'   He looked out of the wheel-house window at the waves building-up under our stern. 'Unfortunately, we have to stay out on station all day because the Royal is flying back home at tea-time, and we can't leave the area until the aircraft is well and truly past our position and back over England. Obviously it's not going to be a very pleasant day, but let's hope nothing goes wrong so that we can get back into harbour before nightfall.' He turned his head for another look out of the window. 'I'm sure you'll be pleased to hear that we are not required to punch our way back to Holyhead against that lot.' He nodded his forehead in the direction of the white-crested waves keeping pace with us. 'We're going to run north to a place named Stranraer where we will stay, at least overnight, and refuel. I don't know how long our stay there will be, but if I can get a guarantee of at least four days you can tell Rigg and Corporal Thorpe I'll do my best to get them a few days leave. Thank you chaps,' he said, by way of a dismissal. 'Please tell the others.'

By ten o'clock we were 'on station' and spent the rest of the day rolling our guts out at dead-slow speed, maintaining our position. When we were steering north, we cork-screwed like a drunken camel with a 15 inch gun barrel up its backside, as the curling green waves washed beneath us. When we turned south, we crashed and pounded head-long into sea after sea, continuously; the whole boat shuddering and jarring. Going east or west, we rolled like a pig's orphan in a beam sea; forty-five degrees either side, over an arc of ninety degrees, our mast clawing circles across the leaden sky.   Standing was almost impossible, and we were seriously uncomfortable. Any movement we made invited knocks and bruises as we were flung about like rag dolls. Half-hour stints, braced in the wheel-house as helmsman/lookout, were as much as a man's aching muscles could stand. Everyone else wedged themselves in a sitting or lying position, wherever space could be found and, with the sole exception of Flight, we all suffered horrendously from 'unseamanlike innards'. The lurching, crashing, and merciless rolling went on endlessly. It was like sitting on a wild Mustang with a thistle under its saddle. HSL's weren't built for this sort of weather. Neither were their crews.

We sat, or lay, in a semi-coma, dreading the thought of standing our 'trick' on the wheel. All we wanted, all we prayed for, was the chance to sit under a tree somewhere, or be left to die peacefully and quickly. Little did Royalty know, or care, of the suffering their little holiday jaunt caused. In my next life I vowed to come back as a rampant revolutionary and behead the lot of them.

At first, we listened to the cheeping of Morse-code from the wireless-room, longing for each message to be our recall but, as time passed, we even lost interest in that. We were lost souls, doomed to die by the unrelenting hand of Mother Nature. Our paper sick-bags were full and overflowing. The nauseous smell of vomit hung like a wet cloak. Please God, let us die.

Flight twitched in an uneasy sleep.

Two or three years later - actually a little after five o'clock that same afternoon - a gaunt, pasty-faced Sparks fell out of his box-like wireless shack, onto the wheel-house deck. 'Recall, Flight' he groaned, and choked on a mouthful of bile.

Like zombies, we each discovered a spark of life deep down inside as we heard those two wonderful words, and dragged ourselves back into the living world. Flight took over the helm and turned our battered bow around onto a northerly course, increasing the engine revs until the boat settled into a comparatively steady swooping motion, running before the grey-green hills of the rolling seas, streaked dirty-white as the wind whipped off their foaming crests. His feet braced wide apart, and with a grim look of determination on his craggy face, he expertly juggled helm and engine speed to give us the safest and most comfortable ride possible in such conditions. One minute we would be surfing down the front of a wave, like a charging rhino, nose-down, stern-up, his experience eyes watching carefully for signs of a broach-to, as he reduced revs to allow the boiling white-caps to surge past. Then increasing speed again as the stern dropped into the following trough, seemingly bringing us to an abrupt stop suspended on the back of the wave, bows pointing skyward, until the next sea lifted the stern up onto its advancing face when the revs would be again reduced to prevent pitch-poling, stern over bow (or in the officer's vernacular - base over apex).

Sheepishly, one by one over the next hour, the rest of us emerged, delicately, from our individual 'chapel of rest,' like debilitated ghosts suffering the chronic plague. At least I was one of the first to recover, and my guilty apology was brushed aside by the indomitable Flight. 'Don't worry lad. You aren't used to small-boat motion.'

My offer to relieve him at the wheel was thankfully declined. No way was he going to trust his boat to anyone in this weather. 'Make a brew if you like' he suggested.

I shuddered at the thought of going back into the vomit smelling foc's'le. 'Shall I leave it a while, until the others recover?' I pleaded, hopefully. He nodded understandingly.

Two hours later - all hands restored to what passed for normality, though still looking haggard and cadaverously pallid - the low-lying coast of Galloway appeared gloomily on our starboard side in the gathering darkness. Shore lights flickered like Morse-code signals as we rose and fell, and they became briefly obscured by the passing wave-tops.

The skipper had been really ill, and had welcomed my offer to help with the navigation. 'Be my guest' he said, waving a weak hand at the small chart-table. So, I was quite chuffed (and not a little surprised) when we raised the Port Patrick light almost exactly where and when expected.

Another half an hour saw us rounding Corsewell Point, coming under the sheltering lee of the land. Then past Milleur Point, to turn South into the relatively calm waters of Loch Ryan, on the last few miles of our voyage to Stranraer, and the end of a bloody awful day.

Moored safely and securely to a solid, unmoving jetty, we thanked God for not granting our earlier death-wish, and loyally hoped the Royal had enjoyed his, or her, day's outing in the knowledge that, had they crashed into the sea, a rescue launch of the Royal Air Force with its paralysed and comatose crew of brave, superb seamen, would probably, and uncaringly, have ignored their plight.

CHAPTER NINE

Laura sat in miserable solitude, propped up by pillows on her bed, staring at the thick brocade curtains that blocked out her view of the dark outside world. Footsteps of passing pedestrians, and the occasional clopping of a weary horse dragging a heavily laden cart to the scrap-yard in the next street, went unheeded and unrecorded, in her mind.

Vehicles rumbled past, rattling the loose-fitting sash-windows, and gusts of March evening wind whistled through every minute gap left in the draught-excluding newspaper rammed hard between the frames, causing the heavy curtain to shimmy like an exhausted Egyptian belly-dancer, and the plastic-shaded ceiling light to swing and turn, imperceptibly.

Jim's recent letters were strewn across the bed covers, having been read again and again. Tears from her wet eyes, squeezed out from between closed lids, trickled down her cheeks to drip onto the night-dress tucked under her chin.

Sobbing quietly, utter misery and despair filled her heart. If only her Jim were here, to comfort and guide her in dealing with the present situation. She didn't know how to cope - or what to do. All because of that creep TOM. God; how she hated that man.

Ever since Jim's last weekend leave, things at the shop had gone from harmless 'accidents' to open harassment. Stupidly, she had told Tom of her efforts to save every penny possible towards a deposit for a house, or flat, for when Jim finished his National Service. Life with Mum was fine while Jim was away - in fact they were company for each other, and had been since Dad died three years ago - but when he was home there was no privacy, no space. Only one small room to call their own despite all of Mum's efforts to be as unobtrusive as possible. It was as though they were a courting couple doing something naughty in the front-room while the parents were upstairs. They could never totally relax and let themselves go. But they did try!

Telling Tom of her house-dream had been a terrible mistake. Overnight, he changed from being a sweet, harmless man. He started giving her small presents, like chocolates and flowers. Each weekly wage-packet would contain an extra shilling or two, most welcome. Frequently, he would say, in a friendly manner, how much she meant to him, how he enjoyed her working there. Then, one day when the shop was empty, he pulled her into the small stock-room behind the counter. The smell of whisky on his breath told her he had drunk some 'Dutch courage'. He took hold of her arm and said that the five-pounds Christmas bonus he had given her could be just a starter, one of many, if she would be nice to him. She was shocked and frightened. He was a Salvation Army Officer, and a Lay-preacher at the Church; A respected figure in the community. He couldn't, he mustn't, act like this. She tried to laugh it off, saying he was drunk, and telling him to stop larking about.

Serious faced, he pulled her against him and she just managed to get her arms and elbows between them. She could feel his heart pounding in his chest. He was becoming excited.

'Sleep with me,' he asked hoarsely, 'and I will give you the house deposit money you want.'

'NO,' she cried angrily, trying to struggle from his grip. 'NEVER.' But he was strong and held her tighter, pressing himself into her.

'You know you don't mean.........' he began, but stopped when the clanging bell over the shop front-door announced the arrival of a customer. He jumped back away from her, took a second or two to compose himself, and then went out to deal with the shopper. She was literally saved by the bell. That customer was followed by another and it was several minutes before he returned to the stock-room to find her sitting on a box, trembling and crying. He took hold of her shoulders and gently lifted her to her feet, trying to put his arms around her, but she shrugged him away.

'Please, please, forgive me Laura,' he begged. 'I don't know what came over me. Please, I'll never do it again. Please don't leave?' He sounded so contrite, so apologetic, so ashamed, but she was too shocked to respond and just stood there, sobbing. 'You stay in here for a while and come out when you are ready luv,' he said, 'but whatever you do, please don't go. I promise it will never happen again. Put it down to an old man's stupidity.' He smiled guiltily as he tenderly sat her back on the box, and went outside.

Ten minutes passed, twenty minutes, half-an-hour. She couldn't go out and face him. She felt cheap and ashamed, as if it were her fault. Had she led him on? .....encouraged him?

Eventually he came back in, carrying a cup of tea for her. 'I can't tell you how sorry I am Laura,' he apologised. 'I am ashamed of myself. Can we make a new start and put it behind us?'

Laura had already considered her options and made up her mind to leave, but he sounded so sincere, so full of remorse, and he *was* a Church-man. She could put it down to a momentary, one-off, aberration, she supposed. And she needed the job. 'Okay' she sniffled, 'but please, never let it happen again.'

He smiled, gratefully, and led her out into the shop where the clanging bell announced another customer.

Three times that evening she started letters to Jim, wanting to pour out her heart, to explain what had happened. She knew he would understand, but would probably insist she left the job. Knowing him, he would most likely hitch a lift down from wherever he was and get himself into trouble with the RAF, just to sort Tom out. She didn't want that. Basically, Tom was okay and she thought she could handle him if he started again. Besides, she liked the job, and needed the money.

She threw the unfinished letters onto the fire, watching them turn brown and curly then burst into flames, odd scraps floating up the chimney. No way could she bring herself to tell him. It would worry him to death.

Tom's promise held good.......for almost a week. Then the bum-touching started again, and each time she would turn to give him a withering look as he held up his hands, palms towards her, apologising with a smile, almost making it a game. She wasn't smiling.

Laura looked down at Jim's letters spread beside her, and was filled with pain and sadness. He wrote that he was worried something was wrong between them and was hurting, badly. She wanted to ease his fears and heart-ache, but how could she explain her feeling of guilt, as if she had been unfaithful to him? How does one put such thoughts into words? So, she took the cowardly way out, and said nothing. Not even how much she still loved him and wanted him.

Her thoughts drifted to his Christmas leave and those few precious moments of his last week-end with her. She tingled at the memory of the hours of love-making, the feeling of him inside her, and the wonder of laying in each others arms afterwards. Fulfilled and exhausted.....until the next time. Her hands drifted down over her stomach, undoing the buttons of her dress and sliding inside but, at that moment, the grinding and rattling of what sounded like a tank passing on the road outside, brought her back to reality. Her dream was broken.

Resting her head back onto the pillow, with damp eyes closed, she wondered where her man was. His last letter, so full of love and concern, was from somewhere in North Wales, but he was expecting to move on again soon, even though he didn't know where to. What was he doing at that very minute? Was he rolling about at sea on his boat, or tucked up in what he laughingly described as his 'pit'. As long as he wasn't womanising somewhere, she thought, with a twinge of jealous concern, knowing full well that was the most unlikely thing on earth.

The one place she wanted him to be was right here, with her. Why couldn't she shed her guilt? If only she had the ability to put her thoughts into words, as he did, she could tell him how much she longed for the feel of his touch, and his body against hers. She could happily give herself to him for ever and ever, but the thought of another man touching her......Ugh!

'You coming out for a cup of cocoa, Laura?' called her Mum, tapping lightly on the door. 'It's poured out ready.'

****

Tom sensed it was the early hours of the morning. It was still pitch dark in the heavily curtained bed-room of his suburban bungalow in the quiet fringes of the City. Beside him, his wife snored in a deep sleep, as she always did when lying on her back. Normally, he would give her an elbowing nudge and she would obediently turn over on her side. Her snoring would stop long enough to enable him to get back to sleep. Tonight was different. Her snoring didn't even register as his eyes swept unseeingly across the black ceiling like twin unlit search-lights. He was afraid. Scared stiff. His years of heavy smoking were at last catching up on him and the very thought of dying started his heart thumping and fluttering. He must make an appointment to see his doctor. He kept putting it off and putting it off, fearful of what he may be told. He didn't need a medical degree to know something was very wrong. Even the slightest exertion made him breathless, and mucus gurgled in his throat and chest like a Turkish hubble-bubble pipe - but it wasn't funny, not to him. He was too young to die. He had so much to live for and one of those things was Laura. The very thought of her made his heart palpitate and, despite his health worries, he began to get an erection. She was so attractive, so desirable, so exciting. He knew he had made a bad error of judgement before, touching her at the wrong time, and being half-drunk, but never let it be said he didn't learn from his mistakes. Next time he would choose the moment, and stay sober. He was sure she felt an interest, just teasing him with pretence denial. She was a healthy young woman who had acquired a taste for sex. Of course she wanted a man, only natural being left on her own after just a few months of marriage, and he was available; more than could be said for her pillock of a husband. He knew she was keen to be touched and wanted, but didn't want to appear too obvious. She was playing hard to get, and he knew how to play that game. After all, he told himself, he was still fairly young, reasonably healthy, with a good body, and knew how to please a woman. There was nothing unnatural, or ungodly, about wanting a woman. Our Lord said 'Go forth and multiply', although, perhaps, he didn't mean with another man's wife he thought, conveniently forgetting the other deadly sins. It was nobody else's business what two consenting adults did. He wanted Laura and he felt sure she wanted him. So, what the heck! It was a matter of choosing the right time to make his approach, when she would be receptive. He could bide his time.

A snorting grunt and slapping of lips, coming from his wife, disturbed his thoughts as she turned over onto her side, away from him, unconsciously farting against his bare thigh.
'Jesus Christ!' he blasphemed like a true Christian. 'It's enough to turn you off women for life, and take up sheep farming.' His thoughts returned to the concern for his health as he tucked the bed-covers tightly under his chin and kicked an opening of the blankets at the side of the bed to release the foul smell. At this rate he'd die of gas poisoning before anything else finished him off.

CHAPTER TEN

We never got to see much of Stranraer. It looked a nice place, good enough for a much needed run-ashore, but so near yet so far. All we saw of it was the quay-side and a small café in the High Street. Except that is, for Doc and Sparks who were despatched into town with a shopping list, compiled by the skipper and Flight to keep us victualled until the powers-that-be decided our next move.

The few hundred yards into town must have been a long, long way, because it was two hours later when our two 'shoppers' returned, laden with plastic bags containing, among other things, the bread and milk we had all been waiting for.

'Get lost?' asked Toby, twisting his mouth in annoyance. The rest of us tried hard to cheerfully welcome their delayed return, but we obviously failed, as did their sense of humour. The prats threw a 'wobbly' and went into a sulk, so we volunteered them to toast the bread.

Meanwhile, the skipper had been ashore, presumably to telephone, (there was nowhere else to go). He returned just as the two 'toasters' started their own slices, having done two for everyone else.

'Right lads,' he announced. 'All ashore for breakfast.'

The two disgruntled 'toasters' threw down their warm bread and managed a dirty look and curled lip between them.

'I'll stay on board, Flight' the skipper continued. 'You take them up to the 'Lowland Café' in the main street.' He handed the NCO a few bank-notes. 'It's all arranged. And mind you bring me a receipt.'

We all stood up; hungrily munching our toast, except of course the two volunteer 'toasters' who had given in, gracelessly.

'Any idea what's 'appenin' to us Sir?' asked Toby as we shuffled crab-wise past the mess-table.

The skipper pulled out a Persil-white handkerchief and wiped his nose. 'I'll tell you the details after you have eaten but basically, weather permitting, we're off to Campbeltown where we will be staying for a week at least, and a few days leave has been authorised for Corporal Thorpe and LAC.Rigg, if they want it.' He raised his eyebrows in their direction and was answered by a whoop from

Donkey and a spitting 'Ach-wheel,' from Jock. 'The two of you can get away from here this morning, before we sail, providing SAC.Jugg is happy to take us over to Campbeltown on his own?'

A big grin split Toby's face from ear to ear. Chief Engineer at last, albeit acting, temporary and unpaid. 'Fine by me, skip.'

The 'Lowland Café' was typical of most that catered for the early morning worker. Outside, its sign hung askew from a rusty bracket. Paint peeled tiredly from the weather-worn door and window frame. A moss-covered stain ran down the external wall from eaves to ground-level, warning of a major leak in the cast-iron guttering, and on the pavement an advertising sandwich-board stood, as though abandoned by its carrier, telling passers-by that the house speciality was ALL DAY BREAKFASTS.

Inside was a warm haven of bare tables and wooden chairs, concealed from the outside by steam-fogged windows resting on sills puddled with condensation. Behind a counter laden with glass-covered cakes, buns and sandwiches, Ben Darren - a former chef on passenger liners - stood bent over a four-ringed gas stove. His balding head shimmering in a cloud of steam and fumes, as he tended the four huge, sizzling frying-pans containing the eggs, bacon, sausages, baked beans, tomatoes and fried bread, ordered by this bonanza of eight starving airmen, who sat waiting patiently, drooling over the aromatic smells wafting around their heads like a fragrant cloud.

'I'm bleedin' famished,' dribbled Sparks, eagerly holding knife and fork upright in his fists on the table.

Ben's wife, a middle-aged, overweight and overworked lady, came from behind the counter bearing a tray. 'Five teas and three coffees,' she declared. 'Who's for what?' Hands shot in the air as she distributed the big china mugs.

'Ah. Nectar!' said Doc, appreciatively cupping his between his hands, and sipping cautiously.

Donkey looked up at him, queryingly, not knowing what nectar is. 'Mine's coffee,' he stated, sniffing at the circling bubbles.

Within minutes, a big plate-full of fried breakfast, was put in front of each of us by the temporarily harassed Mrs. Darren. For a brief moment we stared approvingly at the delicious meal, savouring every second of anticipation, then, as though at a given signal, plunged in like starving wolves. Silence reigned except for the clatter of knives and forks. Mr and Mrs. Darren watched in amazement.

'Them boys was 'ungry luv,' said Ben, mentally counting his unexpected profit.

The wind had dropped to an almost gentle breeze by late morning. Still cool enough to warrant wearing a jersey, but a vast improvement on yesterday's gale. A watery sun tried hard to break through the veil of cloud as I sat alone on the fore-deck in utter misery, watching Jock and Donkey stride jauntily away along the quay, clutching their travel warrants and small attache cases, heading for the railway station and four days leave. God; how I envied them. If only I could get away home to sort out the problem between Laura and me. If only I knew what the problem is. If only! Her last letter, a week ago, was quite short. Only two pages saying she was well and still working hard. There were no loving endearments, no explanations, and no answers to my concerned questions. Nothing; It was almost as bad as a 'Dear John'. At least then I'd know what was what. Not knowing was the awful thing. Had she met someone else? Why doesn't she tell me?

Romeo stepped out of the wheel-house and walked forward to join me; 'No letter yet Lofty?' he asked, sympathetically.

I shook my head, not wanting to speak, not knowing what to say. He sat with me for several minutes, then guessing my need for solitude, placed his hand on my shoulder and squeezed gently, as he stood up.

'It'll work out okay mate, believe me,' he said, turning back aft to the wheel-house where Flight had stuck his head out of the window.

'Stand-by, fore and aft,' came the command.

Grateful for something to do, I got to my feet. Romeo turned around and came forward again, giving me a tight-lipped smile. His station was on the fore-deck. Mine was aft.

'Stand-by engines,' yelled Flight down the engine-room hatch where Toby was revelling in his unsupervised role.

'Ready when you are, Flight Sergeant,' came the answer, in a clear, very precise English voice.

'Ha, bloody Ha,' replied Flight, 'very funny.'

The skipper, standing alongside his coxswain, allowed himself a slight smile. They were a good crowd. 'Okay Flight, let's go.'

There were no letters waiting for me at Campbeltown. Skipper had gone ashore and returned with a hand-full, but none for me. My misery was turning to anger, anger to bitterness. I hadn't had a letter for over two weeks now. Hadn't had a loving one for months. I am now convinced that, for some unknown reason, I have lost her. Why, I don't know, and she won't tell me. I'll not write to her anymore. If that's the way she wants it to be, so be it. I've suffered too much pain, too much heart-ache, over the last few months. It was almost a relief to make such a decision. Until I hear from her with an acceptable reason for being the way she is, I will try to put her out of my mind, out of my heart. How could she deliberately cause me this much grief? She can't love me.

Obviously sensing my depressed mood, Doc, Sparks and Romeo, insisted I join them for a run-ashore that evening.

'I'm broke,' I said as an excuse. I wanted to be left alone to wallow in my self-pity.

'Bollocks,' said Sparks.

'Come on boyo,' sang Romeo. 'We've got plenty.'

Doc practically hauled me to my feet. 'Yea. Get your finger out Lofty; we're wasting good boozin' time.'

Truly reluctant, I gave in. What the hell. Little did I know at that time, that everyone, including the skipper and Flight, had put their hand in their pocket to make a 'kitty' - to take that miserable bastard Lofty ashore and get him pissed.

After the first three or four pints - or was it five or six - I don't remember much about that night-out. I vaguely recall wondering how the other three were managing to stay so sober, whereas I was out of my skull.

Apparently, according to all reports, I behaved abominably. Sang rude words to popular songs, spewed my guts up in the toilets of a pub, and became too friendly with a girl who became offended at first, until my sober mates explained the situation to her, whereupon she became nice and friendly. Understandably, her niceness didn't extend to accepting my invitation to come back aboard or - alternatively - slipping round to the back-yard of the pub for a few minutes. Had she done so she wouldn't have come to any harm. It was said that I could hardly stand.

I had again been saved by my valiant comrades when they explained to a six-foot-three-inch man-mountain that I didn't mean to call him a

'Cowardly Scotch Git' for refusing to step outside with me. And, they apologised to the publican, his customers, and the lady I was holding at the time, when I called for complete silence - then farted loudly.

When I awoke the next morning, it was already late afternoon, and I was tucked up snugly in the fo'c'sle where the others had left me to sleep on, and on, and on, in peace. Alongside my pounding head, stood an empty bucket labelled *Don't piss on the fo'c'sle deck* in large letters so that my unfocused and nomadic eyeballs would get the message.

Nature urged me into consciousness, and I was standing in my crumpled uniform over the bucket, desperately trying to cause an overflow, when Flight entered.

'Ah! Rip Van Winkle has surfaced,' he whispered in a thunderous voice that roared around the inside of my head, putting my brain into bass-drum mode. 'How's the terror of Campbeltown?'

'Piss off, Flight,' said my furry tongue in answer to an uncontrolled signal from my thumping head.

'Empty that, <u>when</u> you're finished,' he said, emphasising the 'when' and nodding towards the steaming bucket. 'Then the skipper wants to see you……. at your convenience of course,' he added sarcastically, with a sadistic smile.

It wasn't easy. My legs were very unsupportive and the bits in the middle - my knees - were wobbly. The sledge-hammering men inside my swollen and fragile head refused to take a break and the brimming bucket was heavy as I got it out on deck, with very little spillage inboard, and emptied its costly contents into the undeserving waters of the harbour, thereby ruining the fish-stock for the next few years.

Blurred faces, smiling secret memories, came and went. Someone thrust a mug of black coffee into my hand as I knocked on the metal door of the skipper's caboose, uncaring about my expected rocket. The door opened and two faces, shimmering like a desert mirage, wavered across my throbbing eyeballs. I wished the blasted boat would keep still.

It lurched, and I thrust a hand out against the bulkhead to save myself a stumble… and missed. The skipper's hands reached out and held me firmly by the shoulders.

'Come in, Highman,' he yelled through an invisible loud-speaker. 'Sit yourself down.' I fell onto the small chair reserved for unwelcome visitors, wishing I could sit my head somewhere too. His two faces merged, momentarily, and his voice dropped half a decibel to a quiet bellow. He was looking at me like an optician doing an eye-test.

'Feeling rough, are we?'

Even my befuddled brain worked out that my condition was nothing to do with <u>we</u>, as I fought to control my leaden optical orbs from wandering around my skull.

'Yes, of course <u>we</u> are feeling rough, you stupid bloody Rupert,' answered my inimical brain; but fortunately for my future well-being, the words that came out were 'Just a bit, Sir.'

I couldn't discern the look on his face through the pounding, blood-red haze that curtained my eyes, but his voice sounded friendly enough; though far too loud. Perhaps he wasn't going to put me on a charge after all?

'You've had all day to recover from last night's binge Highman, and your mates have covered for you in your er - absence,' he began censoriously. 'But it is time to get your finger out and lend a hand. We are moving into accommodation ashore, as we did at Holyhead, so there are things to do. Flight will get you organised. Off you go.'

I stood up from the chair, carefully and gradually, like an octogenarian, taking my weight on hands planted firmly on the edge of his desk, willing my head to follow, as I groped for the non-existing Zimmer frame.

'Thank you, skip.' I grunted, for some obscure reason, as I turned away, missing his amused and unsympathetic grin.

Work and fresh air are guaranteed cures for a hangover, so they say. Wrong! It didn't cure mine.

I was grateful that most of the work had already been done. They were gee-ing me up. Flight said he wanted me to carry the anchor up to the new 'digs' - in case it got stolen. It took ten minutes for it to register as a wind-up.

Time is a great healer, is another wise saying. Bollocks! Two hours later and my head was still suffering an artillery barrage. All I wanted, prayed for, was to lay my head on a pillow, for ever. I certainly wouldn't be going out that night.

Our new accommodation was a former hotel on the sea-front that had been requisitioned, during the war, as an R & R centre for personnel from the near-by Naval Air Station at Machrihanish, and others stationed in Campbeltown itself. Now, a decade later, its twenty bedrooms (nearly always empty) were the responsibility of two desolate looking ex-Navy pensioners who (hoping they'd been forgotten) waited daily for the closing axe to fall. They offered a 'no-frills' service that, in fact, meant no service at all. Our stay was on a B and NBB basis... Bed and no bloody breakfast.

Its dilapidated frontage; exacerbated by the two newly-painted neighbouring private hotels that thrived on pleasure-seeking Glaswegians from across the water, highlighted a total lack of care and maintenance. Over the main entrance, the hotel's name, that had been artistically sign-written back in the nineteen thirties, was almost obliterated by flaking paint-work. Not that it mattered. The 'MONKES PARADISE HOTEL' had long since become universally known as THE NUNNERY by generations of irreverent servicemen. At least the bedrooms were bigger and better than those in THE VALLEY HOTEL at Holyhead. I shared a large twin-bedded room with Romeo that was luxurious by comparison. Okay, the carpets were a bit thread-bare but the beds were spacious, comfortable and clean. And the bathroom was on the same floor!

We even had a beautiful view out over Campbeltown Loch, once we had cleaned the sea-gull crap from the outside of the window and carefully pulled the off-white, crumbling lace-curtains to one side.

I was to spend many a peaceful hour watching the shipping movements in and out of the harbour. The fishing boats, the regular ferries, and once saw the local life-boat shoulder its way out to sea - whether on service or exercise I didn't know. But it was a brave sight, and I for one, am a great admirer of those courageous blokes.

We were victualled at a small café conveniently situated roughly half-way between the boat and the NUNNERY. It was run by two homosexuals who - they said - once worked for Royalty in the Palace of Holyrood House. When our initial, natural, wariness had been overcome, we found them genial hosts who accepted our rough service-style humour with good grace. Their cooking wasn't as Cordon-bleu as the meals-on-wheels we enjoyed at Holyhead but it was good, wholesome and plentiful. Spotted Dick was always referred to as 'suet pudding' to avoid offending their sensitivity and we refrained from making ribald jokes and comments about women and their anatomy, in their hearing. I don't know why. It wasn't arranged that way. It seemed a natural courtesy.

They did get a bit miffed once when they learned we had nick-named their place as 'The cash and carry'. They had named it after their own Christian names, 'THE CHASANDGARRY CAFÉ', and took their revenge by calling us 'The Braindead Brylcream Boys'.

CHAPTER ELEVEN

Laura's mind was in guilty turmoil. She felt like running away to somewhere - anywhere. She wanted to be alone, to think; yet she also longed for a shoulder to cry on; someone to whom she could tell her troubles. Someone who would listen, and advise her what she should do; someone like Jim. Every day for the last week, Tom had been his obnoxious, lecherous self; making sexual innuendo's in a joking, smiling manner. It made her sick, and she hated him.

She looked around the darkened bed-sit room as if seeking answers, or solace, from the flowered wall-paper. Only yesterday, Tom mentioned he'd received a buy-out offer for the shop, from a large grocery chain, that he and his wife were considering accepting. The thought crossed Laura's mind that, maybe, this might be the answer to at least one of her problems, so decided to tolerate Tom's actions, for the sake of her job among other things. Providing he went no further she would grit her teeth and bear it; and see what happened.

That morning, things went from bad to worse. At the first quiet opportunity, Tom not only touched her bum but also squeezed it. She shouted at him to stop, but he laughed in her face. Later, he tried to put his hand up her skirt and she had slapped his face, hard.

'You bitch,' he said lividly. 'One day I'm going to have you.'

'Never,' she answered angrily, 'That day will never come.'

'It will,' he snarled back, almost fighting for breath, 'or I'll sack you and tell everyone what a sex-mad little whore you are. And that will include your precious bloody Jimmy.'

She was stunned; confused. "But you're the sex-mad one. It's <u>you</u> who is molesting me!"

He looked at her, mockingly, spitting as he spoke, saliva drooling from the corner of his mouth. "And who do you think will take your word against mine? I'm a respected, church-going citizen. You're nothing but a cheap slut."

His words hit her like a lead truncheon. How could he say such things? None of it was true. Yet, deep-down, she knew that what he had said would happen, was right. No one would believe her word against his.

'Your wife will believe me,' she cried, desperately clutching at straws, and ran into the stock-room as the door-bell clanged to admit an old lady with a wicker shopping-basket in the crook of her arm.

It was some ten or fifteen minutes later when he opened the stock-room door and Laura was quite alarmed to see his flushed face, and hear his laboured breathing. He looked at her, holding his chest.

'I don't feel well,' he gasped. 'I'm going upstairs to lie down for a bit. You look after the shop, and if I hear anymore from you about telling my wife, or giving in your notice, I will make your life hell around here, and make sure you never get another job.'

He staggered, like a drunk, to the door leading up to the flat above the shop that he and his wife used occasionally during the working week, and climbed the stairs as if he were wearing diver's boots.

Within minutes, Mabel - his wife - stumbled down, heading for the shop's phone. "I'm calling an ambulance" she hooted, her voice full of concern and distress. "He's not at all well!"

The ambulance drew-up outside the shop, attracting a crowd of inquisitive people who stared morbidly as the two ambulance-men carried Tom awkwardly down the steep stairway, strapped and blanketed on a stretcher.

'Is he dead?' asked somebody almost hopefully, stretching to see between the heads in front.

'Na. They ain't covered 'is face,' replied an anonymous voice of experience.

Laura felt sick with guilt as they lifted Tom into the back of the ambulance, closely followed by his tearful wife. Had I caused this? She asked herself. Was it my fault?

With a short, strident ring of its bell, the ambulance pulled away; the crowd reluctantly parting to allow it through. Laura returned into the shop that suddenly filled with customers intent on buying anything of little value, just so that they could ask the question burning in their heads. Laura told them all, she had no idea what had happened. Consequently, the district soon buzzed with speculation. Tom had had a heart-attack. Tom had fallen down the stairs and broke his back. Tom had food-poisoning from his own stock. Tom was drunk. One wildly imaginative rumour suggested he had collapsed with exhaustion during a passionate sex-session. Others, who knew Mabel, found this hard to believe. One or two sceptics wondered if she had been the one involved!

That night was a sleepless one for Laura, or so she thought. She tossed and turned, hour after hour, her brain full of questions without answers, problems without solutions. Despite her abhorrence of Tom she still felt concern. How was he? What was happening to him? It even crossed her mind to wonder if he was still alive. She felt ashamed and evil, having often wished him dead because of his behaviour to her, but that was only a figure of speech. She hadn't really meant it!....Had she?

Then there was the shop, and her job. How would she manage on her own? Would Mabel expect her to do that? Would Mabel help, or allow her to take on a temporary assistant? And what about the offer from the chain of grocers? Would they buy the shop? Tom would almost certainly sell now, because of his health - and where would that leave her? Still employed, or jobless?

All of a sudden she realised, with a shock, that the one person she hadn't given any thought to, was Jim. It was as though she had deliberately put him to the back of her mind, on a back-burner - or even out of it altogether? Over the last months her mind had boggled with troubles and problems, but she was a different person now. More independent, used to living on her own and fighting her own battles. Jim had been in her thoughts less and less. He hadn't been around when she needed him most - not that that was his fault, she conceded, but it wasn't hers either.

Surprisingly, thinking of him now didn't set her body tingling, as it did a month ago. Neither was the longing to be in his arms so intense. Was her body numb to such feelings? Where had those feelings gone? She still loved him dearly......... didn't she? The fact that she even questioned it was horrifying. It frightened her. It was as though he were only a distant memory, a past love, someone who no longer existed. Was there something wrong with her? Was she going mad?

The distant wail of the Dockyard siren, announcing the start of another day for its army of workers (known locally as shirkers), woke Laura.

Daylight filtered through the fabric of the thick curtain, and around its edge like a square halo. Her restless night was over. Thoughts that had tormented her mind during the long hours of the night - before she had obviously and eventually dropped-off - flooded back into her head, like the opening of a sluice-gate. Images of Tom's cold-marble body, sitting upright on a stainless steel morgue slab, shaking a fore-finger at her accusingly, mixed with the vision of his wife floating spectrally overhead, screaming abuse at her, like a banshee. Jim's face, unsmiling and blurred, staring; then turning wordlessly away. The shop, full of ghoulish customers, all poking at her with long blood-red finger nails, and black spiteful tongues.

She shook her head, like shaking rain-drops from an umbrella, endeavouring to rid herself of the hellish nightmare, as she swung her feet out of the warm bed onto the cold lino-covered floor, searching for slippers and dragging a blanket around her bare shoulders against the chill of the early morning. The dull silver-grey light of day flooded into the room as she drew aside the secluding drapes, and gazed across to where the outline of the row of shops opposite stood out, starkly, against the slate-coloured sky. Lonely trees waved bare branches in the Spring breeze and a caped policeman stood sheltering in the Chemist's shop door-way, flexing his knees in anticipation of another seven hours patrolling, as he enjoyed the brief lull in traffic between the swarms of ant-like cyclists converging on the Dockyard gates for the morning In-muster - now all safely enclosed within the prison-like walls of the Naval Base - and the more sedate car and bus-borne office workers.

A movement in the corner of her eye caught her attention and she watched anxiously as the postman (who Jim had dubbed 'the bad-news bag-man', after the delivery of his call-up papers) came slowly along the pavement, stopping at several doors to push his customers good, bad, or indifferent mail, through rattling letter-boxes.

A tatty, foraging, mongrel dog, lifted a hind leg and sprayed the base of a silver-painted street-lamp standard, staining the 'Star and Crescent' motif of the City Council, totally oblivious to Laura's heavy-hearted disappointment as the postman walked straight passed her front-door. It was now over a week since she last heard from Jim.

Desperately unhappy, she stepped away from the window and sat down, heavily, on the bottom of the bed, burying her face in cupped hands and bursting into tears, feeling wretchedly miserable, unloved and unwanted.

Tom's wife came down into the shop from the upstairs flat where she had spent the night to be nearer the hospital. The frosty look on her face was not a good omen as Laura unlocked the front-door, and entered to the accompaniment of the clanging bell.

'I was beginning to think you weren't coming in today,' she snapped, chin up and peering down the length of her sharp-edged nose.

Laura looked up at the big round clock on the wall above the counter. It was twenty-five minutes past eight. 'I'm not late,' she answered, a little annoyed at the reproachful attitude of her employer. Then felt a twinge of sympathy for the desolate woman who must be worried sick. 'Have you heard how Tom is?'

'Comfortable,' said Mabel, petulantly. 'That's all the hospital would say when I phoned half-an-hour ago.' She sniffed, and pursed her heavy lips. 'They said I could go in at ten o'clock, so you'll have to manage as best you can.'

Now was not the time to ask about an assistant, so Laura just nodded and told her not to worry.

The shop had more customers that morning than in the whole of last week, all wanting silly little things like matches, or candles, or a packet of crisps. All fishing for information they could then relay to others, from their newly acquired position of being 'someone in the know'. They weren't concerned for Tom - just being nosy. At this rate, Mabel would have to post a daily-progress bulletin in the shop window.

To Laura, it felt a blessing in disguise having something to occupy her mind, and keep her busy. To save worrying about other things.......Like Jim!

CHAPTER TWELVE

Rain was sheeting down from the swollen cumulus clouds that seemed to have been permanently based over Campbeltown for the last two days. Chilly sou'easterly winds swept up the Loch from the angry sea causing the launch to nudge heavily against her battered fenders as we staggered about her lurching deck, trying to keep our feet, like children playing hop-scotch.

'Tis only Scottish mist,' laughed the oil-skinned figure of the Harbour Master, answering Flight's enquiry about how long this weather was going to last, as he peered down from the other-wise deserted quay-side with rain dripping from the peak of his cap like an overflow from a roof gutter; dutifully checking our well-being, and probably worried about the expertise of Air Force chappies, on boats.

This was our fourth day in harbour. Four days that included a pay day, and I hadn't had another run-ashore. I still felt disgusted with myself over my behaviour on the first night's drunken debacle, and knew that the only way I could rid myself of the shame was to go to the pub and make my apologies in person...........If only I could find the courage.

Secretly, I was concerned that I would make a fool of myself, yet again, should I have another drink. I desperately wanted to drown my sorrow. Try as I might, I couldn't get Laura off my mind.

Doc, Sparks and Romeo, (or the gruesome threesome as I now called them), became quite insistent that I make the effort to return their generosity; as a reward for taking care of me, 'in my hour of need' as Romeo so modestly put it. 'Indeed,' added Doc, trying to keep a serious face 'That's if they allow us back in, after all the damage you caused.'

'Thanks fella's,' I said, submitting gracefully, 'but I want your support in the pub - if I go in.'

'We gave you that when we carried you back on board last time, didn't we?' Doc reminded me with mock severity.

I honestly didn't remember, or recognise, the pub when we entered it later that evening. The curved bar with its highly polished top, gleaming pump-handles and low imitation-beamed ceiling, could have been anywhere. There was no feeling of deja vu. It seemed totally alien, strange that I had been there before creating mayhem, yet with no recollection of it. It wasn't too crowded and we found an empty table, tucked in the corner well away from the jangling fruit machine and ball-clacking bar-billiards table. No one glared at me; I felt no daggers digging into my back. No pointing fingers.

We sat down, and it was several seconds before I self-consciously realised my three companions were staring at me……..

'What?' I queried, raising my eyebrows.

'Your round, innit?' said Sparks, as the other two nodded approvingly.

At the bar, the beefy, long-haired barman had his head down, pulling a series of pints with a tattooed fore-arm the size of pig's back leg, so I stood patiently holding up a pound note like a bidder at an auction, waiting to be spotted. Eventually he looked up and bared his teeth in a smile that seemed to spread across a battered face - obviously he must have been a boxer, or a brawler at some time.

''allo Mate,' he croaked in a surprisingly squeaky voice. 'Never thought to see you in 'ere again so soon.' His aggressive features belied the friendly tone.

'Four pints please,' I ordered, then leaned forward conspiratorially and whispered, 'Sorry about last time.'

He curled his upper lip, thick with scar tissue. 'Nay worries, Laddie. I've seen a damn sight worse, and you weren't that bad, ye ken.'

I paid for the drinks, smiled gratefully at him, and returned to the table, much relieved.

'All right, Lofty?' asked Sparks and Doc together, taking their drinks reverently from one side of the laden tray, almost causing a major spillage.

'Yes,' I answered, restoring the equilibrium of the unbalanced tray and blowing out my cheeks with a sigh. 'That's a load off my mind. Thought he was going to thump me at first. Nasty looking character, don't you think?'

'Got a 'eart of gold he 'as,' commented Romeo, staring vacantly into his glass, as if searching for alien life. 'Looked after you 'e did.'

We sat quietly sipping our drinks, making them last and putting the world to right; debating the rights and wrongs of how our politicians were managing world affairs (and their own). We talked about football, the boat, the Services in general and the RAF in particular. We held an inquest on the dead fly, lying with its legs in the air, in a puddle of beer on our varnished table top - did it drown, or die of alcoholic poisoning? And we questioned the mentality of people who drink standing at the bar, blocking others waiting to be served.

What we didn't discuss - as though by unspoken agreement not to upset me - was the subject of women; a unique experience among a group of men!   So, it came as a bit of a shock when we were interrupted by a female Scottish voice speaking over my shoulder.

'Helloo - remember me?'

The other three looked up over my head and, with mouths open in recognition, rose hesitatingly to their feet with a scraping of chairs, muttering 'Oh!, Hello.'

I turned around on my chair, twisting and tilting to face the girl behind me. I had no idea who she was, but she was certainly a 'good-looker.' About eighteen or nineteen I guessed, with shoulder-length brown hair, and a pert little turned-up nose that was looking down at me with a tight-lipped smile, as if the others didn't exist.

'You don't, do you?' she asked laughing at my apparent confusion, her smile spreading as her strawberry-lips parted to reveal pearly-white teeth.

I stood up, awkwardly. 'No, I'm afraid I................' Then the penny dropped as my cerebral communications department sent me a 'Flash-Priority' signal that said, 'THIS IS HER!'... Followed by another that said 'CLOSE YOUR GAPING MOUTH.'

The blushing started in the region of my Achilles tendon, and shot up like the indicator on a blood-test meter.   No wonder the others recognised her.

'You're not........?'

'Yes, I am. Tessa. Don't you remember me?'

I groaned aloud, praying for an earthquake to swallow me. 'No. So sorry, I don't,' I confessed a little shamefaced. 'But my mates told me how badly I behaved, and I can only apologise.....'

'No need,' she said graciously. 'May I sit down?'

'Please,' I said, motioning with my hand and flashing eye-signals for the others to make friends elsewhere.......Like in Timbuktu. Understandingly (or in fear of wrathful retribution), they made their excuses and moved to the far end of the bar - but not before I reminded them to get the drinks in for Tessa and me.

'Was I really that bad?' I asked fearfully. 'I don't remember a thing.'

She placed a well-manicured hand on mine in the middle of the table-top, and I noticed she wore nothing on her fingers, other than long, painted nails.

'Nothing I couldn't handle,' she answered, giving me a swift once-over survey, as females do when considering the number of 'Brownie-points' to award their victim.

'What did I do?' I pleaded. I had to know just how bad I'd been.

'Well,' she began, holding her free hand up to her chin like a Judge totting-up the number of offences to be considered before passing sentence. 'First, you tried to kiss me. Then when I went to push you away, you put your arms around me and grabbed my bum.'

'Oh! My God,' I interrupted, feeling sick.

'The best is still to come,' she laughed, eyes twinkling mischievously, ''cause then you grabbed my boobs, asking if I was a real woman. But - to give you credit - you did stop when I told you to.' She squeezed my hand comfortingly. 'Later, after you'd been sick, you invited me back to your boat to spend the night with you. To be rocked by the ocean waves - you said - while we made passionate love.' She was enjoying this.

'Aw! Jesus!' I moaned, shaking my head in disbelief and embarrassment, dropping my eyes to our hands, still touching on the table. I couldn't look her in the eye.

'Of course, I refused,' she continued, still smiling ambiguously, 'but then your mates saved me from a fate worse that death when they prevented you from dragging me out into the pub's backyard. For a 'quickie' I think you said.' She laughed aloud, attracting the attention of two bar-stool boozers whose ears were twitching like radar scanners seeking a target. 'Please don't feel bad about it,' she said quietly. 'It was a compliment to me really, even though you were staggering drunk, and I was flattered.' She placed her hands together on the table, sandwiching mine. 'What's your real name?'

I told her it was Jim, and before I knew it I was pouring out my whole pathetic matrimonial problem to her, like a life-long confidant. She listened, sympathetically and silently, sipping her drink, still holding my hand. From across the pub lounge, the three stooges watched happily. Even Romeo, the Don Juan of Carmarthen, felt no jealousy at being bested by a hopeless drunk.

As I finished the whole sorry story, she put her finger tips under my chin and lifted my face until we were looking straight into each others eyes. Hers had a hint of tear in the corners; mine - still a bit blood-shot - sat in hammocks of discoloured, sagging, wrinkles of abused flesh, like a blood-hound with glaucoma.

'Don't worry Jim. It will all turn-out right in the end,' she said prophetically. 'You've both been through a bad few months and need time to sort yourselves out. Give her a while, and then write again.'

I clamped my teeth together tightly, stretching the corners of my mouth, nodding like a dumb parrot. I felt sad, and didn't want to be. Not with Tessa.

'Tell me what you wanted to do in the backyard of the pub?' she said, teasingly, trying to bring back light-heartedness to the conversation. I knew she could read my mind as I considered an answer, but I could never say what I was really thinking.

'Don't know,' I answered nervously. 'Probably needed you to stop me from collapsing in a heap, by all accounts.'

'And what do you think now?' she asked.

'About what?'

'Am I, or am I not, a real woman?'

I looked long and hard at what I could see of her above the level of the table-top. She was no glamour-girl, but without a doubt she was very pretty, attractive and desirable. Her figure was slim and shapely and I knew, instinctively, that out of sight, hidden by the table, were a pair of gorgeous legs. Hormones, alerted by my devouring eyes, became hyper-active, and stirrings started where they shouldn't, as unclean thoughts called my adrenaline pump-men to action stations. My thumping heart, shaking fingers, and rotating eyeballs, gave me away. I was glad she couldn't see beneath the table.

'Oh! you're a real woman okay Tessa,' I whispered, my throat tight with emotion. 'Believe you me.

She gave another of her big, flashing smiles that lit her face and clutched my hand, tightly. 'And.....................?'

'And I fancy you like mad,' I admitted, quickly and urgently. It was obvious the reaction she had hoped for, as she blushed with open pleasure.

'I'm so glad Jim,' she sighed, 'because I felt that way about you the first moment I saw you staggering white-faced towards me in the bar the other night. Drunk or not, the chemistry was there and I've been thinking of you ever since. I even went down to the harbour yesterday afternoon to see your boat, and hopefully you, but you weren't there. Do you think I'm brazen?

'No, I don't,' I answered, honestly. 'I think you are wonderful. And I was on board yesterday. Must have been working down below.'

'I love the sea, and boats,' she said, dreamily. 'If I were a man I'd be a sailor.'

'Don't wish that, whatever you do,' I interrupted sharply. 'I much prefer you being what you are - a very desirable woman.'

'Do you really mean that, Jim?'

I nodded affirmatively. I sure did.

'It's stopped raining now,' she said, turning to look out of the rain-streaked window at the wet yellow-lit road. 'Fancy a walk down to the harbour? You can show me your boat, if you like.'

'Great idea,' I agreed, watching her push back her chair and stand up, my eyes inspecting her from top to toe, absorbing every inch and curve, confirming my image of a pair of gorgeous legs that peeked beneath the hem of her short dress.

'Do I pass?' she asked with a touch of excitement in her voice, noticing my admiring appraisal. I nodded with pursed lips, not trusting myself to say what was going through my mind.

She smiled, knowingly. 'Okay then, I'll just tell my Dad we're off.'

My heart missed a dozen beats. 'WHAT!... WHO?'

'My Dad, over there,' she pointed, 'you don't think I'd come into a pub on my own, do you?'

I shook my head, dumbly. My blood turned to ice.

'Don't worry,' she grinned, seeing the fear in my face. 'He's fine, you'll like him. Would you like to say Hello to him now?'

Jesus, Mary, and Uncle Tom Cobbly. What had I let myself in for? He will hammer me, I thought, as she led me, hand in hand, to a table surrounded by card-players in the far corner of the bar.

'We're just off for a walk Dad.' She leaned over a thin, bespectacled man sat chewing on the stem of an empty pipe, studying the cards in his hand. 'Say Hello to Jim.'

His eyes came up, and a friendly grin spread across the hollow-cheeked face. 'We met the other night lad, didn't we?'

Oh! God, where was the Seventh Cavalry?

'There she is,' I said, proudly pointing down from the quay-side to where the launch was tied-up some fifteen feet below. 'Royal Air Force Air-Sea Rescue Launch Thirty-eight Forty.'

Tessa stretched her neck to peer cautiously down, one foot almost touching the edge of the stone quay. 'It's lovely,' she said wistfully. 'Is it nice?'

I'd never heard a boat described as nice before, but I knew what she meant. 'Fabulous,' I answered, 'and by the way - boats are called SHE not IT.'

She turned to me, frowning. 'Why?'

'It's a long story,' I told her, not wanting to go into the many supposed theories while standing on a chilly dock-side, with rain threatening again.

'Would you like to go on board and look around?'

'How?' she asked, looking for a respectable means of access. I pointed to the iron-rung steps, recessed into the dock wall. She turned to see if I was joking. 'You're not serious, are you?'

'It's the only way,' I told her, 'unless you want to wait for High-water, about three in the morning.'

She looked warily down over the side again. 'You will have to go down first - in case I slip.'

'Fine by me,' I laughed, 'I'll be able to look up your dress.'

For a second, she appeared annoyed, but then she laughed too. 'You would to, wouldn't you, you randy man. What happened to 'gentlemanly conduct?'

Actually I didn't carry out my threat, as much as I would like to have done. I went down first, keeping my face at her waist level, my hands holding the cold, weed-covered rungs either side of her.

Carefully stepping-down one rung at a time, we reached the deck. Courteously, I offered my hand as she elegantly, and unsportingly, clutched her dress tightly around her legs to climb over the guard-rail with dignity intact. The boat lurched slightly with our combined weight and a voice called out, 'Who's that?' as a head and shoulders appeared out of the wheel-house.

'It's only me Toby,' I answered. 'And a friend I'm showing around.'

His eyes popped out when he saw my friend. 'Strewth,' he said admiringly. 'You sure know how to pick 'em, Lofty.'

Tessa rewarded him with a dazzling smile that lit up the gloom - and his face. 'Thank you, kind Sir.'

He ogled her lecherously until I gave him a clear, but silent, indication that he should make himself scarce. Reluctantly, and with a look like a poisoned arrow in my direction, he turned away, clearly disappointed at not being invited to share her company. 'I'll be in the radio shack,' he grunted, sourly.

There's not much to see on an HSL. Tessa looked, without interest, down the engine-room hatch into the dimly-lit space that took up two-thirds of the boat's hull. Her nose wrinkled at the unpleasant smell of oil and fuel, like a cat accidentally sniffing pepper laid as a deterrent by an irate gardener. I smiled at her puckered nose. 'Takes a special sort of bloke to work down there.' She curled her bottom lip. 'Ugh!'

The grandly named 'sick-bay' was of more interest to her. It was a 6ft x 6ft Oxo cube, placed haphazardly on the deck as an afterthought by the builders. It contained two blanket-covered cot-beds with a narrow space between them. Under-bed lockers contained the medical equipment, and overhead - strapped to the deck-head - stretchers (injured for the use of) reduced the head-room to that suitable for hunch-backs, or midgets. This was our 'hospital', the domain of Doc - who she had already met - but the only ones ever to use it were the skipper and the coxswain who commandeered the two cots for over-night sleeping, and the Corporal mechanic who 'kipped' on the deck between them.

She looked back inside again, curling her upper lip distastefully. 'Where do the rest of you sleep?'

I explained the lack of facilities, and our normal use of hotels when necessary, and said I would show her where we 'got our heads down' when we reached the foc's'le (that I eagerly wanted her to see).

Warning her to watch out for her shins, we stepped over the twelve-inch high coaming that kept the water out, and entered the deck superstructure. The skipper's caboose - a small cupboard not grand enough to call a cabin, with room only for two chairs that tucked under a drop-down table - was locked.

'This is the radio-shack', I explained, pointing to another cupboard half filled with radio equipment in front of which sat Toby, like a tired guard crouched in a sentry-box, with a cross-word puzzle book on his lap opened at the 'answers' page. He gave Tessa a grimace in response to her lovely smile, then looked at me with a face like a cleaner clearing a blocked 'bog'.

We spent a few moments in the wheel-house while I described the various bits and pieces of equipment, trying unsuccessfully to hide my lack of technical skills. Neither of us knew what I was talking about. She gave me the feminine 'small man - big toy' look that provided me with the excuse to take her down the half-dozen steps into the foc's'le, with me leading, telling her to come down backwards, facing the steps in the correct manner, allowing me a brief glimpse of stocking-top secured by the button on the dangly bit of her suspender belt...............So far - so good.

At the bottom step she paused to face me. 'Is that really the proper way?' she asked, seeing the twinkle in my eye, 'or just an excuse?' Her eyes were twinkling too as they scrutinised the two six-feet long cushioned seats either side of the corticene-covered table. 'Is this it?' She sounded disappointed.

'Yep,' I said. 'This is home.'

She whistled softly through puckered lips as I folded one side of the table down to make it easier for her to get in. I had no idea what she thought it would be like - probably similar to a liner's cabin - but obviously it wasn't what she expected as I described how five of us slept in here when it was necessary. 'It can be quite comfortable on the seats. Lie down and try it,' I offered hopefully.

She shook her head. 'You sailors are all the same,' she said giggling happily, sliding along the seat to make room for me beside her.

I kept on edging her backwards until she came up against the forward bulkhead. 'I've got you trapped now.' I began to breathe heavily as I put my arm around her. 'You can't escape me now.'

'Oh! Jim,' she panted, melting under my arm and turning her face up. 'I don't want to escape!' The tip of her tongue peeped out like a pink bud to wet her luscious lips, then retired leaving her mouth ever so slightly open as she clung to me..........expectantly? She was irresistible and I wasn't about to fight my own urges. I kissed her hard and she responded, forcing her mouth against mine, opening her hot lips wide, and sucking my tongue passionately as I explored her mouth. My free hand dropped onto her lap, feeling the heat of her leg through the thin dress material. Slowly I move it down to her knee, and there was no resistance. Boldly I moved it up again, under the dress, feeling the sensual texture of silk stockings, then the lace-tops, then the bare smooth skin of naked thigh. Inch by inch, and getting higher, expecting any minute for my hand to be pushed away. But no, she parted her knees several inches, as though in invitation. With my heart pounding like a dinner-gong I eased my sweaty hand over onto the leg nearest me so that my groping fingers were between her trembling thighs, moving higher as her legs opened welcomingly wider. I could hardly contain myself and my breath control went out of the window.

It was just like an electric shock surging through my body, when my shaking fingers touched the silken crotch of her knickers. She gasped, and raised her bottom off the seat as I pulled awkwardly at the knicker-leg to ease my fingers inside, feeling the gossamer fuzz of hair and the hot swollen lips that accepted my fingers as they slipped smoothly into her moistness, her legs now spread wide.

Her husky voice panted sweet nothings in my ear as her hand took hold of my hardness. I thought I was going to burst.

'God, I want you so badly Tessa,' I grunted, then added hopefully 'take him out for me before he rips my trousers.'

She giggled loudly, and I wondered if we could be overheard. 'No darling,' she answered. 'Not here. Not with your friend so near.'

'Shit,' I swore softly in frustrated disappointment, silently cursing Toby for being within ten miles of us.

She placed her forefinger over my lips. 'Shh!' she whispered. 'I want you too, but not here. What about your hotel?' I looked at my watch with renewed hope. 'It's ten o'clock.'

'So what,' she laughed. 'Have you got to be in early?'

Hurriedly we made ourselves decent. I cocked my head to one side thinking that I heard a quiet shuffling noise coming from the wheel-house. I wouldn't put it past that bloody Toby to have had a sneaky 'shufti' at us.

Peeping or not, he made sure he was on deck standing under the iron ladder as we left. I had a good view up Tessa's dress as she climbed warily up onto the quay, so I'm sure he did, even though it was dark.

We hurried through the empty streets. White pools of lighting, hanging from the street lamps, accentuated the surrounding darkness. Small, shallow lakes of black water lay in tarmac depressions on the roadway, and in the distance a girls' voice screeched, like a drunken night-owl. A lonely dog barked, once.

Tessa shuddered as we paused outside the unlit and apparently deserted hotel, its blank-faced windows looking like an ancient sepia photograph. 'Bit weird, isn't it?' she whispered as though not wishing to disturb the decaying interior.

I put my arm around her comfortingly. 'Not five-star maybe, but not too bad.' I'd slept in worse hotels, but couldn't remember where.

The grinding hinge of the front door, the creaking of the foyer floorboards as we crept by the empty reception desk, and the squeaking of the stair treads as we climbed to the first-floor landing like cat-burglars, seemed magnified a hundred-fold in the silence of the dark.

'What the hell are we creeping for?' I whispered. Why was I whispering?

Tessa clung delightfully close to me, as though for protection. It felt good for my masculine ego, even though the quiet ghostly atmosphere was a bit scary, even for me, as we reached the landing and turned along the dark, dismal corridor, lit only by a square of slightly lighter grey from the window at the end. With a twist of the porcelain knob I gently shouldered the door of my room open, hoping desperately, like Daniel entering the lion's den, to find it empty.

'Good.' I breathed a sigh of relief, urgently pulling Tessa into the room and closing the door. 'Romeo's not back yet.'

'What happens if he comes back?' she gurgled, chin tucked in, looking down and undoing the top buttons of her dress. I was already writing 'GO AWAY AND COME BACK IN THE MORNING' on a blank page torn out of a paper-back novel that had been kindly left in a drawer by a previous occupier.

'Wouldn't have a drawing pin on you, would you?'

'Don't think so,' she chuckled, 'Will a safety pin do?'

I straightened it as best I could and used it to pin the notice on the outside of the door, at face level. Romeo would see it and doss-down in the other lad's room. I turned. She was stepping out of her knickers.

'Hold it right there,' I ordered, sitting on Romeo's bed just a foot or two away. She stood upright, unashamedly stark naked; absolutely gorgeous. Every inch of her was perfect. She took her hands away from covering the fabulous cotton-bud of hair between her legs and placed them on her hips, shoulders back and feet apart, like a Roman Centurion surveying an army. 'Will I pass?'

Ripping off my uniform I tossed it neatly into a crumpled heap on the floor, watching in eager anticipation, as she stretched out on the bed, uncovered, enticingly opening and closing her legs. Like a fire-walker I hopped about trying to remove a stubborn sock.

'Hurry up lover,' she cooed. 'I'm getting cold.'

The sock got the better of me and I surrendered to its superiority, stumbling clumsily on top of her, leaving one deserted sock alone on the floor.

The next hour was an erotic paradise. Tessa gave herself to me, hungrily and willingly, in an exciting frenzy of voracious passion that left me in a state of drained exhaustion as we lay spent in each other's arms.

Romeo's drunken return was timed to perfection. He staggered in the door, past the unseen sign, and looked down on the pair of us huddled together on the single bed. Tessa jumped with surprise, then seeing the state of my room-mate, smiled understandingly.

'Allo, boyyo,' he greeted, wavering like a reed in the wind, his eyes trying to focus on the two faces that should only be one. He put one steadying hand onto my side of the bed and leaned over me towards Tessa, frowning and breathing beery fumes. She lifted her shoulders, supported on bent elbows, ignoring the blanket that slipped down from under her chin to uncover the twin moulds of her breasts.

'Hello Romeo,' she said sexily. 'Remember me?'

'Ha! 'tis you my loverly,' he said in a Welsh accent that could be cut with a knife, his eyes fondling her, not even looking at her face as he stumbled around the bed and plumped himself down beside her, right on the edge of the bed. Teasingly she allowed this to pull the blanket even lower to reveal one tantalising pink nipple that attracted his bulging eyes like a magnet. He concentrated on it for some moments, trying to organise his wandering eyeballs, like a scientist adjusting his microscope on an interesting specimen, then with a great deal of effort, tore his glazed eyes away to re-focus on her face.

'Yer a gor - gor - hic - luverly girl, Teresa,' he slurred, getting her name wrong. 'Just what our Lofty needs, look you.' He poked a bent finger close to her face and waggled it. 'You be bloody good to 'im,' he warned, 'or yoowl ansher to me.'

He slipped off the bed and fell heavily to the floor. Tessa leapt out of bed to help him to his feet. He sat up, staring at her. Somewhere at the back of his brain a little man was frantically trying to record the sight of her nakedness, for him to remember - tomorrow.

She put her head under his shoulder and, with an arm around his waist, tried to lift him to his feet. With a look of happy satisfaction his hand shot around her neck, and grasped her breast.

'Ow!' she cried, 'That hurt.'

'Shorry,' he grinned stupidly, relaxing his grip slightly, but not letting go, as I scrambled across the bed to help.

He was a helpless dead-weight but we eventually got him into his bed and stripped off his clothes.

'Brewer's droop,' laughed Tessa, seeing his shrivelled manhood as we covered him. Within seconds he was snoring his head off.

'Suppose I should be getting you home,' I suggested without enthusiasm. It was much warmer spooning with her under the blankets than walking the streets.

'No need,' she called over her shoulder, climbing back under the covers of my narrow bed. 'I'm a big girl now. Dad won't worry. I told him I might not come home, when we left the pub.'

I stared at her in amazement. She was very sure of herself, was this girl.

'Come back to bed and keep me warm,' she invited, snuggling into the pillow.

Obedient, as always, I jumped in beside her, thanking my lucky stars it was only a single bed as she wrapped herself around me. She wasn't cold.

I must have gone out like a light. The next thing I knew the room was full of the dull, grey, morning dawn. I was lying on my back with a warm, smooth, bare leg straddled across me.

'Morning lover,' she breathed in my ear, wriggling over to impale herself on my instant reaction, the bed clothes slipping down around our knees as she cantered above me.

Thankfully I lay still, happy for her to do all the work, wondering where all her energy came from.

Leaning back, facing me with her eyes closed, hands behind holding my thighs, boobs bobbing tantalisingly, she rode me like a child on a rocking-horse, working herself into a frenzy and becoming quite vocal.

'Shhh!' I protested, mildly. 'You'll wake Romeo.'

She dropped her eyes, and a devilish grin spread across her face as she leaned forward to put her mouth next to my ear. 'He's already awake and been watching us for ages darling,' she whispered, returning to her leaning back position. The horny bitch liked being watched. It turned her on! She was an exhibitionist, and surprisingly I liked it. Not that I would ever have let it happen with Laura. That must mean something, I thought, but didn't know what, and gave up trying to analyse it when Tessa howled to a massive climax that drove all thoughts of running water out of my head, and took me past the point of no return.

For several moments, she sat with her eyes closed, like a beautiful marble statue of Venus, with arms. Then, with a sigh, collapsed down onto my chest. Romeo was on his side, facing us, and out of the corner of my eye I saw his lids snap shut, as he saw me turn my head.

The remainder of the week was idyllic. Every night - except for when I was duty ship-keeper - Tessa and I would be together in the hotel. Romeo (bless his heart), when not on duty himself, used the other room and slept in the bed of whichever of the other two were on duty, giving Tessa and me the privacy that I'm sure she would have willingly relinquished.

It was not such a perfect time for the skipper and Flight; they were worried sick. Jock had returned from his short leave, just seconds before his time expired, burbling away to anyone willing to smile or nod whenever they thought his incomprehensible chattering warranted such a response. Unfortunately, there was no sign of Donkey. He was AWOL and the skipper was concerned about how long he could let it go unreported.

'If he's not back by noon tomorrow Flight, I shall have to report him,' he said, putting his own head on the block.

That dead-line came and went. Reluctantly the skipper telephoned whoever his daily contact was. Donkey was now officially AWOL and deep in the proverbial 'SH one T'. Snowdrops would be on his tail, like a ferret after a rabbit.

We heard no more of him - neither did we get a replacement. We parcelled-up his personal gear and sent it back to Bodwinton.

My affair with Tessa was beginning to pall. I didn't love her and she didn't love me.

'I'm not ready for a steady relationship yet,' she told me one evening as we strolled along the sea-front. 'Let's just have fun and enjoy it while you're here.'

It was purely physical. No romance. We couldn't go anywhere or do anything, like real sweethearts do; I had no money. It was just sex, sex and more sex, which was undoubtedly good, but I wanted something more - I wanted someone to love, someone to love me.

As each day came and went I thought more and more about Laura. Wondering what she was doing, what was happening to her. Was <u>she</u> with someone else? It seemed an eternity since I last heard from her. Should I swallow my stupid pride and write again? She was back in my everyday thoughts and the same old question kept repeating itself. Why?

CHAPTER THIRTEEN

The day after Tom's hospitalisation, his wife Mabel authorised Laura to take on an assistant; mainly because she didn't want to demean herself by becoming a shop assistant again after all the years of the good life. Laura already had a girl in mind for the job, and the very next day a grateful eighteen-year old took her place behind the counter. Within hours, Anne proved to be the reliable gem that Laura knew she would be. She was a natural. An excellent assistant; well liked by the customers, and wonderful company. They quickly became firm friends.

That very same afternoon, Mabel barged into the shop almost tearing the jangling doorbell from its coiled spring. 'You!' she snapped viscously, striding angrily across the floor, pulling open the door leading up to the flat and pointing an accusing finger nail at Laura like a blooded dagger. 'Upstairs.'

Laura looked at Anne with raised eyebrows and a turned down mouth. 'Oh! Dear, what have I done now?' she said, meekly following her employer like a chastised child.

Inside the flat, behind closed doors, Laura was at the receiving end of a venomous tirade of abuse that gave her no opportunity to interrupt. Eventually, it became apparent to a bemused Laura, that Tom and his wife had had a long conversation during her visit to the hospital. Tom's condition was weak, barely able to talk, but he knew he was dying, he said, and wanted to tell his darling wife of his devotion to her. He also asked that, if Laura ever said anything bad about him, she was to take no notice. It would be a case of a woman scorned because he had refused her sexual advances.

'You're nothing but a cheap, filthy little whore,' screamed Mabel, thrusting her crooked nose into Laura's face like a bent battering-ram. 'Trying to take advantage of a good, God-fearing man.'

Laura nearly puked at such an unfitting description but her endeavours at denial went unheard and unheeded.

'Well, you'll be out of a job now,' Mabel cackled, like a demented witch, almost foaming at the mouth in uncontrolled temper. ''cause we've sold the shop to Easy-Buys. You'll never get your grubby little hands on my Tom again.' She spat at Laura's feet and slammed out of the room.

Stunned and shocked by the unexpected outburst, Laura was amazed that she had no feeling of anger or animosity towards the woman; only intense sorrow. It must be dreadful to watch your husband die, especially under the circumstances as she believed them to be. She must be distraught, but Laura knew that nothing she could say would change what was implanted in Mabel's mind.

Twenty-four hours later, in mid-afternoon, Laura had cause to remember Mabel's prophetic last words when the shop-keeper next door popped-in with the news that Tom had died during the night. Surprisingly, she felt no sorrow for him, only for his poor wife. As far as he was concerned she felt nothing but relief - and a little guilt for feeling that way.

Even with thoughts of pending redundancy hanging over their heads, like the sword of Damocles, the atmosphere in the shop became much happier. Laura and Anne laughed and joked between themselves and Mabel became conspicuous by her absence, confining herself to her bungalow on the outskirts of the city.

There were no invitations received to attend the funeral so they thought it prudent to stay away, to keep the shop open. They debated whether to send flowers but decided that it would probably upset Mabel unnecessarily if she were to see them and, in any case, it would be hypocritical of Laura if she were to express grief. So, they carried on. Day after day, not knowing what the future held or how long it would be before someone - anyone - came to tell them what to do. Daily 'takings' were locked in a strong cash-box she found upstairs in the flat. Laura had no option. Under whose name could she bank it? Rightly or wrongly, she still placed restocking orders with the suppliers in good faith which, she fervently hoped, would be honoured by the new owners.

Laura was busy in the stock-room when, two days later, Anne called out, 'Someone to see you Laura.' Her visitor was a middle-aged man, mid-thirties she guessed, average build in a smart light-grey business suit with brown hair lightly streaked with grey at the temples. A brief-case dangled casually from his hand.

'Mrs. Highman?'

She nodded with a nervous half-smile, unconsciously patting the curled ends of her hair, very aware of a discreet inspection as his eyes swept over her from top to toe in a split second. He looked like the man from the Pru but she intuitively knew who he was as he offered his open hand.

'Daniel Thorpe,' he announced, introducing himself in a nice, but not posh, educated voice. 'Area manager for Easy-Buy. Can we talk? If it's convenient?'

Laura felt strangely uneasy as she led him upstairs to the vacated flat, leaving Anne - sniggering behind her hand - to look after the shop. It was a long time since she had been alone in a room with an attractive man. She wondered if he could hear her palpitating heart. They sat in the two leather armchairs, facing each other. He, relaxed and composed. She, perched on the edge, self-consciously tucking the sides of her short working skirt around her legs. Again she sensed, rather than saw, his visual examination, feeling girlishly pleased especially when she saw the appreciative gleam in his eyes. What was he thinking? Did he like what he was seeing?

He coughed softly behind a closed fist. 'The position is, Mrs. Highman, as I'm sure you know, we have acquired this property from your former employers. We are now the owners and it is part of the Easy-Buy group.' He paused to lift his brief-case onto his lap and opened it to shuffle through the papers inside. Taking one out, he ran a finger down the page as if looking for something specific. Laura couldn't help noticing his strong, tanned hands and clean, well-shaped finger nails. 'We will,' he continued with a slight tremor in his voice, 'in the very near future, be refurbishing the shop to our own specification, and you should be aware that there will be major changes, both with the shop and with the products.'

Oh! Oh! thought Laura. Here comes the chop.

'The reason you should be aware of these things, he went on, is because we are asking if you would like to stay with us as Manageress, Mrs. Highman?'

Her already fluttering heart missed several beats. She had hoped to be kept on as an assistant but this was totally unexpected.

He lowered his voice, as if concerned. 'Before you answer, there is one stipulation that I'm afraid Easy-Buy insist upon.' He hesitated, as a worried frown wrinkled his forehead, and she was gripped by a cold fear of apprehension and pending disappointment. Then he continued with polite gravity. 'You would be required to live on the premises, in this flat. It would, of course, be rent-free as part of your remuneration.' His eyes looked at her, hopefully, like a dog being teased with a juicy bone.

'Yes, I'd like that,' she replied with a tight throat, trying to keep the excitement out of her response.

'Excellent,' he smiled, the anxiety clearing from his face like a passing cloud, obviously pleased and relieved, as he offered a salary well in excess of her previous wage. 'Is that acceptable?'

Acceptable!!!....She could have kissed him; she was delighted. A new job, a new home and more money. She wanted to throw her arms around him, for more reasons than one, but all she said - as coolly as possible - was, 'Yes, of course; but what about Anne?'

'The girl in the shop?' he queried, flicking again through his papers as though to refresh his instructions. 'You can keep her on at her present wage if you wish but you will certainly need to take on at least one more when the shop alterations are completed. You are the boss now,' he added with a pleasant laugh, looking up from the jumble of papers. His deep-blue penetrating eyes looking right into her soul. 'May I call you Laura?' he asked in a low, sexy voice.

Butterflies exploded in her stomach like startled pheasants at a gun-shoot and a flush burned through her cheeks. 'Please do.'

For the next half-an-hour she sat in a dream-like trance as he detailed other matters, and answered her unasked questions. Controlled chemistry flowed between them like a fast flowing tide, but thoughts remained unspoken.

'I must be off now,' he said reluctantly, glancing briefly at his wrist-watch. 'I'm supposed to be back in Oxford by four o'clock. Not going to make it, am I?' Softly he clicked his brief-case closed and rose to his feet.

'I'll be back tomorrow, about two-ish, if that's convenient. We will have to sort out the bank and that side of thing, and no doubt you'll have more questions by then.' He offered his hand again and she took it apprehensively. If he had taken her in his arms and kissed her she wouldn't have objected. 'It's been really lovely meeting you,' he whispered. 'I'm sure we will make a great team.'

She followed him downstairs, and he nodded a smile at Anne as he clanged out of the door.

'You aren't supposed to have that flushed, glazed look,' said Anne with a wide grin that split her face from ear to ear like a Halloween melon. 'What have you been getting up to?'

Laura lifted her eyebrows high, in mock disdain. 'Mind your own business.'

Anne looked happily at her new friend who was glowing like a light bulb. 'Just remember you are a respectably married woman.'

The well-meant reminder was like being stabbed with an icicle, and guilt surged through Laura as she told her young friend of the new developments.

Despite this wonderful change in her fortune, Laura still felt sad and depressed standing in the window of her Mum's house the next morning, watching the world go by. A humming, battery-powered milk-float, full of empty bottles chattering in their crates, rattled along the road, hugging the kerb and being overtaken by frantically pedalling workers, racing to clock-in. A whistling paper-boy, gratefully finishing his round, kicked an empty fag packet into the gutter, looking forward to breakfast before attending a totally unnecessary day at school. An early-rising old man; standing with the aid of a walking stick on the edge of the pavement, waiting patiently for a half-mile gap in the sparse traffic, before venturing to cross the road. A coal lorry, with its black-faced driver, trundled off to begin deliveries of black gold in sacks, to empty cellars. Across the road, smoke belched unwavering in the windless air from several of the tall chimney pots standing like look-outs on the slate covered roofs. Black at first, then turning grey and white, it rose to join the high light-grey clouds that presaged a fine day.

The long awaited 'bad news bag-man' staggered along the uneven pavement, one shoulder sagging under the weight of his bulging mail-bag, weaving like a lop-sided sailor homing drunkenly back to his ship. It was now weeks since Jim's last letter. She had no idea where he was or what his thoughts were. She couldn't understand why he had stopped writing. Why had he not been supportive and understanding during her problems? It never occurred to her that it might have been her fault in the first place, or that he would retaliate childishly for her lack of effort and consideration towards him and his feelings. Bitterness took over from self-pity and her stubborn streak came to the fore. 'Sod him,' she swore. 'He can't love me very much.'

Nevertheless, her heart pounded in her chest as the postman came through the gate-less gap in the low forecourt wall to shove an envelope into the gleaming brass letter-box. Eagerly, she rushed into the hallway, hope springing eternal, to pick it up with trembling fingers. It was for her but the address was typewritten, so it wasn't from him. Deeply disappointed, she teased open the corner of the flap and tore it open with a finger. It was from a firm of solicitors, Satchley and Satchley, requesting her attendance in their office at a given time and date (the day after tomorrow actually), for the reading of the Will of the late Thomas Bletchworth Dunwell.

Her depression was made worse later that morning when Daniel phoned the shop to say he couldn't make it down for the bank business until the afternoon on the same day as her appointment with the solicitor, which, luckily, was in the morning.

The receptionist at Satchley and Satchley's office was a tall, mousey-haired, unattractive woman obviously selected for the job by an insecure wife. 'Good morning, Mrs. Highman. I am Mr. Satchley's legal secretary,' she announced theatrically. 'Please come through.' She led the way along a short, certificate-lined wall, to a heavy panelled door.

Laura didn't respond to her welcome. Had she done so, she would have said 'and I am a retail executive,' or something equally sarcastic.

Inside, at a huge leather-bound desk littered with ribboned files, obviously displayed to impress and overawe, sat a cadaverous figure whose hairless head protruded from a shirt collar that was six sizes too big for him, and with large overlapping lapels that covered the knot of his funereal tie. He sat under a large gilt-framed portrait of a severe-faced Victorian gentleman whose eyes seemed to stare directly at visitors like cold gimlets, wherever they stood in the room. Elbows on table, he steepled rheumatic fingers to touch the black hairs sprouting from his nostrils like an overflow from a slag-heap.

In front of him, in upright chairs with their backs to Laura, were two other people staring fixedly at the painting on the wall as though waiting for it to speak. One, a uniformed man who hadn't the courtesy to remove his peaked cap, turned out to be a Major in the Salvation Army. The other, sat alongside him, was the unmistakable head of Mabel - Tom's wife. This was going to be fun.

The solicitor flapped an effeminate hand, like the wave of a Royal, to indicate Laura should sit in the vacant chair next to the Major, as he made formal introductions. Neither of the other two acknowledged her presence.

He cleared his throat by coughing up a gob of legal phlegm that he then swallowed, instead of projecting it across the room onto one or other of Laura's two po-faced companions - as she had hoped he would.

Then he began the long, legal preamble that invited all those here present to witness the reading of the Last Will & Testament of the recently departed Thomas Bletchworth Dunwell.

After all the formal, and presumably necessary, mumbo-jumbo, it all boiled down to the fact that the dear departed man, who had made her life such a misery, had left his bungalow, goods, chattels and other possessions, plus the proceeds from the sale of the shop, to his devoted wife. So what's new! What else was expected?

'There are two other small bequests,' the solicitor continued stuffily, and Laura saw both Mabel and the Major stiffen. One with concern, the other with hope.

'One thousand pounds, I bequeath to the City's Salvation Army Citadel,' the solicitor read. The Major bowed his head in a silent prayer of gratitude - or to hide the satisfied grin that spread over his sanctimonious face, 'and I leave to my loyal assistant Laura Highman the sum of five-hundred pounds.' She was stunned. In absolute amazement she turned, just in time to catch the look of pure hate on the face of Mabel, and the soundless movement of her snarling lips mouthing curses in Laura's direction, as the distraught woman stormed out from the office, followed closely by a hurrying Major. It must have been the last straw for the poor woman.

Daniel, the area manager, was waiting for her in the shop, having a good laugh with Anne, when she returned from the hate-filled mustiness of Satchley's. At first, their cheerfulness was annoying after her recent experience but his obvious pleasure at seeing her started a glow deep inside her, as the overworked butterflies began to flap their wings.

Anne saw the look that passed between her two employers and diplomatically moved away, as far as the confines of the shop would permit. She cared deeply for Laura, only wishing her happiness. She knew the hellish months of misery she had suffered but knew little about her marriage problem. She had never met Jim, the husband, or knew the reason for the rift in their short marriage. Her one worry was in case Laura started something she might regret later on, but one look at the radiance in her cheeks, and the twinkle in Mr. Thorpe's eye, as they stood close together was enough. There was a deep attraction and her happiness came first. What the hell! Good luck to them. Who would know? Anne certainly wouldn't be telling anyone.

For one fleeting moment, Laura thought Daniel was going to embrace her as he strode purposefully across the shop, to greet her. He had placed his brief-case on the counter and approached her with both arms outstretched, and a grin spread across his face. At the very last second he dropped one arm to his side and took hold of her hand with the other.

'So sorry I couldn't make it earlier Laura,' he said throatily, 'I had to go to Head Office about this place.' His head swivelled fractionally from side to side to indicate the shop.

The way he said her name made her heart falter. 'No matter,' she said, almost lost for words and returning the gaze of his twinkling eyes. God! What was happening to her? She was shaking like a schoolgirl on her first date.

Reluctantly Daniel turned his eyes away to look across to where Anne stood silently in the corner, trying to minimise her presence. "You all right on your own for a while?" he asked. 'We've an appointment at the bank.'

Anne nodded gratefully; she didn't enjoy being a voyeuristic wall-flower.

During the short walk to the Bank, and the boring meeting with its moribund manager, Daniel was a paragon of virtue - an aloof senior with an unsure junior in tow - but once back at the shop he dropped the officious mask and reverted to being a kind, sensitive, and very attractive man.

'All well?' he greeted Anne, before Laura had a chance to open her mouth.

'Fine,' answered Anne, looking up from the magazine hidden under the counter next to the cash-till. 'Had a hectic half-hour, but it's gone all quiet again now. So you can carry on with your business,' she invited cheekily. 'I'll be okay.'

Daniel opened the door to the upstairs flat and courteously stood back holding it open for Laura. 'May we?' he asked.

For an hour or so they talked shop, or at least Daniel did while Laura sat nervously on the edge of the settee, acutely aware that he rarely took his eyes off of her. Strangely, she felt neither embarrassed nor annoyed.

It came as quite a shock when Anne's voice called up the stairs, 'I'm off now. I have locked up.'

Guiltily, Laura called back 'Okay love, see you tomorrow,' as she looked at the quietly ticking clock on the mantle-shelf over the fire place. It was ten minutes past closing time. Where had the time gone? She turned her eyes back to Daniel, sat relaxed in the armchair. 'Would you like a cup of tea?' she asked, 'or do you have to go?'

He smiled back. 'I'd love a cup of tea. I'm in no hurry.'

He stood behind her in the kitchen as she lit the gas under the kettle with shaking fingers, very conscious of his intimate closeness. 'Tell me about Jim?' he asked.

The unexpectedness of his question stunned her for a moment. 'What do you want to know?'

'Everything. Or as much as you want to tell me.'

For a minute or two she stood silently collecting her thoughts, then the kettle boiled and she occupied herself making the tea. 'Biscuit?' she offered.

He shook his head and carried the two cups into the sitting-room, looking at her strangely as she sat, again right on the edge of the settee, and raised his eyebrows questioningly. 'Well?'

Laura started, awkwardly and hesitantly at first, telling him how she had met Jim, and their early days together. He listened without interruption as she told of the wedding and Jim's call-up for National Service. He shook his head disbelievingly, and smiled without humour at this governmental interference in people's lives, and the typical Service bungling he had heard so much about. She sat staring into the cup of tea, held untouched in her hands, as she related the heart-break and hardships of their parting. Then the saga of Tom's harassment, and of Jim's apparent lack of understanding and support. Tears began to run down her cheeks. Daniel moved across and took the cup from her hands, placing it on the sideboard and then sat beside her on the settee with his arm around her shoulder, comfortingly.

It was as if a damn had burst. Emotion welled-up inside her and she burst into uncontrollable sobbing, burying her face into his chest with an arm around his waist. He let her cry.

Slowly, the tears dried up then, after several minutes of silently holding each other, Laura raised her tear-stained face and looked at him with red pain-filled eyes. He lowered his head and tenderly kissed her wet lips.

At first she did not respond. Neither did she withdraw. Then, like a slow-motion ballet, they embraced, holding each other eagerly, then passionately, as their love-starved libidos erupted. Almost savagely, they devoured each other until, without a word, and as though by mutual consent, they rose and she led him into the bedroom.

Even the bold design of the paper on the wall, a few feet in front of her face, was indiscernible as Laura lay curled up on her side with one open-palmed hand sandwiched between her cheek and the pillow, and the other trapped firmly between her knees. Her wide-awake eyes tried to pierce the stygian darkness but there were no varying shades, no shadows, only total uncompromising black emptiness.

She sensed the unfamiliar surroundings of her new home, and the strangeness of having a man share her bed. His bony knees touching the backs of her thighs, and a hand clenched in the small of her back. His shallow breathing tickled between her shoulder blades, like little wavelets, as he slept the exhausted sleep of a satiated lover. Lucky him! Laura hadn't slept a wink since faking an orgasm to end their unexciting love-making two hours ago. She had too much on her mind to feel sexy. Too many mental conflicts. Her life was one long emotional tug-of-war. There was no time to think, to sort out the muddled confusion of her mind. So much had happened in the last few weeks. Now, after giving herself to Daniel, guilt overwhelmed her and she was ashamed. She felt cheap and unclean. She didn't blame Daniel, it was her fault. No excuses. She had led him on.

Thoughts tumbled around in her mind and, as the grey light of early dawn seeped into the room, she realised she still loved and wanted Jim.

Was it too late for reconciliation? Had she gone too far and lost him forever?

Gently, so as not to disturb Daniel, she eased herself out of the bed and, wrapping herself in a spare blanket from the wardrobe, went out into the sitting-room and curled up on the settee, vowing to herself that she would write to Jim, telling him everything; the whole sordid story. About how she felt and was still feeling. She would hold nothing back, and if any love remained in his heart for her it would be his choice, his decision, as to any future they had together.

Daniel, fully clothed, woke her with a gentle squeeze of her shoulder. 'It's seven o'clock love,' he said, lowering his head and whispering, as though not wishing to be overheard. 'I must be going before Anne arrives.'

She sat up huddled in the blanket, her hair tousled, and looked at his outline, hazy in the half-light of the darkened room, and blurred through her heavy sleepy eyes. 'I'm sorry, Daniel,' she said apologetically. 'It should never have happened.'

His hand squeezed her shoulder again, and he smiled sadly. 'It never happened Laura, but I shall never forget you.' He gave her one last loving look then straightened and turned towards the doorway. 'Good luck with Jim,' he said his voice thick with emotion.

CHAPTER FOURTEEN

Campbeltown is a lovely town for holiday makers and, undoubtedly, for the natives too, but for us lonely, bored and almost penniless ASR launch crew it held few delights. The novelty of our uniforms had worn off among the local girls and there was little to do that did not cost money.

Week after week went by with the only break in the unrecorded monotony being a short two or three hour run-out into the Loch every few days for engine warm-up trials. Each morning the skipper went ashore for his telephone call to base, and each time he returned dispiritedly shaking his head. No news. Why were we being kept waiting? Had the powers that be forgotten us?

Luckily for us the summer weather made life a little less tedious. Long hot days encouraged us to undertake wild adventurous past-times, such as going for walks and paddling in rock-pools. Everyone tried their hardest to maintain harmonious relation and any dissent was quickly defused. We were a friendly and easy going bunch, determined to make life as bearable as possible, but we had too much time to think!

'Fancy a walk up to get the mail Lofty?' asked Sparks, poking his ugly face out of the wheel-house window and disturbing my peaceful day-dreams of Laura.

Despite the passing of time, my mind remained in turmoil about her. I had no doubts that I still loved her as much as ever but the recurring question occupied my mind - Why? Why had our love deteriorated so quickly and easily? I was desperate to learn the reason. It tormented me. There was so much I did not know, so much I needed to know. I wanted to write and ask, but too worried what her answer would be.

'Well!..... Yes or bloody No?' said Sparks, testily.

Weary with inactivity, I rose from my seat on the top of the after cabin, where I had been enjoying the weak, but surprisingly warm, sunshine.

'Why?' I mumbled sotto voce, "need someone to hold your hand?"

Together we climbed the iron rung ladder up onto the quay, and strolled listlessly into town. One or two of the locals bid us 'good morning' as they went about their business, but mostly we were ignored as we sauntered past open-doored shops with their owners, or assistants, busily organising the display of their wares for the early morning shoppers.

A young girl in a striped apron, leaning awkwardly over the white marble slab inside a fishmongers' window, suggestively offered an eel to us as we passed, then poked a cheeky tongue out in response to our bent elbowed fist.

I followed Sparks into the Post Office and stood back, like a look-out on a bank robbery, as he joined the queue at the counter. A young mother, standing patiently waiting her turn, gave me a lovely smile, then turned her back and provocatively bent over her baby's pram. Her tight trousers, stretched even tighter by the bending, left little to the imagination but, instead of lecherous thoughts of her, I pictured my Laura.

'One for you Lofty,' called Sparks, walking towards me holding an envelope under his nose from the small bundle in his hand. 'Mmmm...smells nice too.'

Eagerly I snatched it from him, immediately recognising Laura's hand-writing as I tore it open. There were a number of pages inside. It seemed to be a long letter.

'You push off back to the boat, Sparks,' I said, my heart pumping ten to the dozen. 'I'm going to the park to read this in peace. Tell Flight I'll be back soon.'

He nodded understandingly, 'Yea, take your time Mate.'

The two minute walk was an eternity with the letter burning a hole in my pocket. What did it contain? Was it a 'Dear John'?

The park was empty, except for the ubiquitous sparrows and blackbirds foraging on the concrete paths and patchy grass; and an old pensioner being towed along by an equally ancient dog eager to get back to its comfy basket, and favourite bone. I chose a bench-seat, speckled with bird droppings, in a secluded corner under a tired tree, and sat staring at the raggedly opened envelope, torn between wanting to know what she had written and fears for what it may contain. Was this the ending?.......or an explanation.

146

With sweating hands and trembling fingers I withdrew the pale-blue sheets, opened them out on my lap, and began to read.

Flight sat quietly on a quay-side bollard, looking down at the grey-decked launch gently rubbing its fenders against the green sea-weed covered side of the granite stone quay, feeling the cold from the iron seat seep through his serge trousers. 'Good way to get piles', he thought to himself as his professional eye surveyed 'his' boat from stem to stern, noticing that part of the identifying numbers painted on the fore-deck had peeled off and a triangle of dirt had accumulated in the corner of the scuppers where the side joined the transom - a job for someone.

'Enjoying the sun, Flight?'
The NCO raised his head to find his skipper standing over him, a wide grin splitting his face from ear to ear.
'Good news, Sir?' he asked, expectantly, seeing the officer's happy look.
'Yes, Flight. At long last they have remembered we exist. We're off to Mallaig in the morning to pick up a brass-hat who wants to be taken on a visit to the missile firing range in the Outer Hebrides.'
The Flight Sergeant felt a small surge of adrenaline. At last. He was fed up with the aimless dreary routine of trying to keep the lads busy. There was only so much to do on such a small craft. They needed to be kept occupied.
'I'd better get the lads organised then, Sir.'

Carefully, I folded the curling pages of her letter and eased them back into the envelope, having read them three times. The first time left me shocked, as though my whole life had come to a shattering end. She had written of her problems with her boss Tom, and the hellish nightmare he had put her through, and of the reason why she could not bring herself to tell me about it, but all I could think of was her confession. She had had an affair! It was all my mind could focus upon. The very thought of it - of her giving herself to another man - tore me to pieces. I felt like screaming. I wanted to hurt somebody, anybody. Anger boiled up inside me, then slowly subsided as tears came and I cried, my head buried in my hands, oblivious to any passer-by.

147

I do not know how long I sat there in the early summer sun-shine. I had lost count of time, but my anger and pain were now fused into a leaden ache. My entire body felt heavy, spineless, as I read those pages for a second time, trying to understand now that I knew the whole story. She had been through a bad time, I appreciated that, but it did not excuse the affair. Perhaps it would not have happened had I been more supportive in the first place, and stood by her; but I had thought she had stopped loving me! She should have told me of her problems in the beginning. Marriage is about sharing the bad, as well as the good. Had I known, I would have done my best to help - applied for compassionate leave if necessary - but to have an affair!!!! That was unforgivable, and unforgettable. Frantically, I tried to control the maelstrom of my frenzied thoughts, desperately seeking to find a reason that would enable me to excuse her behaviour.

It was only after the third reading that logic and common sense returned to my confused mind, and I began to analyse the situation. She had been overwhelmed by circumstances, without anyone to turn to. Her motives in not telling me were to save me from hurt and anxiety. She had been through a stressful hell, alone. I had reacted badly, and wrongly, to a misconstrued situation. Nevertheless, one big problem filled my head like a big bold newspaper head-line. SHE HAD HAD AN AFFAIR!

Then it hit me like a lightning strike - I had not given it a thought up to now - SO HAD I! I was just as guilty, just as wrong and just as unfaithful; more so in fact. Mine was more than a one-off.

I began to feel bad, very bad. Not just mentally, but physically as well. I wanted to be sick. I was full of a mixture of pain, guilt, sorrow, self-pity and, I suppose, a shattered male ego.

It was at this point I was brought back to earth, back to reality.

'Jesus, Lofty,' panted Sparks, as he stopped in front of me. 'I've been looking all over the bleeding park for you. Flight wants you back on board, now.' He looked down at the envelope still clutched tightly in my hands. 'You all right?'

I stood up, tucking the letter into the breast pocket of my jacket. 'I am now.'

The journey to Mallaig was the sort of trip that holiday-makers would pay a fortune for; the scenery unbelievable. It was also a navigational challenge, so when skipper asked if I would like to be involved - as a check on his admitted limited experience - I readily accepted.

We sailed from Campbeltown at six in the morning, causing our usual disruption, and a little after an hour later rounded the Mull of Kintyre, unconsciously humming Scottish traditional songs as we turned north, cleaving through a calm sea at a steady sixteen knots. During the three-and-a-half hour run up to the infamous Gulf of Corryvrechan where, at times, the tidal race fills the narrow stretch of water with dangerous over-falls making it look like a witches' cauldron, I had the time to think seriously about Laura, and to mentally compose a letter to her while pretending to study the local chart. The other less skilled 'erks' mashed the tea and organised toast and bacon sandwiches. The not-to-efficient electric heater worked over-time, and it was a joy to be served my breakfast by a non-navigational nobody who, I was sure, would get his own back at the earliest opportunity.

An hour later, a sharp left turn past Duart Point, brought us to the entrance of the beautiful Sound of Mull where the luscious green forests grew right down to the water's edge. Surely a painter's, or photographer's, paradise, especially the quaint picturesque little fishing village of Tobermory at the far end of the Sound. I could almost smell the Spanish gold, until Flight mentioned that, during World War Two, it had been a major Naval training base, packed with warships and thronged with matelots. Somehow that ruined my romantic dream. The sunken treasure galleons were probably covered with a layer of empty tins and bottles by now.

Rounding the next headland, and passing the delightfully named Isle of Muck and its big brother Eigg, we continued on the last sixteen mile run to arrive at our destination a little after six in the evening. Skipper and I congratulated each other on our navigational skills as though we were Cabot and Magellan. He felt pleased he hadn't needed to call too much on my expertise, whereas I knew my presence was the only factor that prevented us from running disastrously aground.

The busy harbour of Mallaig, set in very attractive surroundings, is no place for penniless servicemen. Its drawbacks being the distinct lack of pubs, the obvious scarcity of lasses, and the hundreds of sheep that roam freely on the road, in people's gardens, and even sleeping on their doorsteps. They were everywhere, so were their droppings. It required a clear, sober head to negotiate a path between the little lumps that covered every surface, like daisies in a meadow, only not so sweet smelling.

The only building of note was the hotel that stood in all its weather-beaten, Victorian splendour, at the top of the sloping road from the harbour. Resting motor coaches relaxed tiredly at its entrance, having disgorged their passengers for a night's stay before boarding the morning ferry to Skye. Our one venture into its plush public lounge was welcomed with true Scottish hospitality, until they realised we weren't rich pickings. A half-pint of Bitter each was not going to fill their coffers so we upped anchor and returned back on board, calling at the General Store in the one and only street, for a meagre supply of bottled beer, to sustain our flagging spirits.

The advantage of this quiet back-water was that it gave me the opportunity to think and reflect. Laura's letter had changed everything. We were just victims of circumstances. Being separated, and unable to talk face-to-face, we had both gone off on false tangents, believing what we wrongly perceived to be the situation. We had not been married long enough to build a trust strong enough to withstand the pressures of such an early separation.......or was I looking for excuses? We were supposed to love each other! Deep down - well not too deep - I knew I had never stopped loving her. She had hurt my male ego I suppose, and I had taken it out on her, instead of being the rock she needed. The more I thought about it the more I realised I was the one at fault - what a prat!

In this mood, I found myself a quiet retreat on a wooden bench-seat on the grass-covered high ground overlooking the peaceful harbour - now almost empty of its fishing fleet - surrounded by the ubiquitous and inquisitive sheep, and their droppings; losing myself for an hour or more in the warm sunshine, writing to Laura. Putting into words the thoughts in my mind as honestly as I could; including my infidelity with Tessa. If we truly loved each other, and wanted to start afresh, at least we would do so with a clean sheet - or so I thought - as I posted the envelope at the village post office.

'Chop, chop, you lazy shower,' bawled the Flight Sergeant, rudely awakening us from our mid-day siesta, indolently sprawled on the fore-deck drinking tea in the soporific sun-shine. 'Skipper's back, we've got to get our fingers out.'

Drowsily, we contemplated him through heavy lidded eyes, not exactly leaping to our feet at his command. We had seen the skipper's return and noted, without interest, his lighter than usual step. Slowly we rose to our feet, weary with inactive exhaustion. Dregs of tea dripped onto the deck from our enamel mugs dangling carelessly from hooked fingers. Unfinished cigarettes, flicked overboard, arced into the placid waters of the harbour, exciting the hunch-backed gulls into launching themselves from their look-out perches to inspect the prospect of an early snack as they patiently awaited the return of the fishing boats; and a proper meal.

Disappointed at the non-edible quality of the flotsam they returned to their vigil with eyes glaring hatefully at our launch, and its annoying crew.

'The Air Vice-Marshal has arrived,' said the skipper gathering the crew together, in and around the wheel-house.

I could see the new sparkle in his eyes; of exhilaration or anxiety? Whatever it was it immediately aroused everyone's interest and I edged closer, peering between Sparks's tangled hair and the pimply neck of Doc.

'He is at the hotel now,' continued our officer, 'and will come aboard in the morning for the trip over to the Outer Hebrides.' He hesitated, somewhat nervously I thought, as he plucked at his unbuttoned breast pocket, like a reconnoitring pick-pocket. 'He has requested no unnecessary bull and wishes to be treated as an ordinary passenger, not as a high-ranking VIP. However..........' He looked around at each of us in turn to emphasise his next words. 'He is an AVM and I require you, and the boat, to be immaculate in every respect. I know you won't let me down,' he said, then added with a tight smile, 'God help you if you do.'

'Good morning, gentlemen,' said the grey-haired, slightly overweight AVM as he stepped aboard dressed in civilian clothes, accompanied by the skipper in his best bib-and-tucker uniform.

'Good morning, Sir,' we chorused like schoolboys greeting their Head-master at Assembly.

A brief smile creased his ageing face as he noted our new, Persil-white jerseys, and then carefully made his way into the wheel-house guided by our attentive coxswain.

The skipper had gone up to the hotel earlier that morning, and walked back to the launch with the AVM who was shadowed by his over-burdened flunky carrying a largish case, a cap box, and two suit-covers presumably containing his officer's uniform. We were going to be a bit crowded.

Without the customary acknowledgement from our incomprehensible engineer, the engines burst into life with their usual explosions that shook every building, rattled every window and brain, and scared the living daylights out of every sheep and sea-bird within hearing. The town's road and verges would be even more heavily manured now.

The skipper took off his uniform cap and absent-mindedly placed it over the compass repeater, from where it was discreetly removed by the AVM, as our valiant commander put his head out of the wheel-house window and called out 'Let go forrard' to where Toby (unused to receiving such a command) had pre-empted the order by a few seconds.

'All gone forrard,' called Toby.

'Let go aft.'

We were greeted, at the Outer Hebrides Guided Weapons Range pier, by a phalanx of military - headed by the Royal Artillery Commanding Officer - that included everyone but the duty toilet cleaner. Our passenger, now dressed in his braided and be-medalled uniform, stepped ashore to a barrage of hand salutes. The only things missing were the mounted Household Cavalry and the band of the Royal Marines.

It was a barren looking, God forsaken place, suitable only for sheep, scavenging gulls, and exiled politicians. Miles from anywhere, it had no recreation facilities, other than a small NAAFI club, and I wondered what crime a serviceman had to commit to be posted to such a dump.

We were there for two days, bumping and grinding against the pier, flattening our fenders in the swell that came up the small Loch from the Atlantic Ocean. Apart from a two-man duty watch, we lived ashore; eating with the other service personnel in their mess and sleeping in a draughty, barely heated Nissen hut. A neatly painted sign, hung inside the hut door by an obviously talented but bored artist, declared it as 'STALAG BELSEN'. That, and the damp smelling blankets, told us it was rarely visited by anyone in authority.

The evening before our departure, the skipper told us the news, just received, that, after returning the AVM to Mallaig we would be sailing back south to Bodwinton.

'Before you get too excited,' he added quickly, 'the bad news is that Bodwinton base is being closed down, and the two HSL's, 3840 and 3848, are being taken out of service as part of the ASR reduction program.' This announcement was greeted by a stunned silence. 'I have no idea what will happen to any of you,' he went on. 'Presumably, you'll be posted elsewhere within ASR, or re-mustered.'

Like the rest of the crew, my immediate concern was for myself. I still had more than a year to serve. What would happen to me?... would it all go pear-shaped just as things might be about to improve between Laura and me? ...... would I end up as an Admin.Orderly out in the Far East, or somewhere equally as distant?

After a sleepless night of worrying, the faces that greeted the AVM next morning were glum. He appeared glad that the official 'pomp and ceremony' of his visit was over, as he relaxed in the launch's comparatively homely atmosphere. According to Flight, he seemed genuinely sorry to hear of our bad news and regretted that, being an Engineer Officer, he was in no position to influence the outcome.

That same evening, back in Mallaig and having disembarked our VIP, we were busy refuelling and re-storing for our next morning departure, when a messenger from the hotel arrived with an order from our skipper to say I was required at the hotel, immediately.
With jibes of 'Who's been a naughty boy then?' ringing in my ears, and panicking like a prisoner appearing before a Judge for sentencing, I ran up the sloping road dodging most of the piles of bloated currants, arriving breathless and worried at the paint-peeling front door entrance. 'What had I done?'
The AVM's flunky ushered me into the lounge where the great man and my skipper sat comfortably in large-cushioned armchairs, holding balloon glasses of brandy, like hand-warmers. I stood to attention, remembering at the last second not to salute bare-headed officers.

'Ha, Highman,' said the AVM, waving his hand in the direction of another armchair. 'Please sit down.'

Self consciously, I collapsed awkwardly into the over-soft cushions, my knees embarrassingly close to my chin, almost like sitting on the floor with my elbows high up on the arm rests. I felt like a Cormorant drying its wings. A fleeting smile passed over the skipper's face.

'Flight Lieutenant Harrison tells me you were a navigating officer in the Merchant Navy prior to being called-up for your National Service.'

'Yes, Sir.'....... (so?).

He looked at me, chin supported on the edge of his glass. I stared at his forehead.

'Mmm,' he muttered, turning his head to inspect immaculate finger nails. 'I wonder if you would be interested in an idea of mine, now that your present posting will soon be ended?' He raised a hairy eyebrow.

I nodded a slight gesture of affirmation, saying nothing. What was I supposed to say?.... 'Yes'... 'No'... 'Get knotted'. Did it matter what I said? I had little respect for service officers.

'How would you like to join my personal staff?' he asked, then continued without waiting for an answer. 'You see, I have a small yacht - a 25ft sloop - which I intend to sail across to the Channel Islands next season with my step-daughter, Janet. In all probability I'll not have time to sail her back again, and although Janet is a good sailor she couldn't navigate her way along a canal. So, if you are interested, you could sail across with us, or fly over, and sail her back with Janet as crew.' He paused, giving me a quizzical look; then answered my unspoken question. 'In the meanwhile, you can look after *Astra* and give her a winter overhaul, and crew for me whenever I get time to sail her. It should be a pleasant way of spending the remainder of your two years, eh?'

It sounded fantastic. 'Where do you normally keep her, Sir? Her permanent berth I mean.'

'Well, that's another reason why you may be interested,' he smiled. 'She's in a marina at Gosport and I understand your home is in Portsmouth, so you could probably live at home on a 'Live-out Allowance', if you wished.'

My heart thumped like an African drum. I could be back permanently with Laura, if she'd have me.

'No need to give me an answer now,' said the AVM, 'but let Flight Lieutenant Harrison know as soon as possible so that I can get it

arranged before you get back to your base.......Bodwinton is it?' This
last he addressed to my skipper.

'Yes, Sir. That is correct.'

'I can give my answer now Sir, if I may,' I said.

The AVM tilted his head slightly to one side and nodded.

'I would be very pleased and grateful to accept, Sir.'

Bodwinton was like a graveyard as we motored slowly up the creek
to our old berth, trailing a chevron of rippling wavelets that caused the
bank-side reeds to sway like drunken choristers. Resting moorhens
and coots raised indignant eyes as we chuntered by. A pair of swans
waved their webbed feet underwater to glide effortlessly out of our
way, heads swivelling on long white necks, beady eyes saying *'We
thought you lot had gone'*.

Flight eased the boat alongside, hardly denting the fenders, as Doc
stepped casually onto the wooden decking of the deserted jetty to
secure our lines. We felt like a raiding party, covertly making a silent
amphibious assault.

The journey down from Mallaig had been uneventful and, in the
end, somewhat boring. We called at the same places as on our
northward run but only stayed overnight at each, for fuel and fresh
victuals. There were no comfortable hotels; no warm, soft beds to
enjoy. Mattresses in the fo'c'sle had been the order of the day (or
night, should I say?). It was a routine of arriving during the evening
and sailing early next morning, which was good. I had no wish to
renew any 'old acquaintances'.

I had posted another letter to Laura from Campbeltown telling her
of my new posting, hoping it would be good news for her, and asking
for the shop's telephone number so that I could ring her.

We had had a quick half-pint and fish and chips in Holyhead, but
were far too shattered to even go ashore in Milford Haven. Everyone
(except for me) felt depressed, miserable and lifeless. The only topic of
conversation was their future... or lack of! For one reason or another
we were glad to be back at our West Country base.

"I'm going to see what is what, Flight" said the skipper, climbing
onto the jetty in his semi-uniform of battle-dress blouse and flannel
trousers and disappearing up the sloping path, under the archway of
leafy trees.

The silence was eerie. Even the birds were quiet. It was as though we had landed on a deserted island.

'Like a bleeding ghost town, innit,' ventured Sparks, almost reverently. 'Perhaps they've all gone already.'

Flight sniffed. 'No, there's bound to be a skeleton staff left....just for us.'

'Can we go up, Flight?' I asked.

'No. Best wait for the skipper.'

'Or the skeletons,' suggested Sparks.

We made a brew, and were sitting around staring into empty mugs, seeking consolation, by the time skipper returned looking very displeased. Expectantly, we looked up from our tea-leaf studies.

'The bastards have gone and left us nothing.' He swore uncharacteristically. 'Nothing except a fuel bowser, and a message.' He swung his leg over the guard-rail and fisted the wheel-house in angry frustration. 'Everything's locked-up and everyone's gone except for a Police Corporal in the Guardroom and the bowser driver. We've got to refuel and go on to Plymouth in the morning.' He was really upset. 'The only good news is that the SWO has arranged a meal for us at the pub in the village, but I'm afraid it's mattresses again tonight lads.'

The reception at our Plymouth base was somewhat different, and not just because we had a white-belted 'snowdrop' standing on deck to give us the appearance of being a military police launch (or, as Romeo suggested, an ASR launch under arrest).

We had sailed, with mixed emotions, early that morning, leaving the desolate, deserted Bodwinton base to the wreckers who would, no doubt, soon be breaking down the gates, dismantling the buildings, and returning the ground to Mother Nature. It wasn't a tear-jerking departure. No one had been in love with the place but it had been our home, for a while. As far as postings were concerned, there were better. There were also a bloody sight worse!

Three other ASR launches lay alongside the base jetty, looking pristine with smartly dressed crews on deck. A fourth launch was the sorry looking '3848' already in an advanced state of being decommissioned and de-serviced, ready for sale. Everything movable had been removed from her. All Service signs and insignia, including the huge 'call-sign' numbers on her fore-deck had been painted over. Canvas hoods covered her ventilators, upper bridge binnacle, and the holes where aerials had been. She looked a sorry state. An unkempt empty shell - which she was - and it sadly crossed our minds that '3840' would soon look the same.

On the concrete jetty a small group of people, mostly officers, welcomed our arrival. Our skipper was greeted like a long-lost son. The rest of us were ignored by everyone except a haggard looking Corporal with orders that we should take ourselves, and our personal belongings, to the 'transit' billet that was to be our home for the present. Flight and our NCO engineer would, of course, be accommodated in the Senior and Junior NCO's quarters, respectively.

Not only did we look a weary dishevelled shower of 'erks' as we stumbled along the jetty, heavily laden with cases and kit-bags, we were also told so by a well-ironed base Corporal who made us stand to attention as he officiously mentioned his uncomplimentary opinion of us......or at least he *was* doing so, until our own Flight Sergeant approached and told him to take his boots (the Corporal's) to the nearest latrine, making sure he was still wearing them.

CHAPTER FIFTEEN

'You all right Laura?' called Anne, opening the door in the shop leading up to the flat. 'Laura, you there?.......You okay?' She waited anxiously for several seconds, looking up the gloomy, unlit stairway, and was about to go up when the door at the top opened, silhouetting her boss.

'Yes, I'm okay love,' answered Laura, thankful that the semi-darkness and back-lighting hid her red-rimmed eyes. 'Will you open up and manage without me for a while? I'll be down shortly.' The last thing she wanted was for anyone to see her at the moment. She turned back into the flat, shutting the door quietly behind her. Back to Jim's letter.

He had opened his heart in what appeared, at first, to be a loving letter. He wrote saying how much he still loved her and wanted her, how much he missed being with her, how stupid he had been. It made her so happy, so full of love for him. She wanted the whole world to know. The weeks of Hell were over............until she turned the next page. Then her wonderful new world collapsed. He too had had an affair! Not just a mad, drunken, one-night stand, instantly regretted, but a full-blown <u>week-long</u> sexual relationship that probably only ended when he had to sail away. She couldn't get her head around it. It couldn't be true. Not her Jim! He didn't love the girl, he said, full of remorse. He had felt so miserable, so lost, so alone. All the usual excuses men make when they were guiltily ashamed. How could he! She collapsed side-ways on the bed, burying her face in the pillow sobbing uncontrollably, letting her tears soak into the downy softness.

A hand clutched her shoulder, shaking it gently, and she awoke with a start. Anne was standing over her holding a china mug, and returning memory made her stomach heave.

'I did knock,' said Anne apologetically, and was about to add ' *but you were dead to the world,*' when she saw the red puffed eyes and grief-filled expression on Laura's face. 'Here's a coffee. I can't stop. I've got to keep an eye on the shop.'

'Oh, my God!' cried Laura, looking at her watch, horrified to see it was nearly ten o'clock. 'I'm so sorry, Anne. I'll be down in a Sec.' But Anne was already half-way down the stairs feeling disturbed and concerned for her boss, and friend. Obviously something nasty had happened, probably between her and her husband she guessed - or maybe it was Daniel? If Laura wanted her to know she would tell her.

True to her word, Laura came down to the shop after a splash of water and a hurried repair job to her haggard face, and began to serve the back-log of waiting customers, whispering a quick 'Sorry,' to her harassed assistant.

The particular section of 'Sod's Law', as applied to the retail grocery trade, reads; '*Customers will flood in at precisely the time when a quiet spell is longed for.*' And so, in accordance with '*Sod's*' the two girls were kept busy until well into the afternoon. This came as a relief for Laura as it kept her mind occupied, but for Anne it was torment. She desperately wanted to help and comfort her wretched friend and at the same time her feminine inquisitiveness needed to know what it was all about. Her imagination ran wild until she was convinced that Daniel was involved, somehow. So, it came as something of a surprise to learn the truth.......and she was late getting home.

It came out in dribs and drabs, in between customers, and at one time Laura had broken down and rushed out to the toilet, in tears. Only after they shut up shop for the day were they able to talk fully, and uninterrupted, over a cup of tea in the upstairs flat. For nearly an hour Laura poured out the whole painful story from beginning to end, even showing Anne part of Jim's letter. Anne listened, silently and attentively, her heart going out to the unhappy girl sat opposite, so full of sorrow. She loved her friend dearly and had never met Jim but, in all honesty, she could see his point of view. Not that she condoned his affair - not for one single moment. Anne tried hard to remain dispassionate, neutral even, so that she could be honest and fair should Laura ask her opinion. Determined not to say anything, advice or otherwise, unless asked.

It was a relief for Laura to get it off her chest. There was no one in the world she trusted more than Anne. She was lucky to have such a good friend and felt much better for having told her everything, no holds barred. She sat for a while staring vacantly at Jim's letter held tightly in her lap, not knowing what else to say. She had told it all and felt more composed, having been able to talk about it. In some ways her sorrowful load seemed lighter, as though she had unburdened some of it on her young friend's shoulders. Laura raised her head to see the solicitous frown on Anne's worried face. 'What do you think?' she asked, longing for a crumb of comfort, a life-saving solution to her heart-ache.

The question was a dilemma for Anne. Was it a call for help? A need to hear hollow words of re-assurance to ease her pain? Or a sincere plea for an unbiased view from a trusted friend? Knowing her as she did, she thought it certain to be the latter, but it would be hard not to be biased in Laura's favour, and harder still to find the right words. She studied her nails, without finding inspiration. Honesty was not always easy. 'I could be wrong,' she said, taking a deep breath for courage. 'But, from what you've told me, I think the two of you need your heads banging together.'

Laura was leaning forward, elbows on knees, hands clasped and head bowed as if in prayer - or awaiting an executioner's axe.

Anne looked at the top of her friend's head knowing she could never begin to imagine the anguish going on inside it. 'But I have to say,' she continued nervously, 'that, initially at least, I think it was your fault.'

Laura's head jerked up in surprise, eyes flooded with tears, 'Why?'

"Cause you should have told him the truth in the first place; confided in him. He's your husband for Christ's sake! Whether he could do anything about it or not, he was entitled to know about Tom. At least by telling him, you would also be saying that what happened was against your wishes. Jesus, Laura! The poor bloke was miles away from home, loving you like mad and missing you like crazy..... and what do you do? You stop writing and stop telling him how much you love and miss him! What was the poor bloke to think?' She stopped. Had she gone too far? She wasn't being of much comfort. 'What happened then was definitely his fault though,' Anne said, trying to save any possibility of alienating her distraught friend. 'I can understand what happened between you and Daniel; it was the situation. A spur of the moment thing that you instantly regretted; whereas Jim's affair lasted a week before he came to his senses. But he did come to his senses, Laura. Men are different to us. They're weak. Instead of facing a problem they turn to drink - or sex. It's only a passing fancy, to take their minds off other things; to forget their problems. They bury their heads in the sand, like bloody ostriches.

161

Unless they are in love - like Jim is with you - one woman is the same as any other. Like another pint of beer on the table. Like ships that pass in the night. Sex doesn't mean the same to them as it does to us.'

Laura's head, still bowed, was cradled in cupped hands.

'If you want my advice love, you should write to him. Tell him you still love and want him too. Tell him you want to put all this behind you and start afresh. Clearly he loves you, and wants to do exactly that. You're two silly people who have hurt each other deeply. Now he wants to kiss and make up, with no hidden secrets. He didn't <u>have</u> to tell you. He's offering you his hand again. Don't miss the opportunity love; take it.'

As they say in literary circles, there was a long, pregnant pause. Then Laura rose from her chair and leaned stoopingly across to put her arms around Anne's neck. They stood up together in a tight embrace, both crying. 'You're right again, as always, you clever bitch,' said Laura, laughing unsurely through her tears.

CHAPTER SIXTEEN

It was lonely and miserable sat in the empty transit billet with only eleven vacant iron-framed beds for company. Nothing to do, nowhere to go, just sat waiting - for what? I could have gone walk-about around the buildings and quays of the Plymouth base; even gone aboard one of the H.S.L's for a chat, but that might mean missing anyone coming to look for me with my new orders. For the last twenty-four hours I had been on my own, seeing no one, other than at meal-times in the canteen. Not even a visiting NCO to pester me into keeping the billet clean and tidy. Had I been forgotten?

Within hours of our arrival at Plymouth, (was it only four days ago?), Sparks had been posted off to a Wireless School somewhere, on a SAC's qualifying course, without even getting a night's sleep with us. The next morning, Doc Broome was sent off on leave, with orders to report to an RAF Station in the Midlands on completion. In the afternoon Toby received orders to proceed to Dover, to relieve one of the HSL crewmen there. Then Romeo and I had to report to the Orderly Room where he received a travel warrant for home leave without notification of his new posting that he would be given 'in due course'.

My call had been in error, and I felt pretty low as I trudged back with Romeo to the billet and watched, with envy, as he packed his gear and strode off to his transport, happily promising to keep in touch.

I had set my heart, and hopes, on hearing from Laura by now. It was more than a fortnight since I wrote to her; plenty of time for her to decide what she wanted to do. What if my 'home' posting came through and she didn't want me? ...... What if?...What if?

How long I had sat on my bed, sunk deep in self pity, I'd no idea. It was as if I were in a boat, at sea in a fog, aimlessly drifting, waiting - for what? Perhaps I might even have nodded off, I don't know, but the crash of the billet door banging open against an iron bedstead, made me jump.

'You Highman?' queried the scruffy looking 'erk' standing in the open doorway.

'Yes.' I stood up expectantly. Orders at last?

'Mail,' he said, tossing two envelopes onto the bare springs of the bed he had just clobbered. 'Been in the Post Room for two days. Only just found out who you are.' He turned and went out, slamming the long-suffering door behind him as I leapt across the intervening four beds, cracking a shin on one in my eagerness.

The envelope lying on the bed-springs was addressed in Laura's hand and a flood of joy surged through me as I picked it up, scrabbling under the bed for the other that had fallen through to lie face down on the floor. Both were from her and my hands shook, hoping they contained good news, as I stumbled back to my bed-space completely forgetting my earlier misery, my painful shin, and the resentment I felt towards the Postal Clerk; I <u>had</u> called at the mail-room on each of the four days I had been here!

Thankfully, my weak knees gave way as I collapsed onto my bed, not even heeding the lumpy mattress and twanging springs as I tore at the envelope flap with trembling fingers. The first was a short note to say that she had posted a letter to me the previous day and then received my second one telling her of my 'home' posting. *'Goods news'* she had written *'Hope to see you soon. Love Laura'*. My heart sank. Not 'Wonderful news' or 'Longing to see you.' Hastily, I ripped open the second envelope and withdrew the light-blue sheets, faintly perfumed with her erotic scent that always sent my heart-beat racing. Had she done it on purpose?

Quickly, I scanned each page, not even getting the gist of what she had to say; looking for any sign of a 'Dear John'. There was none, but she had signed it *'Love, Laura,'* which eased my concern as I returned to the first page, to read it through from the beginning:-

Dear Jim,

Received your letter a couple of days ago and I have to tell you I am deeply hurt and shocked at what you said. I know I did something stupid and it is no excuse to say it was only a 'one-off' but that's exactly what it was and it was regretted immediately afterwards. I find it hard to believe that your feelings could have been the same. You continued seeing that girl for a whole week and would probably still be in her bed now if you had stayed in that place. You must have wanted to keep seeing her. You could not have felt any regret, or remorse, as I did. I felt I had let you and myself down. That I had dishonoured you, and my vows. Even that one time would never have happened had I had the strength of your love to hang on to. Perhaps we have both been at fault during the last six months, and had your affair been a 'one-

off' the blame would have been equal and perhaps easier to accept. However, it wasn't, was it!

I am very grateful for your honesty, and I'm sure you mean it when you say you still love me and want us to be together again. To forgive and forget.

In my heart I know I still love you, you are my husband, and maybe - one day - I will be able to forgive, as you have done. The question is, can I forget?

I need to see you. We need to talk, face to face if possible, to see if we can resolve this mess. Can you get any leave? If not, will you phone me one evening after shop hours? I have a phone in the shop and I've written the number at the end of this letter.

I look forward to hearing from you soon.

Love Laura.

...........Well, it wasn't what I had hoped for but at least there was a sign of promise even though she hadn't sent any kisses. I put my hand into my trouser pocket, pulling out a handkerchief, then delving deeper, pulled the pocket inside out and emptied the crumbs and contents onto the palm of my hand; a pencil stub, a sixpenny piece, and a penny. Seven pence was my worldly fortune. Would it be enough to phone Laura? I couldn't remember the last time I had used a telephone. I had no idea of how much it would cost.

My wrist-watch showed half-past-three and I remembered from way back that Laura said the shop closed at five... or was it six? It was going to be a long couple of hours, at least.

I read her letter again. It made me feel no better, or worse. I put on my battle-dress jacket and beret and walked out into the late afternoon sunshine - to think.

'Do your jacket up, Airman,' ordered a florid faced, rotund Sergeant who probably had nothing else to do with his boring life but to chastise erks like me, in between cups of tea. Automatically, I raised my eyes from their study of the tatty toe-caps of my boots that hadn't seen polish for quite a few days and buttoned the offending blouse as ordered, silently muttering "Bollocks". His tone was not unfriendly so I hoped he wouldn't fall off the quay-side and contaminate the fish as I ambled inattentively towards the Orderly Room; lost in thought, and worried.

'Outside the Main Gate, turn left, about a hundred yards up on the left,' said the Orderly Room Corporal in response to my enquiry about the nearest public telephone booth. 'Gets busy in the evening. You'll probably have to queue.'

With nothing else better to do I walked - unchallenged - out of the base, passing the striped pole that officiously blocked the road outside of the Guardroom, intending to locate the phone booth.

'Lofty!' called a voice.

I turned. Corporal Browning, the police NCO from Bodwinton, stood in the Guardroom doorway, his arm outstretched like a saluting Nazi. He beckoned me over and invited me into his daunting military sanctum; much to the inquisitive concern of the Duty Guard who were not used to seeing a 'snowdrop' drinking tea with an 'erk'.

He listened, interested, as I brought him up to date on what had happened to the others, and of my endless wait for the promised 'home' posting.

'Jammy bastard,' he said enviously. 'AVM's personal staff, eh! I'll be saluting you next.'

We went on to talk of other things. I mentioned that I would be phoning Laura later that evening and asked if he would lend me a few pennies as I only had seven pence to my name and didn't think that would be enough for more that a few seconds chat.

'Can do better than that mate,' he said. 'If you promise not to tell a soul, I can get you an outside line from here later on, providing you don't hog it and take too long.'

'Christ. That would be great Corp. You have my word; I will not mention it to a soul.'

'Okay then. Make it about seven. I go off at eight. Come straight in here,' he indicated the room where we were, 'and wait if I'm busy.'

CHAPTER SEVENTEEN

The bed felt as if it were vibrating, but Laura knew it was her that was trembling as she lay propped up by the pillows, filing her nails, preparing herself for Jim's expected call, planning and rehearsing what she would say. She knew she still loved him - of course she did - but promised herself not to let it show..... Well, not too obviously. It had been a long six months and many things had happened. She knew in her heart she would forgive him and take him back, but she wouldn't make it too easy. 'Don't be a door-mat Laura,' she said to herself. 'Be strong'.

The strident ringing of the shop phone made her jump and she rushed downstairs, sliding her hands down the rails either side of the narrow stairway, feet hardly touching the carpeted treads; heart pounding as she snatched at the phone. As soon as she heard his voice it knocked her for six and all her good intentions were forgotten. His words came out in a rush. In the little time he had, he said how much he loved and wanted her. How much he missed her, and longed to hold her. Breathlessly, he asked her forgiveness and vowed it would never ever happen again. He had been a fool, an absolute idiot. Briefly - his time was running out - he told her he was waiting for the 'home' posting that should come through any moment. He would phone again the minute it did and he'd be on the first train home....if she would have him? She couldn't get a word in edgewise, barely had time to say 'Yes' before he had to hang-up.

For several seconds she stood in the darkened shop - her mind in a whirl - looking at the black bakelite telephone now resting silently on its cradle, trying to imagine him at the other end, wondering if he felt as wretched as she did. He said he loved her, but did he? Were his words sincere? She thought they were, she *hoped* they were. She so wanted to believe him.

Lost in thought, she returned tiredly up the dismal stairs, her energy drained after the sudden adrenaline rush, and looked around at the flat that, over the months, she had made her home. Her choice of pictures hung on the walls, the choice of decor reflected her personality. It was almost as she wanted it, except for the worn settee that would be replaced when funds permitted. Yet, it still lacked something, and she knew perfectly well what it was ....love.

She walked across the newly carpeted floor that had nearly broke the bank despite being fairly inexpensive, and pushed open the bedroom door with its flower-patterned porcelain knob. It was the only room still waiting to be decorated. She knew exactly what she planned to do with it, when she could afford it, and first on the agenda was the bed. That just <u>had</u> to go, for several reasons. It was old and uncomfortable. It had been the Dunnell's before she moved in, and she hated the thought of that, even though she had bought a cheap new mattress. And last, but not least, was that it reminded her of the night spent in it with Daniel. One part of her wanted to forget him; to erase what happened from her mind, forever. To pretend it never happened. The other part recalled the tenderness of his love-making, so fantastically wonderful. At first she had been so turned-on by his body, so aroused, so excited. Desperately, she had wanted to please him, and he had done things to her that she had only ever fantasised about.

With Jim, sex had always been sensational; satisfying yes, but unadventurous in a deeply loving way that always left her with a warm glow of being his adored wife. Her response to Daniel had been different. She had wanted to be his whore-in-bed; anything to please, so many varying positions, so fabulous. Until guilt overcame her emotions, and the man between her legs suddenly became nothing but an invited rapist. This was not love - only lust. It had hit her like a cold shower. She had wanted it over quickly, like NOW; so she'd faked a noisy orgasm knowing it would bring him to a climax.

Nevertheless, she thought - looking down pensively at the bed that had, at the time, been so rumpled and wet with sweat - it had been a tremendous thrill. Something she would never forget... could never forget; a skeleton in her cupboard, and in her conscience. Yet, her sense of decency rebelled against letting her share that same bed with Jim who, no doubt, would assume that is where it had happened. It wouldn't be fair to him. She would buy a complete new bed for Jim and her. It would have to be on the never-never, and delivered quickly. It was the least she could do, a job for first thing in the morning. She wanted to be a proper wife again.

'Bad night?' remarked Anne, raising her eyebrows questioningly at Laura's haggard appearance as she hung her coat in the storeroom that doubled as a temporary staff rest-room. 'Looks like you've been out on the tiles all night.'

Laura's face cracked into a lacklustre grimace. She felt so tired and jaded after a sleepless night worrying about her marriage. 'Gee, thanks,' she said, 'Just what I needed to be told.'

Busying herself around the shop in preparation to opening, Anne could not help feeling concern. She could see the dark rings under her friend's dull eyes and the strain on her face. It didn't need an Einstein to know something was wrong........again. They had a deep bond between them and, knowing Laura as she did, she knew when not to ask questions. If Laura wanted her to know she would tell her in her own good time. 'Why don't you go back to bed for an hour. I can manage, as long as you're down by 10.30, for the interviews.'

Laura stood behind the counter, unlocking the till and checking the cash 'float'. She looked up in surprise. 'What interviews?'

Anne turned, fists on hips, tight mouthed in mock annoyance. 'You are seeing three applicants for the new assistants job......remember?'

'Oh, Christ! I'd forgotten all about that.'

CHAPTER EIGHTEEN

AIR MINISTRY. LONDON.

'Air Vice-Marshall Roley to see you, Sir,' announced the young Waaf officer, flicking the switch of the intercom on her littered desk and waiting for a response. Absent-mindedly, she looked at the second-hand of the bland-faced clock, hanging crookedly on the office wall facing her, nervously watching it twitching its tired circuit to nowhere. Only eleven o'clock and already she felt mentally and physically exhausted. Could she stay awake until lunch-time? The back-log of paperwork in her 'IN' tray didn't seem to lessen in ratio to the increasing pile in her 'OUT' tray, and last night's party with its romantic aftermath didn't help matters. 'Bloody Aussie pilots' she smiled to herself, nostalgically.

'Ask him to come in please.'

She nodded permission to the back of the elderly officer who, having already heard the invitation was already disappearing through the heavy panelled door. She tried to image what he had looked like as a young man, and decided he must have been rather dishy. Not that she fancied older men. Still.......he had a nice bum.

'Ha! Gerald,' greeted the Air Marshall, rising out of his soft leather swivel chair from behind an enormous polished desk; his extended hand with upward facing palm indicating towards one of the pair of slightly less luxurious chairs. 'Good of you to come at such short notice. Don't get much chance to see you these days. Too bloody busy, what! How's Joyce?'

'Fine thank you, Sir,' replied the grey-haired visitor, not deigning to correct his pompous, self opinionated superior. His wife's name was June, not Joyce, and she had died two years ago from the dreaded 'C'. He settled himself, expectantly, wondering what this was all about.

'Won't keep you long, old chap,' said the resonant voice from out of a luxuriant handle-bar moustache. 'Care for a snort?'

The AVM shook his head, wondering why this pathetic, and rather aged officer, insisted on still talking like a teenage pilot. 'No thank you, Sir.'

'It's about this National Service chappie you've requested for your personal staff,' continued the Air Marshall, pompously leaning back in his chair, his steepled fingers caressing the tip of his nose and fondling the greying, regulation *Biggles* moustache.

The AVM remained silent, thinking. So that was the reason for this 'urgent' call. Why was an Air Marshall involving himself in staff postings? Someone running to him with tales? Someone jealously begrudging him a 'perk'?

'I am led to believe that you want him to look after your private yacht?' His inflection rose at the end making it into a question, and he lifted a heavy eyebrow, theatrically. 'Is that correct?'

'Yes, that is absolutely correct,' said the AVM, determined not to give his obnoxious chief the pleasure of seeing him annoyed. 'He lost his job in ASR when two launches were de-serviced. He is a qualified Merchant Marine navigating officer with, I think, ten years sea experience and I thought it best he be employed usefully for the remainder of his two years; for his benefit and that of the Royal Air Force. Better that, than white-washing lumps of coal to decorate a Station Commander's house somewhere.' He leaned forward, opening his eyes wider. 'I believe, as a senior officer - albeit a non-flying engineer type - that I am entitled to an occasional perquisite?'

The moustache bristled, clearly annoyed. Being surrounded by obsequious staff all day he was unused to such a response. 'Mm. Yes Gerald, I don't deny that, but it's the political issues that concern me. The media would have a field day with it.'

'Why?' asked the AVM, stubbornly. 'It's no different than having a private driver, or a personal servant, or a gardener for that matter.' He knew the be-medalled Air Marshall had all three. 'And who would think it necessary to inform the media? Unless of course, it would be your informant.'

The AM's face reddened under the twitching whiskers and he placed his elbows on the desk, fingers cradled, controlling his anger. 'Not the same,' he snapped, (although - if asked, he could not have stated the difference). 'We cannot be seen to be using conscripts in such a manner. I'm afraid I must deny your request.'

The AVM's unflinching blue eyes momentarily stared across the desk, quietly angry. Then he stood, white knuckles resting either side of a model Spitfire adorning the table top. 'If that is your final decision, Sir,' he said, emphasising the last word, 'then of course there is nothing further to be said. But I fail to understand why an officer of your seniority should bother with such trifling details as appointments and postings. I myself am far too busy to get involve with minor items. I could have done with his, and your, help.'

'I think you have made your point, and said enough, Gerald,' said the irate, hirsute face.

'Yes, I agree,' replied the unbowed AVM as he turned, walked across the plush carpet, and quietly closed the heavy door behind him.

The Waaf officer didn't see him go. She was too deep in thought and worry, huddled over her desk, staring at a broken finger nail. She had drunk too much last night and couldn't remember if the Aussie had used any precaution. Blasted Colonials, couldn't be gentlemen if they tried. She tried to remember his face, but the image eluded her.

Outside, fuming silently, the AVM returned the salute of a passing airman who was shocked to hear such a senior officer mutter 'Stupid bloody prat.' The poor lad looked down at his uniform. No buttons undone, everything looked all right. His cap was on square, he'd saluted with the right hand. What had he done that was wrong? Bloody officers. All bloody barmy.

CHAPTER NINETEEN

The long-suffering springs of the unmade bed twanged, and crunched, as I twisted around onto my side. Propping myself up on an elbow, I looked at the tattered calendar stuck to the side of the steel locker beside the bed with adhesive tape, by an unknown airman who had occupied this space before me. He had neatly crossed out every day of the whole of July, and the first two weeks of August. The following four days were unmarked, like laundered football shirts hanging from a clothes' line.

I had started my own marking by blanking out the whole of each day's square; no neat and tidy crosses for me. That was a week ago. Seven wasted days out of my life. Seven days spent on my back, waiting for something to happen.

I stared, disinterested, at the scantily clad blonde, sitting provocatively astride a colourful motor-cycle in the picture that filled the top half of the calendar, and wondered if its previous owner had felt as forlorn and forgotten as I did. Where was he now?....Posted to some God-forsaken unit?....In a cushy billet enjoying himself?....or maybe even demobbed and back in civvy street?

I laid back, hands cushioning my head, thoughts wandering aimlessly, thinking about the past; dreaming about the uncertain future, and my Laura.

Tired of gazing up at the strutted, un-ceilinged roof of the billet, and the hypnotic swing of the shaded light-bulbs swaying in the pervasive draughts among the rafters, my heavy eyelids closed droopily over unfocussed eyeballs that had begun to trend uncontrollably inwards towards each other, as I drifted off into dreamland.

She was running away from me, looking back fearfully over her shoulder, her long golden hair streaming across her face. I tried to call to her to tell her not to be afraid, but the words wouldn't come out; I was dumb. I ran faster, but wasn't moving. It was as though I was running through glue as I reached out for her, but my boneless arms sagged uselessly. I felt myself falling forward; face down into the glutinous ooze that surrounded me. She stopped, turned around and beckoned to me, but I was sinking.

175

'OY! Highman,' shouted a voice in my ear. 'You're wanted in Admin.'

I awoke with a start, and automatically swung my stockinged feet off the crumpled grey blanket, almost kicking the surprised erk who stood over me. 'Right,' I answered, not really knowing if it was Christmas Day or the Autumnal Equinox, as I followed him to the door. His disapproving look, as he went out, warned me something wasn't right. I returned to my bed to put on my battle-dress blouse, beret and boots and was half-way to the door again before realising that my braces were dangling down around my legs like a Cossacks sword-belt. My mouth tasted like the bottom of a parrot's cage and I had a throat like a gravel path. I must have fallen asleep with my mouth open. I felt as dry as a dead camel and would have willingly killed for a drink.

'Think you were forgotten did you, Highman,' greeted the Admin. Flight Sergeant, as I entered his cluttered office.

The refreshing spring air had been a tonic during the short walk from my billet. I'd feel better in a decade, or two.

He handed me my orders and, to save me reading them said, 'You're going to RAF Grassmere as a Safety Equipment Assistant. It's a Fighter Command Station so should be a cushy little number for you.' Little did he know his words devastated me. What had happened to my AVM's staff posting? Everything was falling to pieces - yet again.

'Here's your travel warrant,' he said, holding it out to me. 'You haven't got to report until Monday, so if you get away sharpish tomorrow, you could break your journey and have a few days at home..... Pompey, isn't it?

'Yes, Flight. Thanks, Flight,' I answered, still trying to get my head around the shock of the disappointment as he handed me another envelope.

'Letter for you. From the Air Ministry,' he smiled, with some curiosity. 'Got an Uncle who's an Air Marshal, have we?' He arched his eyebrows and waited, expectantly, for the enlightenment that wasn't forthcoming then, after a short pause, said, 'You could get most of your clearing routine done this afternoon and just leave the bedding store, and us, for the morning.' He was referring to the routine of going around the various sections on the Station, getting signatures from those in charge as proof there was nothing outstanding between the departing airman and that section. 'Come back before five and I'll let you know the train times for tomorrow morning and........' he added jokingly, 'if you give me a big kiss, I'll arrange transport to the Railway Station for you.'

Outside, I tore open the letter with shaking fingers and opened the hand-written, officially headed pages.

My dear Highman, (it read).

I am taking this unusual step of writing to you because I think you are entitled to know why, after the promises made, I am unable to take you onto my personal staff. Those in higher office (Yes, I too have seniors whom I am required to answer to) have deemed it inappropriate that I should use a National Serviceman for the purpose we discussed. However, I am not beaten yet, and I sincerely hope you will find the posting I have managed to arrange for you will, in some small way, make amends.

I wish you good luck.

Gerald Roley.

Air Vice- Marshal.

The thoughtfulness of the man made me feel a bit better, but not much. I had really been looking forward to the job and living at home with Laura. Still, it could have been worse. Grassmere wasn't too far away. Bloody sight better that the Far East, or the Outer Hebrides. I suppose I should count my blessings.

One of the places I had to obtain a clearance signature from was the Guardroom, and fortunately my friend Corporal 'Gravy' Browning was on duty. 'Any chance of a quick phone call later this evening Corp?' I asked, hopefully. 'Just to let the wife know I'm coming home. Give her time to get rid of the lodger.'

He stuck out his lower lip and shrugged. 'No problem. But if anyone's in here with me when you come, have your message already written out and hand it to me. Then I'll phone it through later.'

'Great,' I said, offering my hand. 'and in case I don't get to see you in the morning, or get a chance tonight, thanks for everything.'

He took my hand and shook it, heartily. 'Been nice knowing you, Lofty, and the best of luck. Let me know how you get on 'cause it looks as though I'll be here until Jesus arrives.'

I walked away with a heavy heart and after a couple of dozen paces turned to look back. He was still standing at the Guardroom door, and gave me a salute. I did not see him again after that evening, although I did write as promised. He never answered, maybe he didn't receive it. Wonder where he is now?

CHAPTER TWENTY

The upholstered seat in the compartment was as hard as a slab of solid rubber, barely indented by my eleven-and-a-half stone body-weight, and my long suffering bottom felt like the bruised toes of a ballerina after hours of practising her points on blocks. I looked, unsympathetically, at the empty seat opposite, with its covering ripped and slashed by a mindless moron, probably bored out his skull with being human - or maybe by a trainee surgeon revising for an appendectomy exam. The knife, or scalpel, would surely have been well and truly blunted.

Happily, the smiling bikini-clad beauty, protruding from the advert above the seat that invited everyone to visit sunny Bognor, gazed down on the torn seat forgivingly; despite her Hitlerian moustache added by a budding artist. Next to her, a similar holiday advert extolled the virtues of Scunthorpe from which an exponent of the English language had erased the first letter, and the last five, presumably an attempt to describe himself.

Twisting to ease the pressure on one buttock, and to increase the suffering of the other, I looked out of the window; unconsciously trying to count the telegraph poles being snatched past every second or two, each one taking me that much nearer to home, blindly indifferent to the background patchwork of the multi-shaded green Dorset countryside being alternately lit by the bright Autumn sunshine, then darkened by the shadows of fluffy grey-white cumulus clouds racing across the face of a glowing sun that was still trying to give warmth to the land after a cool night.

Cows stood endlessly chewing the cud; like bored housewives discussing "Her up the road and her flash new boy friend" over a demarcating fence, while critically surveying each others less-than-white washing hanging limply from sagging clothes lines, and certainly not failing to note the state of her neighbours bedroom lace curtains that concealed God-knows-what happenings within.

Even the sight of a weary farmer, draped sleepily over the wheel of his bouncing tractor as it led a cloud of hovering sea birds diving noisily for juicy worms along the furrows of newly ploughed earth, failed to register in my mind as the train rushed through the dividing fields towards Southampton where I had to change trains. All I could see was the reflection of my own miserable face staring back at me. I was going home for a few days; I should be happy. Why wasn't I happy? Because I was bloody miserable, that's why!

I had phoned Laura the previous evening from the Guardroom, to tell her of my new posting and that I would be home the next day, then waited hopefully for an excited response. After a few seconds worrying pause she had said, 'Any idea what time you will arrive?' So cool, so unloving; as if she had something else arranged.

'About sixish I think.... all being well.'

'You'll want some tea then?'

'Yes please,' I said, and then added for some reason, 'If that's okay.'

'Yes, fine. See you about six then.'

I took the hand-set away from my ear as it clicked off before I had finished saying goodbye and looked, angrily, at the mouthpiece; shocked at her abruptness. Was she really going to make things difficult? Trying to be deliberately hurtful? Was there to be no forgiving? I would soon know.

I got off the train at Fratton Station just as the big hand of the platform clock clunked noisily to cover the figure twelve. Bang on six o'clock and I still had at least a twenty minute walk over the bridge and along Goldsmith Avenue (probably longer carrying a case and heavy kit-bag slung across my shoulders), but I had no option without the price of a bus fare in my pocket.

The Avenue itself was busy, mostly with late workers cycling home, as I staggered - heavily laden - along the pavement, thinking of the other connotation put to the saying *'Getting off at Fratton'* and wondering who first applied it to the act of a man withdrawing from his partner during sex and just before reaching his climax, if not wearing a Durex, in the hope of preventing an unwanted pregnancy. Of course, an officer would call it *'Coitus Interruptus.'*

'Want a lift chum?' called a voice from the cab of a small open truck as it drew up alongside me; heaven sent.

'Please. I'm only going as far as the White House pub.'

'S'right. Hop in,' he invited, leaning across his cab to open the near-side door. 'Put your gear in the back.... It is clean.'

It only took three minutes to cover the distance, during which time he treated me to a quick resume of his service career in the Army. I listened attentively and politely. I was very grateful.

'Done lots of hitch-hiking in my time,' he reminisced wistfully, pulling up at the Milton junction to let me off, waving away my gratitude as he crunched his engine back into gear. 'Good luck, mate,' he called cheerily; his good deed for the day done.

I must admit to being a mite apprehensive as I turned the corner. It seemed very strange to be going to the shop instead of to her Mum's house. How would I be received? Surely our marriage was not irreconcilable? We hadn't even talked 'properly' yet. I would give anything to turn the clock back and undo the wrongs….. Would she?

I looked up under the peak of my cap, head tilted sideways by the shouldered kit-bag. There was no twitching of the curtains covering the shop windows. There was no one looking to see if I was coming.

Nervously, I dropped my case and bag at the door, and knocked. Obviously Laura wasn't waiting behind it, as it took some seconds before she answered - or was she purposely making me sweat?

I heard the bolt click, and the door slowly opened, jangling the bell on its hanging spring. It wasn't exactly flung open in ecstasy, neither did she greet me with a huge excited grin, or fling herself into my arms and smother me with kisses, as I had hopelessly wished. She just stood back against the wall, holding the door open for me.

'Hello,' she welcomed, with a small tight smile. 'I've only just shut up the shop.'

I picked up my gear and crabbed sideways past her, feeling like an unwelcome 'late' customer.

Laura pointed to the panelled door at the far end of the counter. 'That door there,' she said. 'Up to the flat'.

Sod it, I thought. One of us has to make the first move, so I dropped my gear to the floor and held out my arms to her, with a smile and a pleading look.

Carefully, and deliberately, as though to give herself time to think, she closed and bolted the door then turned and, after a slight hesitation, walked towards me; but not into my arms. Her outstretched hands took hold of mine and held them down at our sides as she tilted her head up and to the side, inviting a kiss on the cheek. God! She was so beautiful. Emotion boiled up inside me. I snatched my hands away from hers and wrapped my arms around her, pulling her tightly to me. I felt her stiffen, her arms remaining at her side. I nuzzled into her neck, smelling the sweetness of her hair, tears flooding my eyes, and whispered in her ear, 'I love you so much darling.'

We stood like that for several minutes, totally unmoving; then she slowly lifted her hands to my elbows in a silent gesture - of acceptance?

I took my arms away and cradled her face in my hands. She felt so good. Her eyes were moist, her lips so inviting. I couldn't stop myself from kissing her.

At first, the lips that looked so warm and soft were cold and hard, but then she seemed to melt slightly, and began to respond. Our kissing became more intense, it was fantastic; she was mine again. I wanted it to last forever as we clung passionately to each other, but then my male-type wiring switched-on and my libido went into overdrive. I became aroused, and too amorous. Suddenly, as quickly as I had switched-on, she switched-off; pushing me away from her with her hands flat against my chest and muttering 'No, No, No.'

Rejected and dejected, my ardour and ego deflated rapidly. I felt stupid. I had blown it, yet again.

'Sorry. Sorry,' I pleaded, as she broke away, through the door and up the stairs to the flat.

I must have sat on my case downstairs for a good five minutes, trying to compose myself and come to terms with Laura's reaction. Her feelings were becoming crystal clear. She didn't love me any more....did she?

I picked up my gear again, deciding to play it cool from now on. Let her take the lead, if she wanted to. She knew how I felt; now it was up to her.

'Can I bring my gear up?' I called.

She came to the top of the stairs. I could see she had been crying. 'Yes, of course you can,' she said, 'it's your home too.'

My heart and hopes came back from under my boots. Hope springs eternal.

Laura showed me around the flat as if she were an estate agent trying to make a sale. It was wonderful. Everything had her touch. It was where she lived and slept, but I had to fight off the memory that this was also where she had made love with someone else.

Desperately I tried to concentrate my thoughts on other matters. How could I ask her to forgive me unless I forgave her?

'Put your stuff in the second bedroom' she said, pushing open its door. 'It's hardly worth unpacking as you are only staying a few days.'

I didn't quite know how to take that. What did she mean? I decided not to ask; I might not like the answer.

'The bathroom's in there if you want to freshen up,' she offered, indication the pine door next to her bedroom.

I felt much better after having a wash, and a welcome change into my old 'civvies'. It was good to get out of uniform.

After an embarrassingly quiet tea of delicious scones and delicate sandwiches, we sat together on the settee in front of the empty fireplace and silent radio, sharing a bottle of white wine brought up from the shop.

At first, we 'small-talked' about her job, and the shop, and her hopes for its future. I admired the success she had made of her life and told her how proud I was of her for doing it all on her own. Whether it was this compliment that made her glow or the wine, I don't know. Probably the wine, because as the level in the bottle dropped lower, our shyness and reserve lessened. Talking became much easier until, quite late in the evening and after another bottle had mysteriously appeared from downstairs, the dreaded subject that we had both been studiously avoiding, cropped up. In turn, we told the details of our infidelity. I was as honest and open as I could be, and I think she was the same.

Somehow - I suppose the numbing influence of the wine had a lot to do with it - hearing the facts first hand of why, and how, was not so horrendously hurtful. In fact, I think Laura felt as relieved as I was to get it out into the open. We sat holding hands, listening, talking and commiserating with each other. Trying hard to understand the difficulties we had both been through. Neither of us asked for, or sought, forgiveness. The moment was just for honest explanation and admission. The time for forgiveness and forgetting would be in the future, if at all. That would be up to the two of us now that our cards were on the table; face up.

It was past midnight when we decided it was time for bed. Both bottles were empty and we were mentally and physically exhausted.

After two attempts I managed to get to my feet and stay there, hovering over Laura like a tethered barrage balloon in a strong wind as

I tried to choose which of her four hands would be best to haul her to her feet with. Eventually, with a lot of giggling, we stood holding on to each other for mutual support, waiting for our eyes to settle. I said something about seeing her to her bedroom then going to sleep in the second room - or on the settee (if I remember correctly). She didn't answer. Her unfocused eyes roamed over my face, frowning heavily, then she broke away holding on to one of my hands, and towed me, weaving, across to her bedroom. She fell through the door onto her knees. I bent over to help but became top-heavy and ended up knelt beside her, both of us laughing like a couple of hysterical school girls after their first illicit taste of champagne

'Yewrr my hosbant' she slurred, staring wide-eyed at something alien on the tip of my nose, 'and you sleep, hic, with me.'

A little man in the back of my head, wearing three stripes and with a mouth like a coal hole, roared 'Always obey the last order.' I thought he was lovely.

With great difficulty, our sides splitting with laughter, and with tears running down our cheeks, we levered ourselves up on our feet and with great concentration, shuffled towards the bed. Laura put one knee up on it then collapsed face down into the quilt. Feeling my way around to the other side, I stood looking down on her as though from a great height, then taking several deep breaths, like an athlete preparing for a tug-of-war, I took hold of her hands and dragged her fully onto the bed.

After a five minute Naafi break, to recover and let the room settle down, I started to undress her, lifting and rolling her dead-weight around to remove each item that I then threw neatly into the corner of the room. My blurred vision, and clumsy uncoordinated fingers, made a hash of the more intimate bits, such as unbuttoning her stockings and unclipping the suspender belt and bra, (I wasn't used to women's webbing); but perseverance prevailed and at last I rolled her naked body between the sheets, without a single sexual thought in my head. My clothes joined hers in the corner with an accuracy that would have delighted a darts player striving for double-top.

Eyes closed, and completely shattered, I slid into bed beside her; then immediately sat up and climbed out again, stubbing my little toe painfully as I felt my way around the supportive walls, to the toilet where my aim was a bit erratic, so I made a mental note to get up before Laura in the morning, to clean up the mess.

Back in bed, flaked out on my back too shattered to turn over on my side, my eyelids glittering with shooting stars, I was just about to slide into a deep black hole when Laura turned over towards me and threw a warm leg and arm across me. She tried to push her nose into my ear and whispered 'Iz a new bed. Only came yesterday.'

'Pardon' I asked, uncomprehendingly. But she was already asleep.

It was the muffled thud of a closing drawer that woke me in the morning, and I cautiously opened one sticky eye to test my brain's response. Daylight, peeping from the sides of the heavy curtains and playing over the edges of the papered wall, lit the dim room like a square corona; casting shadows. The little three-striped man in the back of my head beat his bass drum with sadistic glee. Wine drinking was not my forte.

The thought of wine recalled the events of last evening and, despite a hazy memory of its last hours, the vision of Laura's naked loveliness as I put her to bed, was as clear and vivid as a flash photograph. Gingerly, I turned to look at the pillow beside me; it was empty. Nothing but an indentation; there was no Laura. I began to panic.

Forgetting the malevolent drummer, I raised my heavy head and myopically scanned the gloomy room. Then I saw, and recognised, Laura's shadowy figure cross the foot of the bed, her hands groping up between her shoulder blades fiddling with a recalcitrant bra fastener. Like a tideway, my panic ebbed away and relief flowed in. It wasn't all a dream.

'Morning,' I grated, with a mouth like a coal-miner's jockstrap.

She came to stand beside me, like a beautiful angel surrounded in an aura of half-light, and bent over, leaning her hands on the bed, her hair tumbling down around her face.

'Sorry. Did I wake you?'

The vision of her standing there, the whiteness of her bra and brief hipster knickers glowing almost luminously, was the most erotic sight I have ever seen and it will be etched in my memory until my dying day. My hormones started to react and the little three-striper hastily threw away his drum and started to shout and bawl in my ear, ordering me to control myself, to remember to play it cool and not to blow it again.

'Yes, you did,' I answered her, holding out a hand, dearly wanting to place it on her thigh - or somewhere. 'But thank you. I wouldn't have missed the view for anything.'

She laughed. 'Behave yourself and go back to sleep. I have got to go downstairs now. It's twenty-to-eight and the girls will be here any minute. I'll open the shop and get them sorted; then come back up to do you something for breakfast.' She gave me a quick chicken-peck on the cheek then moved away, to finish dressing in her working skirt and blouse. 'See you in a minute.'

I laid back, hands behind my head trying to pacify and de-stress my little overworked three-striped alter ego; and cursed my luck. I had forgotten Laura would have to work.

Quickly exhausting my vocabulary of Anglo-Saxon expletives, I stared blindly up at the polystyrene ceiling-tiles that were all the rage at the time. For twenty minutes or so, I drifted in and out of sleep, fantasising about my gorgeous Laura - then the bloody shop-door bell started. Clang-clang, clang-clang. Every time a customer came in or out of the shop. Every two minutes. Clang-clang, Clang-clang; like a town crier who wouldn't move on. It was getting on my nerves. What did they want the bloody thing for? Surely they could see customers coming in!

I pulled the pillow over my face in vain. I could still hear every maddening, tinny chime... but I couldn't breathe. Exasperated, I flung off the bed covers and got out of bed. Clang-bloody-clang. Even in the kitchen, with the toaster going full blast and the radio blaring, there was no respite. Clang-bloody-clang. I was going to silence that illegitimate bell if it was the last thing I ever did.

'You're up,' said Laura with surprise as she joined me in the kitchen. 'I've come up to do your breakfast.'

'I'm fine,' I answered, waving my Marmite toast. 'This'll do me.'

She dropped her chin and looked up at me from under raised eyebrows, sensing my anger. 'Something wrong?'

'Yeah! That bloody door bell is driving me up the wall.'

'Is that all?' she laughed gently, her eyes twinkling. 'I thought it was something serious.'

'ALL! I snapped back with a half smile to take the sting out of my outburst. 'It is serious. I feel like flippin' Quasimodo.'

'Tea?' she asked, pointedly turning down the volume of the radio and spooning tea-leaves from the caddy into a pot without waiting for my reply as I cut myself another slice of bread from the loaf and dropped it into the toaster.

I turned around to see Laura poised over the stove, her back to me, watching the kettle boil. My leering eyes scanned her from top to toe, feasting on every inch while I ignored the feverish knocking of my little three-striper as he tried to gain my attention. Her soft sandy-coloured hair had an almost golden sheen as it curled across her shoulders, and a bra-strap peeped sexily through the work blouse. From her narrow waist, the black skirt stretched tightly over the firm roundness of her shapely bum, and curving inwards to mould clingingly around her thighs. Vaguely (or was it my visual fallacy), the outline of her knickers, and the small lump of a suspender button, showed provocatively through the material, super-heating my libido despite the frantic remonstrations from my three-striper.

Replacing my eyeballs for a few seconds, I continued my lustful survey of her figure, down to the skirt's hem that ended trendily three or four inches above her knees, to show a pair of perfectly shaped nylon-clad legs that swept curvaceously to slender, delicate ankles; and sensible two-inch heeled work-shoes. Every part of her was fantastic, and my lecherous mind worked overtime with impure thoughts; I trembled uncontrollably. She looked so ravishing, and I was ravenous for her. How the hell could I have ever wanted anyone else?

Levering myself away from the kitchen work-top, I only managed half-a-step towards her before I felt the grip of a Half-Nelson stranglehold around my neck and heard the snarling voice of my guardian angel three-striper yelling urgently in my ear, telling me to 'Cool it, pal. Don't be a prat all your life.' The tinkling sound of a stirring spoon brought me back to my senses.

'You all right?' asked Laura, handing me a steaming mug. 'You look quite pale.'

I suppose that her female intuition, and the look on my face, told her what the problem was. She was all woman, and certainly no fool. Twisting sideways, she placed her cup back on the work-top and came towards me, reaching for my mug and taking it from me to place alongside hers. 'Oh, darling!' she said, wrapping her arms around my neck and pressing the whole length of her body tightly to mine. 'What have we done to each other?'

I clung to her, passionately, never wanting to let her go; wanting her so much, longing for her to want me; my obvious need pressing into her as she returned the pressure. I felt about to explode.

'I don't know, my love,' I panted, kissing her neck, 'but I know what you are doing to me.'

Gently, and I hope reluctantly, she eased herself away, her face flushed. 'Me too,' she giggled, her limpid blue eyes dropping to the bulge that seemed to join our separated bodies. 'But mine doesn't show.'

She turned, and taking hold of my hand led me, crouching in discomfort, towards the bedroom. 'We'll have to be fairly quick, Jim,' she said huskily. 'I don't have much time.'

CHAPTER TWENTY ONE

The Monday morning train journey would have given me the opportunity to reflect back over the fantastic weekend, had it not been for the middle-aged ex-soldier who shared my compartment and insisted on giving me a run-down on his war service - mainly in North Africa and Italy - that in spite of two fairly minor wounds and months of hardship and deprivation, he had, in hindsight, thoroughly enjoyed !!!   From the time we pulled out of Fratton station, until the moment I slammed the carriage door shut on arrival at Hilchester, he did not stop his continuous chattering. If I as much as glanced out of the window for one second he would lean forward and touch my knee to command attention. I found it hard not to rudely ignore him. I didn't want to offend the poor chap who had served his country - and was proud of it - but he was such a bore; not even interesting to listen to.

'Think your self lucky, lad,' he said on more than one occasion. 'I wish I was still in. I remember.....,' and off he would go again. I wished he was still in; in my place!

Luckily, the journey was a short one, and I felt gratefully relieved to step out onto the platform, to leave the old soldier to his dreams.

'The bus stop is over there,' said the genial ticket-collector, pointing across the road. 'Leaves every half-hour. Ask them to drop you off at Boxley; then it's only a short walk to Grassmere.'

I staggered to the indicated stop, virtually dragging my kit-bag over the tarmac, too weary after an energetic weekend to hump it up onto my shoulders.   No one noticed me; no one looked.   Uniformed servicemen were a ten-a-penny sight. Listlessly I sat on the edge of my canvas case, leaning back against the upright kit-bag, alongside the bus stop. The time- table holder hung drunkenly, on one rusted bolt, from the standard that doubled as a lamppost, the paper schedule of bus times all soggy, stained and unreadable through the broken glass front. Fortunately, it was a lovely sunny day with cotton-white clouds being snatched across a blue sky by the warm breeze, and I thanked Saint Globface - the patron saint of pissed-off airmen - that it wasn't pouring with rain.

My twenty-minute wait, and the ensuing short distance bus journey, that took over half-an-hour, seemingly stopping at every other house along the route, gave me time to recapture the last few days with my wonderful Laura.

Our love-making, on that first morning, had been a mixture of shyness, pent-up passion and lustful need. But after the first few hesitant moments of nervous modesty, Laura surrendered herself completely, and for ten hectic minutes we thrashed around on the bed in a frenzy, all thoughts of infidelity banished from our minds; hopefully for ever.

'I must go down now' she panted breathlessly, retrieving her knickers after a short search, and scrabbling around for the rest of her strewn clothing. 'The girls will be wondering what I've been up to.'

I laughed, thinking back over the noise she and the bed had been making. 'I think they'll know, don't you? It must have sounded like World War Two from downstairs.'

She stopped finger-combing her hair and clapped both hands over her open mouth, in a sort of coy shock. 'Wee' she said, 'You don't think they heard anything - do you?'

'Of course not' I assured her; then added with a suggestive grin, 'Unless they were deliberately listening.' She fled.

It was an hour or more before I went downstairs to meet the girls and unscrew that bloody clanging bell from the door. Jenny, the new girl, was busy serving a customer while Laura and Anne stood in animated discussion, sorting the contents of the shelving. I opened the door at the bottom of the stairs and entered the shop; all eyes seemed to turn on me. I felt like some sort of horrible apparition.

Laura, her face still glowing like a blushing bride, dragged Anne towards me. 'Hello, darling, this is Anne.'

Before I could answer, Anne came close and put her arms around my neck and kissed me full on the lips. Stunned, I looked guiltily over to where Laura was standing with a smile of approval spread across her face, watching as the pretty girl - in her late teens I would guess - embraced her husband. Obviously, a great bond of trust and friendship existed between them.

Anne stepped back and surveyed me at arm's length, her eyes twinkling knowingly, as she studied the bags of exhaustion under my eyes. Then, placing the tip of her forefinger on my lips said, 'Oh sorry! Did I hurt you Jim?' Obviously a reference to my bruised lips.

Still flabbergasted, I remained speechless.

'I've heard *so much* about you Jim,' she whispered in a mock sexy voice loud enough for Laura to hear, and trying successfully to act like a Mata Hari. 'I've been longing to meet you.......' Seductively she fluttered her long eyelashes then added, '.......in the flesh.'

Laura burst out laughing, holding her hand to her mouth. Jenny and the customer turned their heads inquisitively. Then I realised it was a wind-up.

Recovering my equilibrium I responded with a vengeance, wrapping my arms around Anne's waist and lifting her off her feet. 'And I've heard you're a wanton hussy who flaunts herself to all the male customers.'

She giggled delightfully as I put her down and kissed Laura, who then turned to the startled customer and introduced me as her husband. A ghost of a smile flitted over the old lady's face as she recognised the light-hearted atmosphere.

'And this is Jenny,' said Laura, holding out her hand to the young teenager whose mouth still drooped open, gob-smacked; wondering what to make of it all.

I lifted my hand in a sort of salute. 'Hi, Jenny.'

'You two can go back upstairs if you want,' said Anne, mischievously. 'We can manage, can't we Jen!'

'Stop it!' warned Laura, pointing an admonishing finger, aware of her friend's innuendo, 'or the unemployment figures will be going up- by one!'

I walked across the shop holding the screw-driver like an officer's sword "at the salute". 'Thanks for the offer love' I answered appreciatively, 'but I've an appointment with a doorbell.'

Later that evening, with the shop shut-up for the night, Laura and I were curled up on the settee in a companionable cuddle; she nursing a cup of tea and me with a glass of beer; gazing into the unlit fireplace. Her head rested on my shoulder lovingly as I buried my nose in her sweet smelling hair.

'Darling,' she said without moving her head. 'Was I very drunk last night?'

'Very,' I mumbled into her hair.

'Were you?' she asked.

'Mmmm, so, so.'

'And did you undress me and put me to bed?'

The memory switched-on my hormones and lust stirred in my naughty parts. 'I sure did.'

She tilted her face up to mine. 'Then why didn't you take my stockings off as well. They were down around my ankles in the morning... and ruined.'

We both chuckled, but for the life of me I couldn't imagine anyone less like a wrinkled-stocking washerwoman, than my gorgeous girl.

Tactfully, she didn't mention the wet mess on the toilet floor that she had certainly cleaned up.

'Boxley,' called the bus conductor, bringing me back from my reverie. 'Your stop, lad. Go straight down there.' He pointed to the narrow road turning off on the opposite side.

'Thanks,' I said, not really meaning it, as I dragged my gear off the platform onto the grass verge. He had interrupted a beautiful dream and left me standing beneath a broken signpost arrowing into the ground. "RAF Grassmere" it read. 'Much obliged.'

Thankfully, the railway station's ticket-collector had been right. It was only a short hike - about a quarter mile - before I arrived, like an over-loaded donkey, at the curved white-washed walls that narrowed into the main gate. A snowdrop, resplendent in white cap, webbing and revolver holster to match the walls, stood in the warm sunshine, feet apart like a miniature *Colossus of Rhodes*, outside of the Guardroom on which a huge sign advised anyone who may have been misdirected that, within these portals was, RAF. GRASSMERE. 11 Group Fighter Command.

I approached the guardian of military law with some trepidation. Was he from the Hednesford mould, or Bodwinton? Dumping my gear at his feet I reported, 'New bod, Corp. For the safety equipment section.'

His stern face regarded me for some seconds and then surprisingly, as though in recognition, his face contorted into his version of a smile, the corners of his mouth curving upwards, seeking his ear lobes. I was soon to learn the reason for such a friendly welcome.

'Inside and sign-in, mate,' he said, nodding towards the immaculate Guardroom, itself guarded by blood-red fire buckets full of sand, a brilliantly polished ship-type bell with a virginal-white rope, and numerous white-washed boulders. 'You can leave your gear in the

192

cells and collect it later if you want,' he invited, 'while you report at the Admin office.'

I was duly impressed.

After booking-in at Admin, almost like an hotel guest, and being advised of the necessary joining routine, I was directed to the S.E.Section that would be my place of work. It was a brick-built oblong building, back along the road towards the Guardroom and adjacent to the imposing, but almost engineless, WW2 Spitfire fighter plane, that stood as an awesome reminder of the Station's wartime importance as one of the main Battle of Britain airfields.

Without knocking (I was an old hand now), I opened the door and found myself in a small reception area consisting of a counter and nothing else except a telephone and a few box files. There was no sign of life. I banged on the counter, whistled and called out, for attention. No response. With the confidence of my vast service experience I lifted the counter-flap and stepped through to another door. I knocked again. Still nothing, so I opened it and walked into a work-shop that occupied about one half of the building. There were a number of work tables, store cupboards and various machines, but no bodies. At the far end there was another door. This time my knock was answered by a meaningless grunt, so I opened the door of what was obviously a store area. There were two men playing cards at a small table being watched by a third. They looked up, disinterested, as I entered. One, the spectator, with two chevrons of a Corporal on his arm band, raised an enquiring eyebrow as the other two returned their attention to a battered crib board.

'Highman' I said, by way of introduction. 'Come to join this section.'

Three pairs of eyes became suddenly interested, as the cards were placed face down on the table, to be continued later.

The NCO, a swarthy, balding man in his early thirties, stood and extended his hand. 'Dave C********' he said, announcing a surname that sounded totally incomprehensible (I later saw it in writing. It appeared to be about a dozen consonants, mainly Z's, Y's and K's). I wasn't surprised to learn he was of Polish origin and known to everyone, officers and airmen alike, as either Corporal or Ziggy. A trained S.E. fitter, he had been on the station for longer than anyone could remember, and I soon became aware that, as far as the station was concerned, he was Mr. Fixit. If you wanted anything, he could get it. A loan, a piece of equipment, an article of clothing, a travel warrant or leave pass, a girl, a duty stand-in. Apparently nothing was beyond him - for a price. His services were available to officers and men, and very discreet. It was rumoured that, if someone wanted another out of the way, Ziggy could supply the assassin, but I think that was an exaggeration; he was too nice a guy.

Only a very small minority were treated by Ziggy with privileged favour. The Station Warrant Officer, and the Station Police, and the Flight Sergeants i/c the Main Stores and Cookhouse. Not one officer was included. It was not hard to reason this selection. Apart from these few, everyone seemed to be in his debt to some degree, hence I suppose, why he managed to stay where he was.

'This' he said, pointing to the skinny teenager with a nose like a doorknob, 'is Robbie Burns.' The youngster grinned. 'And this,' he nodded to the second card player, 'is Wiggy Bennet.'

The red-cheeked, rotund, obviously over-weight lad, asked if I played crib and seemed delighted when I said I did.

'They're both conscripts,' continued the Corporal, a little contemptuously, 'and can't wait to get out.' I got the impression they were not highly regarded by him.

'I'm National Service too Corp,' I admitted before he made any more disparaging remarks.

He frowned to reduce his high forehead. 'Blimey. At your age? How come?'

I repeated the often quoted blurb about my sea service and his eyes lit up with enthusiasm. 'Must know a bit about safety equipment then?' he asked with a look of hope on his sallow face.

'Yes, a bit,' I agreed, 'only maritime stuff though.'

'More than enough,' he grinned. 'You can be my 2 i/c.'

It was the turn of my eyebrows to join my hairline as I looked towards the other two. He saw the direction of my gaze. 'Don't worry about those two idle bastards' he said, 'they're bleeding useless.'

The lads showed no resentment. They had returned to their game and probably hadn't even heard.

'Come on then,' he said, leading me out of the building with his arms chummily around my shoulders. 'Let's get your gear up to the billet and get your joining routine done.'

I was clearly accepted - by him at least.

Back at the Admin office; having overheard me say to the clerk that I came from Portsmouth, he asked, 'Why don't you live out?' -

Meaning why didn't I claim the permitted allowance to live (and eat) at home and come into work each day. 'It's less than twenty miles away.'

'No transport,' I answered disconsolately, and thought no more about it until two days later when I entered the section workshop and found Ziggy in the middle of the floor, standing alongside a BSA Bantam motor-bike, looking like a cat that had got the cream. The bike looked brand new - or nearly so.

'Yours' he grinned. 'Sixty quid, and you can live out.'

I looked at the bike, with longing at first, then disappointment. 'Christ, Ziggy. I can't afford that. I only get twenty-eight bob a fortnight.'

His face fell for a moment and his hand came up to rub his chin. Clearly he wanted to please me. Then he came alive again. 'Five bob a week and give the bike back to me when you go.'

I was sorely tempted, but money was very tight. I had to consult Laura. 'Can you wait until the weekend?' I asked. 'I'll have to ask the Missus.'

Laura was delighted with the prospect of having me home every night, nearly jumping down my throat with glee. 'Of course we can afford five shillings a week love,' she said, 'and a bit more for the petrol.'

Many years were to pass before she told me about the five hundred pounds left to her by Tom Dunwell. She was worried in case I misinterpreted the reason. I always thought it was money she had saved from her salary.

Ziggy was absolutely chuffed when I told him.

'All I have to do now,' I reminded him, 'is to get the okay to "live-out".'

'No problem' he answered. 'Go down to Admin. It's all arranged.'

I was amazed. Was there no limit to what he could organise?

And so, every day I commuted between home and Grassmere. Getting to know all the short cuts as I pop-popped happily along the uncongested roads; not even worried if circumstances made me late. No one would query it. Ziggy would sort it; he could sort anything.

Every weekend was spent at home. Christmas came and went in a haze of happiness and love, as Laura and I cemented our new found relationship. Work was a doddle. With only three operational squadrons flying from the station our work-load was light, to say the least. In fact, the last thing the section needed was an additional hand. I did all the work- what there was of it - and the two lads made the tea, kept the place tidy, played crib and did any chores that came our way. Ziggy was a happy man; nothing to do, except concentrate on his business.

Under the circumstances life was idyllic, and for the next eight months my daily routine consisted of the ride from home, a couple of hours work, then the rest of the day loafing about waiting to go back home again. We did no guard, or fire-watch duties, courtesy of Ziggy's "arrangements". No one dared put our names on a roster without incurring his wrath, and the dire consequences that would inevitably follow.

Ziggy continued to amass his fortune, and reputation, while I lived the life of Riley with my precious Laura. What a way to live! I could easily spend the rest of my days enduring this life-style; but only if the financial rewards were to be vastly increased to a liveable level.

In early August, with only three months left to demob, I received a letter, via the Station Adjutant, from Air Vice Marshal Roley, to say he was sailing *Astra* (his yacht) over to Jersey in the Channel Islands with his daughter in the next week or two and would I still be interested in going over to sail the boat back? If so, I should inform the Station Adjutant who would then make the necessary arrangements, on his behalf.

Laura, knowing how much I would like to do it, urged me to agree. 'It won't take you long' she said, 'and you'll enjoy it. You may never get such an opportunity again.'

The Adjutant accepted my affirmation with a rather stern face. Probably he didn't like the idea of "erks" getting letters from AVM's, but had little option other than to obey his superior who, in any case, was a friend of the Station's Commanding Officer.

Ziggy was impressed. Under his highly arched eyebrows his wide owl-like eyes appraised me in astonishment. 'And I thought I had contacts and influence,' he said in respectful admiration. 'An AVM, no less!'

He was even more amazed, several days later, when he saw my travel orders, instructing me to report to HM.Gunwharf, inside HMS.Vernon, the naval shore establishment at Portsmouth, at a given time and date, to embark on the War Department vessel *HSL Grand Parade*, for onward transportation to Jersey where I was to locate the *Astra*, berthed in the marina.

'Jesus H. Christ and General Jackson,' blasphemed Ziggy over my shoulder, addressing the empty work-shop. 'They've even laid-on a private bleeding speedboat for him!' I went up several notches in his estimation.

On the appointed day, shouldering a kit-bag now bulging with sea-going gear, I walked nonchalantly up to the main-gate of HMS.Vernon and found myself the centre of attraction of the hundreds of sailors going in and out, most of whom probably had never seen an airman entering the place, and considered the RAF as "The Gentleman's Service" for some obscure reason, full of "Brylcream boys". In typical matelot fashion, they gave a couple of wolf-whistles, not knowing that I had wrung more sea water out of my sea-boot socks than they had ever sailed on.

'What do you want, mate?' asked the white-gaitered sailor leaning nonchalantly against the window of the guardroom, his blue collar flapping in the breeze.

I offered him my travel papers saying, 'Gunwharf please,' but he waved them away, not even interested, as he pointed to a road opposite that followed the inside of *Vernon's* boundary wall.

'Down there, chum,' he said, amiably. 'Gunwharf's at the end, just before you fall into the 'oggin.'

Thanking him, and shouldering my kit-bag, I crossed the road. I had hardly taken a dozen steps when a shouted command blared out behind me. 'Oy you! Airman! Where do you think you're going?'

Being the only Raff bod within spitting distance I knew someone was referring to me. I turned around stiffly, swinging my kit-bag, to see what could only be described as a caricature. From under a peaked cap, a florid face with frog-like eyes appeared to be joined, neckless, onto a brass-buttoned uniform that had gold badges on the tunic collar. It stood in the guardroom doorway like a failed dysentery sufferer who hadn't quite made it to the toilet.

The first sailor said something to him as I called out 'Gunwharf,' and I could almost see him deflate, foiled. 'Well, smarten your bloody self up,' he screamed, determined, like all of his ilk, to have the last word and establish his authority.

Tactfully, under my breath, I likened him to my testicles, but thinking they were a damn sight more useful.

As I turned the last bend in the road from *Vernon's* gate the sight that greeted me would have delighted the eyes of any sailor. Scores of small craft, all in a uniform light grey paint, were huddled together like newly hatched chicks, cradled between a strutted jetty on the right that jutted out into Portsmouth harbour, and a wide quay to the left on top of which several craft were chocked-up, high and dry, against the tall walls that were *Vernon's* perimeter buildings. This was H.M.Gunwharf, the home of the Army's Navy.

Alongside both the jetty and the quay, vessels were tied-up, three and four abreast, so that only a narrow gap between the outside ones on each side prevented a crossing from one side to the other. The variety of craft was amazing. From small forty-foot general purpose launches, to sleek HSL's, to powerful sturdy craft like naval MTB's, to a couple of one thousand ton coasters and a trawler. Grand-daddy of them all was a tank landing craft with the letters ADC painted on either bow that, it was later explained, stood for Ammunition Dumping Craft; one of the multifarious tasks undertaken by the War Department Fleet.

As I past a covered workshop at the head of a slip-way, I noticed a building at the seaward end of the quay and decided to make my way towards it. There wasn't a soldier in sight, but striding purposefully in my direction came a figure dressed in navy-blue battle-dress and wearing a sailor's cap with *War Department* on its tallyband. As he neared I could see that on each shoulder of his blouse he wore a small blue ensign defaced with crossed swords. It was the same flag that the vessels were flying.

'Any idea where I can find *Grand Parade*,' I asked him, hopefully.

He stopped suddenly, as though surprised out of a day dream, and looked at me as if I were from Mars; then turned his head to scan knowingly over the fleet. 'There she is,' he said, pointing seaward. 'Layin' outside of the ADC.'

I looked. She was small by comparison with the larger vessel. About fifty feet long and sleek, like a racing greyhound. 'Cheers mate.'

Clambering awkwardly across the ADC, I dropped my kit-bag onto the spotless scrubbed deck of the launch, causing a lurch that brought an enquiring head and shoulders to poke out of the wheel-house door.

'You Highman?' it asked.

'Yes, I......'

'Move it then Chum, we are late.'

'I'm early....' I said, but the head had disappeared and a voice called 'Start her up, Jim.'

The engines burst into life with a cloud of blue-black exhaust fumes that reminded me of the old 3840 and two blue battle-dressed crewmen came out on deck. One went forward and the other aft, as I staggered along the side-deck to squeeze myself, and my baggage, through the narrow door and down the two steps into the cramped wheel-house.

I watched, in admiration, as the launch was driven, stern first, out of Gunwharf in a creditable feat of boat-handling, then being turned seaward to pass out of the harbour entrance at a rate that exceeded the regulation speed limit by just enough to avoid incurring the wrath of the authorities.

Once past the Outer Spit buoy, Sam - the skipper - a thick set jovial-faced man in his forties, pushed the throttles to their stops and *Grand Parade* leapt forward like a thorough-bred, speeding over the wavelets with a smooth growl, heading for Nab Tower and the open sea, as the two deck-hands joined us in the wheel-house.

It was only then that the skipper seemed to remember my presence. 'Sorry about that chum,' he said, offering his hand. 'Welcome aboard. We're a bit adrift you see. We expected you earlier.'

I took his hand and explained that I was aboard ten minutes earlier than ordered.

He smiled; his face lighting up. 'Never mind, eh! You're here now.' He gave me the impression of being an action man. He would face a problem, deal with it, and then put it out of his mind. He introduced his two crewmen, Bill and Sid, who clearly wanted to move away to somewhere less confined, and explained that Jim, the engineer, was below with his box of tricks and would probably stay there for the whole trip. 'He doesn't like fresh air, does our Jim.'

The cross-channel trip was marvellous, just rough enough to be interesting but not bad enough to be uncomfortable. The crew were a good bunch and accepted me as one of their own once they learned I was a seaman first, and an airman second. They also made a terrific cup of tea, frequently.

The five hour voyage passed far too quickly. Sam told me about the War Department Fleet, that he had joined as a Boy Seaman. I was surprised to learn how big it was, in numbers, and that even though it was the Army's navy, the crews were mainly civilian merchant seamen; not soldiers, as I imagined. I told him of my situation and the purpose of my journey to Jersey, and he laughed at my disappointment when he explained that his boat hadn't been "laid-on" especially for me. My lift was a coincidence, no doubt arranged by wheels-within-wheels and the old school-tie. Sam's orders were to proceed to St. Helier where he was to place himself, and the boat, at the convenience of some General or other, who required to go to St. Malo on army business - or, as Sam so prophetically put it, 'On a piss-up with the French Army using us as his private bleeding yacht, I expect.'

CHAPTER TWENTY TWO

I felt truly sad saying goodbye to Sam and his lads when *Grand Parade* tied up in the St.Helier yacht marina; they had been good company and I had to admit to envying their life-style.

With the umbilical kit-bag slung uncomfortably across my shoulders like a dead deer, I stepped ashore to begin the search for *Astra* up and down the numerous pontoons. I had a rough idea what the boat looked like and in all probability her name would be prominently displayed - hopefully.

In accordance with Sod's Law she was at the last pontoon. Had I turned right instead of left in the first place she would have been among the first. I uttered my appreciation of that ancient Law. Her cabin hatch was shut, but not locked. Down below, on the cabin table, I found a note left for me by the AVM, saying his step-daughter Janet - who was living ashore in the Yacht Club - had the boat's keys. He said I should live aboard the boat but to use the marina's facilities and eat at the Yacht Club where arrangements had been made for me to sign for anything I wanted, to be put on his bill. The Club would know me only as Mr.Highman, his yacht skipper. Sounds good to me, I thought, as I unpacked my gear and made-up a bed for myself in the quarter-berth and climbed in. It was still early, just gone eight, but I felt dog-tired. It had been a long day.

I awoke with a start. *Astra* rocked, and footsteps on deck heralded the arrival of someone on board. I wriggled out of the quarter-berth and struggled into trousers as I heard the cabin hatchway being pushed back and the doors opened. My heart pounded as I searched around for a weapon. A female giggle made me look up. The hatch slid open, and from the darkness beyond, a pair of thick, heavy-boned bare legs, emerging from a short flared skirt, were descending the three steps down into the cabin. For someone whose eyes were accustomed to Laura's long slender legs the sight was far from exciting. Thick thighs, followed by a podgy backside, that looked like the stern of the *Vanguard* and should have been covered by a tent rather than a skimpy pelmet, stepped down to reveal a short-haired, broad shouldered girl in her mid-twenties whose huge bosoms were heaving breathlessly from her efforts.

She stared glassily at me from hooded unsteady eyes, trying to concentrate her nomadic eyeballs on the dim shimmering shadow standing before her.

'Who the f*** are you?' she slurred drunkenly, like the lady she obviously wasn't.

'Miss Rowley?' I asked, ignoring her question.

' 'Course,' she said, 'Who the f*** were you 'specting?'

Before I could answer, we were joined by another pair of legs, this time in trousers, topped by a skinny body in a blazer jacket sporting some sort of yacht club badge on the breast pocket. In the gloomy darkness he looked a typical public-school chinless wonder.

The fact that I was bare-footed and stripped to the waist didn't seem to register in her befuddled mind. 'Piss off,' she said, spraying me with saliva from her slack lips. 'This is my boat.'

'I am Highman, Miss Rowley,' I said, trying to reason with her. 'You were expecting me.'

She opened her drooling mouth to say something and then snapped it shut as if forgetting the question. Then lost her balance and sat down heavily on the cushioned locker-seat that creaked under the onslaught.

'Do as the lady tells you,' ordered the trousered prat, in a tone used by cowardly officers when speaking to men whom they knew couldn't respond in kind.

I fixed him with my best Burt Lancaster belligerent glare. 'Miss Rowley is the owner's step-daughter,' I informed him contemptuously, 'and as such I shall do my best to comply with her wishes - when she is sober. Meanwhile, I am the skipper of this boat, put in charge by her father Air Vice-Marshal Rowley, to whom I am responsible. You......' I emphasised the last word pompously, 'are nobody as far as I am concerned, and I reserve the right to put you ashore, or over the side, if I wish. So don't tell me what I should, or should not, do.'

'Oh! I say,' he answered through pursed lips, as though kissing some superior's back-side, completely taken aback by my reaction.

Janet Rowley lifted her Mongolian features from her knees, desperately trying to steady her wildly gyrating world. 'I told you to f*** off,' she spat at the brass barometer which stood on the cabin shelf alongside its sister clock that luminously gave the time as ten to eleven.

I knew she meant me, but I had nowhere to go, so, gathering my shirt and bed-clothes, and with one last despising scowl in the direction of the effeminate Rupert, I retreated to the fore-peak berth, closing the separating door behind me. This berth was wider than the quarter-berth but with no headroom to speak of, so I lay angrily staring up at the underside of the fore-deck less than ten inches above my nose, like a corpse in a coffin.

The banging, crashing and giggling, coming from the main cabin was no lullaby, and I guessed they had already forgotten my existence and were drunkenly trying to lower the cabin table to the level of the surrounding locker-seats to convert it to its other use, as a double bed. Then, apart from shuffling noises, all went quiet for a while until the pair began to grunt and groan in pain, or ecstasy; I suspected the latter. The boat started to rock, and a rhythmic thumping began. 'Harder, harder,' screamed Madam, in decibels that must have been heard all over the marina. I felt sure we would be receiving annoyed visitors before long.

The Rupert might have been effeminate in appearance but his performance proved otherwise. I thought he would go on all night as the banging orchestrated with her grunts, groans and pleadings. It seemed ages before he announced to the marina that he was coming. I heartily wished he were going, and eventually fell asleep to the clinking of bottles against glasses, and the soft mutterings of Laurel and Hardy on the other side of the partitioning door.

All was peaceful and serene as the slapping of water against the hull, and the tapping of halyards against the aluminium mast, woke me. I must have gone out like a light. I reached up in the darkness, like a miner in a tunnel, and awkwardly unscrewed the knurled nuts of the fore-deck hatch, less than the length of my fore-arm, above my face. Blinding daylight flooded my tomb-like berth as I eased the hatch open to let the thick foul air escape. I could almost hear the hiss as it rushed out to be replaced by a funny smell, soon to be recognised by my ruined olfactory organs as fresh air. It was half-past-seven; I had been battened down in a space, not much bigger than my own body, for eight hours. No wonder I had a head like an elephant's tambourine.

I lay there, gratefully sucking in the sweet sea-air, for some time, allowing the fetid stench to clear from my head and lungs, gradually easing the pounding in my oxygen-starved brain. By the time I judged myself to be about ten percent normal; I wormed my stiffened body up through the hatch and onto the fore-deck. It was a cool, breezy morning. God, it felt good. I appreciated how submariners must feel on surfacing after an extended dive.

Careful of my still drumming head, I groped my way aft to the cockpit to see if my visitors of last night were still on board. They weren't, but the lazy drunken buggers had not only left the cabin hatch and doors wide open but also left the cabin itself looking like a bomb had hit it. At least the open hatch had allowed most of the smell to escape, but it still stunk like a brothel soaked in booze; not that I had ever personally experienced such a situation, of course.

The table was still down in double-bed mode, and covered in a wrinkled sheet stained with God knows what. I rolled it up and bundled it into a paper sack ready to be dumped in the litter bin ashore. No way was I going to wash it. If anyone asked where it was I would bloody well tell them!

I opened every porthole and aperture I could find, to let clean air flow through the boat, while I collected the debris of last night's orgy. Two empty wine bottles, two drained beer cans, four glasses (two of them broken), a pair of men's socks, an overflowing ash-tray, and an empty syringe. Jesus! If they were shooting dope into themselves on top of all that alcohol they'd be inviting trouble. I searched the cabin, holding a pair of tweezers from the first-aid box, for any used Durex, but thankfully didn't find any. Serves her right if she ends up in the pudding club, I thought maliciously as I climbed ashore in shirt and shorts, clutching my toilet bag, towel and litter bag, to visit the marina's luxurious ablutions.

Washed, shaved, and changed into a shirt and long trousers, I called in at the Yacht Club to make my number. It was nine-thirty. A member of staff greeted me with a hearty 'Good morning, Sir,' as he advised that I was too late for breakfast. He answered my starving, crestfallen face by saying he could 'organise a cup of tea and a bacon sandwich Sir, if you are desperate.' I was, and it felt really good to be treated with respect, like a human-being again, after so long as an insignificant minion and skivvy.

'Yes, Sir,' said the staffy in reply to my question, when he returned to the veranda overlooking the marina, bearing the goodies I had so earnestly been waiting for. 'The Air Marshal has instructed we afford you every facility during your stay.'

'Does that include telephone calls?'

'Yes, of course, Sir,' he bowed, ever so slightly. 'There are booths in the hallway. Give the Air Marshal's name to the receptionist; she will give you a line.'

Laura answered almost at the first ring. 'Hello darling,' she whispered, and I realised that she probably had a shop full of customers at this time of the day, and wouldn't want to be kept talking for long. Quickly, I told her of my trip across, safe arrival, and the situation here in Jersey, before telling her how much I loved her and missed her, promising to phone again that same evening after she had closed the shop. I left out the bit about the orgy in case she might think I had been involved in some way. Women are funny creatures. They're wired differently.

Back on board *Astra*, and looking at her in daylight, convinced me that the AVM must have left her in a hurry soon after arriving in the marina. He was not the sort to leave her in such a state. The foresail had been rolled untidily onto the fore stay, and needed re-doing. The main still hung loosely in ties on the boom; no attempt had been made at a harbour stow or jacketing. The RAF light-blue ensign, with its RAFYC motif, hung almost at half mast over the stern while, from the cross-trees, the club's burgee and the AVM's personal flag, sagged on loose halyards. Sheets and sail halyards were bundled like Bosun's nightmares in heaps on the deck, wherever they had been dropped, and the mooring lines needed adjusting. There was a lot to be done.

Despite my annoyance at finding her in such a state, I enjoyed working in the sunshine putting her right, making her ship-shape and Bristol fashion. Several neighbouring yachties called out greetings and a couple stayed for a quick chat. Was I imagining things or did they give me funny looks. Had they heard last night's noises and think I was some sort of sex maniac? Was their brief chat just being friendly, or hiding their annoyance, or just wanting to be voyeuristically inquisitive? Perhaps my concerned mind was working unnecessary overtime.

By three o'clock in the afternoon I had finished. *Astra* looked smart and seamanlike again and I felt pleased with my efforts. I had enjoyed a good lunch at the club and a cooling pint of lager, courtesy of the AVM. I felt at peace with the world and looking forward to lazing in the cockpit, soaking up the sunshine and catching up on some of last night's lost sleep.

Unfortunately, Saint Globface let me down; he must have been on leave. Caught in the act of removing my shirt, Madam climbed aboard. I stood up politely. 'Good afternoon, Miss.'

Ignoring me completely, she stepped into the cockpit and looked down into the cabin, like a ferret checking for rabbits. After a few minutes - I thought she had fallen asleep - she spun around and gave me the sort of look a rodent inspector would give when locating the decaying remains of a dead rat. If I was expecting an embarrassed apology from her, or a pitiful plea for my silence, then I was sadly mistaken. Her pugilistic face was tight with anger as she gave me the benefit of her unladylike vocabulary. This time she was sober.

'You keep your f****** mouth shut about last night, do you hear?' she warned. Well, at least she remembered; that was something.

'Of course, Miss.'

'What I do is none of your f****** business,' she continued, hissing like a hooded cobra, as if I had done something wrong. 'And, if you mention any of it to my father, or anyone else for that matter, you will wish you had never been f****** well born.'

'You're right Miss, it's none of my business,' I assured her diplomatically. 'If your father finds out, it won't be from me.'

She sniffed, and went down into the cabin like a rat down a drainpipe. A minute later she re-appeared at the foot of the steps and looked up. 'Did you clear up?' she snapped, without an ounce of gratitude in her voice.

'Yes, Miss.' (who did she think did it.....the bloody fairies?).

'Did you find anything?'

'Only empty bottles and cans, Miss, that I've dumped ashore.'

She climbed up out of the cabin, stepped onto the pontoon and walked away stiff legged, her backside wobbling grotesquely, muttering to herself under her breath, 'That bastard ran off with my knickers.' I decided that now was not the appropriate time to broach the subject of the return trip home.

That evening, after a gentlemanly three course dinner at the club, followed by my call to Laura, I strolled around the delightful town of St. Helier. It was packed with tourists wearing gaudy shirts and dresses that they wouldn't have dared wear at home. Well, the British ones wouldn't. It was hard to visualise such a pleasant place being the only part of Britain to be occupied by Jerry during the war, and I wondered what the locals thought about it? No doubt most would have hated it, but probably there were others that went with the flow. How would we have behaved on the mainland if it had happened to us? Thank goodness we would never know. I dragged my musing away from such depressing thoughts and looked around at the promenading throng, all presumably enjoying themselves. I had never seen so many jewellers' shops! Every other building seemed to be one. It had to be a Mecca for holiday-making women; and a drain on the pockets of their men-folk. Still, I thought, as I wandered back to the yacht club for a well-deserved pint of cool lager, that's better than wasting money on booze! I crossed myself, and silently asked for divine forgiveness for making such a blasphemous utterance.

Saint Globface returned from leave and gave me an undisturbed night's sleep in the quarter-berth. With everything open that could be opened, a relieving breeze drifted through the boat. Tomorrow, I thought, as I dropped off into a dreamless sleep, I would tackle The Rhino (as I had dubbed her ladyship) about sailing for home. She could come or stay, I couldn't care less. I'd be quite happy doing it solo.

Next morning, just as I finished my breakfast coffee at the club, the same member of staff who had been so obliging on that first morning, came to my table and bent forward, conspiratorially.

'Could I have a word, Sir?' he whispered, looking around as though checking for an eavesdropping spy. 'In the lounge, if you'd be so kind, Sir. It's quieter in there.'

I followed him as he led the way into that deserted room, wondering what the hell I had done wrong.

'It is Miss Rowley, Sir,' he said, apologetically. 'I wondered if you might have a quiet word with her?' His eyebrows lifted like an air balloon that had broken its cable.

I looked him straight in the eyes, trying hard not to laugh. The thought of me having a quiet word with The Rhino was hilarious.

Keeping a straight face with extreme difficulty, I tilted my head, listening, waiting. The poor bloke was clearly very concerned about something.

'We have been receiving complaints from other guests, Sir,' he cleared his throat. He was finding his task embarrassingly distasteful. 'Apparently, Sir, Miss Rowley has been entertaining - er - gentlemen, in her room at night and disturbing other residents with loud banging, shouting and - er - other noises, Sir.' He was finding it hard to find acceptable words. 'Naturally, the Club would be extremely reluctant to take any direct action. She is, after all, the daughter of a very respected and valued member, Sir, and we appreciate that young people need to enjoy themselves, but we have our other members and guests to consider, as you will appreciate. May we hope for your discreet intervention, Sir?' He had the look of a prisoner awaiting sentence.

'Leave it with me,' I replied, magnanimously, inwardly bubbling with joy. Now I had ammunition to fire back at the toffee-nosed bitch.

'Most kind, Sir. Most kind I am sure.'

I scribbled a note on the club's notepaper. "*Meet me at the boat at your earliest convenience. Urgent. Highman.*", and placed it in an envelope, also provided by the club.

'Will you have this delivered to Miss Roley, please?' I asked.

'Certainly, sir. And thank you.'

It was another five hours before I saw her strutting arrogantly along the pontoon, her weight making it sway from side to side, just like the rolls of fat around her waistline. Had she fallen in, the resulting tidal wave would have swamped every boat within fifty yards. I didn't like the girl.

'Welcome aboard,' I invited with false cordiality, trying to keep sarcasm from my voice as I reluctantly watched her heave her bulk over the guard-rail, causing *Astra* to list several degrees.

Without a word she thumped into the cockpit and manoeuvred herself down the hatch to the cabin, sitting on the locker seat with elbows inelegantly pressing down on the protesting table top.

After a few moments venomous eye contact she broke the silence with gracious gentility. 'Well..... What the f*** do you want?'

I smiled, knowing it would annoy. 'Civility would be nice, for a start.'

'WHAT!' she exploded, hopefully as a prelude to an epileptic fit. 'Who the hell do you think.......'

I stopped her, placing the palm of my hand a few inches from her bulbous nose, like a policeman stopping traffic. 'Shut up, you cocky bitch. Keep your filthy mouth shut for a minute and listen, for a change.'

Her mouth dropped open - not a pretty sight - stunned in quiescence. No one had ever dared speak to her like that.

Taking advantage of her speechless state I related, with a little innocent embellishment, the complaint from the yacht club, adding as a frightener, that they intended to forward their displeasure to her father unless I undertook to remove her from the club, forthwith. Whether she believed me or not, by the time I had finished she was a different person, pale faced and subdued, blaming everything on the dope she had been given, pleading with me not to tell her father.

'Sorry,' I said, trying to hide how chuffed I felt, 'but the damage has been done now, the only way to save your back-side is to get all your gear from the club, book-out, and come back aboard now, this afternoon. I'll check the tides and weather. Perhaps we can get away sometime tomorrow and get you home, away from your problems.'

Meekly she nodded, and for one fleeting moment - that lasted all of a milli-second - I felt sorry for her. She looked devastated, but it served her right. Perhaps a lesson had been learned; you can't treat people like trash and expect to get away with it.

By five o'clock she had returned with two heavy suitcases. It was a wonder she hadn't got a flunky to carry them down for her. She wasn't hungry, she said, (or perhaps couldn't face the club members and staff), so I left her unpacking her things, while I went for a celebratory meal at the club where I received a welcome fit for a King. I had avoided an unpleasant scandal and was the best thing since sliced bread, in their book.

Laura was delighted to hear I would soon be on my way back, and told me to hurry home. I felt on top of the world and didn't want to chance spoiling anything, so didn't mention Janet the Rhino, at this juncture. Laura was a woman and therefore wouldn't understand, or would misinterpret the situation. I'd explain everything when I got home.

CHAPTER TWENTY THREE

The frantic tap-tapping of halyards against mast, the whistling of the wind through every tiny gap, and the plopping of wavelets splashing against *Astra's* hull, was my reveille next morning. That and the snoring coming from the hump of bedding on the "double bed" a few feet away and just forward of where I lay in the quarter berth. Last night I had refused, point-blank, to inter myself in the grave-like fore-peak berth. Even the prospect of sleeping in the close proximity of The Rhino was better than that, but only marginally so. She said it didn't worry her - why should it? I wouldn't touch her with a high-jumper's vaulting pole. Given the choice, I'd have preferred sleeping with a sex-mad, naked, three-badge AB, than with her; thoughts don't come much more revolting than that.
I wriggled out from the quarter berth and slipped my trousers on quickly, in case she woke up and got ideas that would require all my karate defence skills. Daylight filled the cabin as I pulled the hatch back, and opened the doors. Daylight, yes. Sunshine, no.
Lowering clouds, the colour of a coal-miner's face flannel, were being dragged across the sky by a stiff sou'westerly breeze, already an estimated Force Four and heading for the forecasted Force Six that, provided it stayed that way, would give us a fair wind all the way home.
Edging along the narrow side decking I sat down, pushing my legs under the guard-rail, reaching for the sea with my bare feet. I needed a pee and didn't want to wake madam by using the clanging pump of the inboard toilet. There's something very soothing and satisfying in "pumping-ship" nature's way, as long as you aren't seen by anyone; especially marina officials, or maybe Greenpeace?
Much relieved, I returned to the cockpit and called down the hatch. 'Wakey, wakey, Miss.' I looked long enough to ensure she was awake, then turned away to attend to some unnecessary task to avoid the sight that would likely put me off women - and whale blubber - for life.
After ten minutes, fiddling with trivial adjustments to ropes and rigging, I saw what appeared to be a round, water-logged, rope fender, emerging from the hatch. She was awake.

'Good morning, Miss,' I smiled to infuriate her, as her crab-like eyes fell away from me to survey the early morning scene. It was probably the first time she had seen the world before noon. 'If you want any breakfast you'll have to rustle up something for us both,' I said as she submerged back down again like a geriatric walrus. 'Otherwise I'll go to the club for mine.'

An answering grunt rumbled up, like flatulence.

'I'll take that as a "yes" shall I?'

After feasting on a plate of tepid baked beans and charred toast, that would have been a gourmet meal in an open-boat after a hundred days adrift, I visited the marina ablutions for a wash and brush-up. The delicious aroma of frying bacon wafted out of the restaurant as I past by, and my taste-buds went into orbit. I couldn't resist it and covered the hundred yards back to *Astra* in four seconds flat, to dump my toilet bag and put on a respectable shirt.

'Just going ashore to telephone,' I called to Madam, lying through my teeth as I dashed back to the club, leaving her with burnt toast hanging grimly to the corner of her mouth.

I returned aboard, replenished by a good fry-up, to be regarded suspiciously by my enforced companion. Forestalling the question forming somewhere in her befuddled brain I said, 'I want to be away by ten.' I spoke slowly to avoid taxing her confused mind, 'to get best use of the tides.' She probably didn't have a clue what I was talking about. 'Any chance of you clearing up the cabin while I get her ready?'

She nodded, slowly. Well, more like a slow-motion ducking of her head; obviously suffering from self- inflicted withdrawal symptoms! 'Give me a minute and I'll be up,' she drawled, like someone who has had a stroke.

Nearly an hour later, true to her word, she joined me on deck. It was a few seconds before ten o'clock. I must admit she looked a darn sight better. There was a spark of life in her eyes and she actually recognised me.

'Sorry,' she said, 'I'll be all right now.'

It didn't need a trick-cyclist to see she was fighting quite a battle with her inner self, and slowly winning. Was that a small flicker of admiration for her that crossed my mind? I went below and cranked-up the Volvo diesel-engine that fortunately (I'm no mechanic) started easily and ran sweetly.

'I'm going to motor out of harbour and across the bay, until we can get her close-hauled,' I said decisively, like a real skipper. 'Hopefully, that'll be before we reach Corbiere. Will you take the helm?'

A few yachties, on boats moored in the marina, waved us farewell - or was it good riddance - as we chuntered out west-bound across St. Aubins Bay that was already busy with early morning sailing boats whipping around like scattered confetti. Madam seemed quite confident and at ease as she manoeuvred among them. So far, so good.

As we drew abeam of Portelet bay I was delighted to see *Grand Parade* race by on our starboard side heading in the opposite direction towards St. Helier. She looked so sleek and graceful as I wondered where she had been. Coming from that direction it couldn't have been St. Malo.

I waved, madly, at the shadowy shapes in her wheel-house, but no one responded. Either they weren't looking, or wondering what the hell that lunatic yachtie was doing, prancing around like a fire-walker on hot embers. Nevertheless, she was a grand sight and brought a lump to my throat.

'Bring her round into the wind a bit, Miss. I'll get some sail on her.'

'Okay, Jim,' she acknowledged.

JIM!!! .... had I heard right? Did she actually use my name? I saw her chubby face smiling at my astonishment, her cheeks coloured from the breeze and clean salt-air. She looked as if she was enjoying herself.

'I'm feeling better already,' she called after me as I crabbed over the cabin roof undoing the sail-ties and dropping them down into the cabin to join the jacket I'd removed before leaving harbour. Reaching the mast and bracing my feet wide apart, I hoisted the mains'l, cranking it taut with the mast-winch handle and easing off the topping-lift. Without being told, Madam overhauled the mainsheet as I sweated the slack of the kicking-strap into its jamming cleat. *Astra* listed as the wind filled her sail.

Back in the cockpit I slackened off the weather fore-sheet and winched in on the lee sheet, drawing the huge fores'l from the roller-reefing fore-stay. *Astra* heeled even more as we finely tuned the sheets until she was creaming along, gunnels under, close-hauled through the choppy sea, faster than the engine could drive her. Thankfully, I shut the engine down.

Apart from the thumping of waves hitting against her bow, the swish of sea-water rushing along her sides, and the soft whistling of wind in the rigging, the silence was wonderful. So peaceful, yet so exhilarating. One look at Madam's face showed she was enjoying it just as much as me.

I lowered the log's spinner into our bubbling wake and paid out the plaited line, watching for several minutes to let it settle down to give an accurate reading - nearly seven knots. We were racing towards Corbiere. This is the life I thought, at sea and on my way home to Laura. Perfect!

By lunch time, with Corbiere Point now on our starboard quarter, I took over the helm and gybed *Astra* onto a northerly course across the expanse of St. Ouen's Bay. Madam (I no longer thought of her as The Rhino, and hadn't been invited to call her Janet), went below to heat up the contents a few tins for what became a passable meal; very much an improvement on her efforts at breakfast time.

We ate together, balancing the plates on our laps in the cockpit, me with a forkful of something in one hand and the kicking tiller in the other. One eye trying to guide the fork mouthwards, the other watching the sails and surrounding sea. It wasn't easy. No wonder I was cross-eyed.

Astra ran before what was now a strong breeze, dipping and corkscrewing in a following sea with the log ranging between seven and eight knots. She handled well. I wished she were mine.

With the remains of the meal cleared away, Madam relieved me at the helm so that I could take a few bearings of Grosnez Point for a running fix that put us two miles off.

'Do you feel happy about taking her up to Cap de la Hague so that I can get some kip?' I asked. 'With this wind and tide we should be abeam of the light before dusk; then I'll take her for the night.'

'Sure. No problem.' She was in her element.

'I know you are a good sailor,' I said, a little embarrassed, 'but you will promise to call me if you're in the slightest doubt, won't you?'

"Course I will,' she laughed, 'now go and get some sleep.'

Laid out in my berth, fully clothed, sleep evaded me; I wasn't all that tired. Responsibility weighed heavily, yet I felt concern rather than worry. Madam seemed perfectly capable, so far, but still an unknown factor. I had to keep an eye on her. I would never be able to sleep - or so I thought.

A thump, heavier than usual, woke me and I felt *Astra* heel. I peered at the luminous hands of my wrist-watch. Christ! It was gone eight! Rushing up on deck, expecting to find disaster, I missed a step and grazed my shin. Madam sat cradling the tiller like a baby, and humming softly to her self, completely happy. She'd been at the helm for six hours.

'Why didn't you wake me earlier?' I shouted angrily, looking around in the rapidly fading light and seeing a flash on our starboard quarter. 'Where the bloody hell are we?'

'Tut, tut. Such language,' she mocked with a grin, (That was good coming from her, then I realised I hadn't heard her swear since yesterday). 'I didn't call you before because there was no need, and you have a long watch ahead of you,' she said, 'and that flashing light is Cape Haigh. You should know; you're the navigator.'

'It's pronounce Cap de la Hague,' I corrected peevishly as I returned below to fetch the hand-bearing compass. I took a bearing of the light but with no other land, or light in view, I could only estimate our position as being somewhere along the line of that bearing. I was annoyed. 'What if I hadn't woken up,' I snapped, irritably. 'We'd have gone sailing off into the blue not knowing where the hell we were. I needed a good fix on that light.'

'Oops, sorry Captain,' she grinned, 'but if we keep on going in this direction aren't we bound to arrive at England?'

Typical woman's logic I thought as we changed places, wisely deciding not to get into an argument. She went below.

Twenty minutes later she came back up again, carrying a very acceptable hot concoction of tinned meat and tinned veg that she held for me as I scooped it into my mouth, inelegantly, in between *Astra's* jerky rolls and dips.

'Sorry, Jim,' she apologised with sincerity, 'I realise it was silly of me, but I did it for the best.'

'Yeah, well!' I was lost for words. This girl was changing by the minute. Perhaps the last few days <u>had</u> taught her a lesson. 'In future just do as you're told.'

'Aye, aye, Captain,' she said, saluting with the wrong hand. 'I'll get my supper now and make you a flask for the night.' She yawned behind her hand. 'Tea, or coffee?'

The night flew by. In no time at all, it seemed, dawn began to light up the eastern horizon to starboard. There was just a gradual lightening of the grey at first, followed by marble-like streaks spreading wider to reveal the ragged skyline of heaving waves. The wind had-if anything-dropped slightly but the swell coming up channel from the Atlantic had *Astra* rolling and weaving like a drunk. I had seen the steaming lights of numerous ships during the night, moving east and west across my bow, but none came near enough to warrant taking avoiding action. Had they done so I would have scarpered, fast. Despite the rule that says steam shall give way to sail, I would never chance *Astra's* right of way against a bloody great super-tanker.

Madam, now looking almost human, poked her tousled head above the open hatchway. 'Morning,' she greeted, still half asleep. 'What time is it?'

'Good morning. It's nearly seven.'

'Jesus!' she cursed, and disappeared again.

By eight o'clock I began to hopefully scan ahead for a sight of land. The horizon was vague and misty, like a distant fog, but visibility appeared to be about three or four miles. I had little idea where we were. What with the vagaries of wind and tide, and the lack of a good departure fix of Cap de la Hague, my dead-reckoning could give us a land-fall anywhere between Durleston Head and Selsey Bill. To end up with St. Catherines Point dead ahead, as planned, would be an absolute miracle.

Madam woke for the second time. Titillating smells began to chimney up from the hatch and I was soon gratefully munching beans on toast, chatting away with Madam, with one arm crooked over the tiller while keeping a weather-eye open for land; trying not to let my anxiety show. Despite my keen vigil, Madam spotted something first.

'What's that?' she asked, pointing ahead.

'Where?'

'Ahead, just to port.'

I looked hard, seeing nothing but a haze in the distance. 'Can't see anything.'

'There!' she said, jabbing with her finger as if poking someone's eye out.

Then I saw it; just a ghostly shadow slightly darker than the lighter mist. She had bloody good eyesight. Frowning, I stared until my eyes watered. I couldn't make it out. It looked like a ship, head on, coming towards us.   Then the mist lifted, fractionally, sufficient for me to identify it. 'Christ! It's the Nab Tower!' I couldn't believe it. We must be more than a dozen miles off course to the eastward and missed the Isle of Wight completely.   How could anyone miss the Isle of Wight?' So much for my navigation.

'Do you know where we are now?' Madam asked, having tactfully avoided the question for the last few hours.

'Yes. Spot on,' I lied.

She was impressed. I was bloody relieved.

We dropped the sails at Outer Spit buoy and wound-up the Volvo to motor through the entrance channel into Pompey harbour. I felt like we had returned from a round-the-world voyage, but no one gave us a welcoming wave or a second glance.   Even the dozen or so people stood sight-seeing on the Round Tower ignored us.   We were insignificant. Just a piddling little yacht. They had much better things to look at.

We entered the harbour, sneaking past an Isle of Wight ferry paddle-steamer that looked the size of an aircraft carrier in comparison. I hoped <u>her</u> skipper knew where the Island was.

It was lucky for me that Madam was on board as we turned into the marina. She was able to direct me straight to the AVM's berth. I had no idea where it was.   Once we had *Astra* secured alongside the pontoon, Madam busied herself clearing up below decks and packing her bags while I gave *Astra* a neat harbour stow. God knows when, or if, I would see either of them again.

'I'm off, Jim,' she announced some time later as she humped her gear onto the pontoon. 'I'll ring Daddy from the marina office to let him know we've arrived, then get a taxi to the ferry and a train home from Portsmouth.' She held out her hand. 'Thanks for everything, Jim.'

I felt the lump back in my throat again. I was just beginning to like the fat ugly cow. 'Bye, Miss.'

The Gosport marina pontoons rocked exactly like those at St. Helier.

Up at the marina ablutions, having washed and shaved, I sat on the toilet - contemplating. Grassmere didn't know I was back, they didn't know where the hell I was. Probably didn't care either. I could go home and take a few days off and no one would know.   Then I remembered that Madam had told her Dad. Surely he wouldn't begrudge me a few days?

I cursed as I stood and adjusted my dress in compliance with the notice plastered over the urinal. Did I have enough money to get me home?

Back on board, I spread my worldly wealth across the table. There were more copper coins than silver but, even discounting the trouser button, it was sufficient with just enough left over for me to phone Laura and let her know I was on my way.

CHAPTER TWENTY FOUR

'So?' asked Ziggy, leaning forward eagerly onto the edge of his rickety wooden chair, elbows on knees, chin cupped in his cradling hands. 'Then what happened?'

I smiled at his blatant curiosity. His preoccupation with making money had dominated his world, even to the detriment of having a love-life. Now that his interest - among other things - had been aroused, he craved for the slightest sexy detail, like a vicarious voyeur peeping into other people's windows. 'Nothing, mate,' I answered, shaking my head and looking around the back room of the Section hut, trying to look nonchalant and worldly. 'She just packed her bags and went off home to tell Daddy what a horrible erk that Highman was.'

'But what about when you got home. How was things with you and Laura?' His eyes glistened.

'Oh, that!' I said, with pretended naivety at his innuendo. 'That was fine.'

He fidgeted, irritable and annoyed. He was dying to hear the juicy details, and I felt sorry for this man who, for all his wealth and omnipotence, was clearly a lonely man, probably craving for the love of a woman. She would have to be some very special sort of lady.

'Well?' he persisted.

I wasn't about to tantalise his carnal thoughts by teasing him with details of my passionate few days at home, but it didn't stop my memory from recalling every precious moment.

The shop blinds twitched the moment I entered the street, and a second later the door opened and she was standing there, smiling, beautiful and waiting. I barely had time to drop my kit-bag to the ground before she threw her arms around my neck, hugging me tight.

'Hello, darling,' she whispered ticklingly in my ear. She felt so good, and smelled fantastic. This was what I call a welcome home. I couldn't wait to get her inside and upstairs, even though it was difficult; I didn't want to let her go.

It was quite a few hours later and very dark, before we came up for air. Laura made a pot of tea while I lay, exhausted, on the bed. How come women are so full of energy afterwards? Was it something to do with transfer of energy? Is that why we men are left completely shattered?

We talked until the early hours. She wanted to know everything, and kept shaking me awake until she knew all the gory details. The last thing I remember, as I collapsed languidly into a deep bottomless pit, was of Laura giggling at the thought of me sleeping close to The Rhino.

The next day was a working day for Laura. I had hoped to spend it relaxed and restful, to recuperate from the previous night, but Laura thought otherwise. Halfway through the morning, and again in the middle of the afternoon, she came upstairs to have a cuppa with me, but the only tea I tasted was when I made it myself - after she had gone back down to the shop. Luckily, at lunch-time, we did stop long enough to make a quick sandwich. How she expected me to keep up the required strength on a bloody sandwich was beyond me. She was insatiable; what did she think I was - a machine? It was dreadful, and I loved every minute, as we made up for all the lost time we had spent apart. It wasn't just sex. It was the togetherness, the closeness, the belonging to each other. Even when we weren't making love it was wonderful, just to lay together, feeling the warmth and softness of her nakedness against me. Or sitting quietly, cuddled up on the settee, getting to know each other again.

Only once, during the whole three days I was at home, did we go out. I hadn't suggested doing so as I hadn't a bean in my pocket, but on the Saturday evening Laura said 'Let's go out for a drink.' Seeing the look on my face she added, 'My treat.'

It was a fabulous evening. I felt so proud to be seen with my beautiful wife and to see the envious looks of other men. She wore a fashionable, white, tight fitting dress, that showed her gorgeous figure to perfection and - as is my want - I grew all amorous thinking of all the things I had done with that fantastic body; and all it had done to me.

In the pub, more than one pair of eyes were glued upon her, and her every movement attracted more, especially when she crossed, or uncrossed, those lovely legs. She seemed totally unaware of being a focal point, or of the lecherous stares, as we sat close together. I wasn't jealous. I felt ten feet tall and my male ego was bursting at the seams. She was mine. I wanted to shout out 'Look, but don't touch.'

Rather than get bloated on beer, and suffer the dreaded "Brewer's droop", Laura persuaded me to drink shorts. What the hell! I was on leave - albeit unofficially. So, whisky it was. I preferred rum but Laura didn't like the smell of it and I, being the dutiful husband, complied with her wishes while she enjoyed her "Bloody Mary".

One guy, who had amassed a lot of courage through smelling the barmaid's apron, came over to our table and made a complimentary remark which, although understandable, was a little unacceptable. He looked a bit shocked when I stood and politely requested he returned himself to the bar, for his health reasons. I didn't do it to impress anyone. He annoyed me. He should never have underestimated the opposition. Laura was a bit tipsy and said how proud she was of her protector. At first, I wondered whom she was talking about, then both brain cells in my Bacchanalian brain became intimate and I realised, she meant me. I was her hero, her knight in shining armour, her saviour. I was chuffed, even though I hadn't meant to appear that way. It was a natural reaction. Whisky is a great drink.

We stayed until closing time, undisturbed and very much in love. Our eyes - slightly unfocussed - were only for each other, and we sat whispering sweet nothings until the landlord swung, like a demented monkey, on the rope below the ship's bell hanging forlornly behind the bar. 'Time gentlemen, please.'

'That means we can both stay,' I giggled. Laura didn't get the joke so I took the next ten minutes to explain it, as she upended her empty glass, for the third time.

Standing, unsteadily, I waited for the bar to stop carouselling around, concentrating, one eye at a time, on a dart-board shimmering on the wall, it's three darts - or was it eight - stuck in double-top. Laura helped me to help her to her feet, and we staggered back home supporting each other across the full width of the pavement, like an 'A'frame.

After circumnavigating the keyhole of the shop door a half-a-dozen times, I eventually got it open and assisted her upstairs by using a mixture of a rugby scrum position and fireman's lift, and heaved her unceremoniously onto the bed. She was dead-o, and it took the last of my reserves of energy to get her undressed and under the sheets where I joined her - fully clothed. My last thought being, 'Thank God it is Sunday tomorrow.'

I was not a happy bunny when I awoke. My brain thumped painfully against the inside of my skull, as if wanting to get out. I couldn't blame it. I had a mouth like a cat's litter tray and a throat like a carpenter's rasp. To make matters worse, Laura's soft singing voice was drowning the blaring wireless in the kitchen. Why did she have to sound so bloody cheerful?

'Wake up, Sir Lancelot,' she shouted, as she banged a cup of tea down on the bed-side cabinet, with a thud that would send a seismograph needle trembling, in Australia. You can go off people you know.

By noon, I was working at getting my other eye open, while Laura cleaned the flat and prepared what in any other circumstances, would be a delicious roast dinner. The room had steadied to a slow waver and a milk bottle full of aspirin had quietened my head to a thunderous roar. I sat up on the edge of the bed and contemplated my crumpled trousers, then, with a great deal of effort, mumbled to myself, like an orator from Uzbekistan, 'I'd better change.'

'You'd better have a bath too,' said Laura lovingly, as she overhead my one-way conversation. 'You smell like a brewery.'

Don't self-righteous people annoy you?

Bathed, shaved, and changed into something that didn't resemble a crunched-up ball of discarded wrapping paper; I sat at the table girding my loins for the task of eating. The meal was perfection. I love my roast dinners. Unfortunately, it was spoilt when Laura asked, 'Would you like a beer, darling?' I nearly threw-up.

It was nearly six o'clock the next morning - Monday - two hours prior to leaving for Grassmere, before my abused body could react to the demands placed upon it. Even then, it was a case of laying back and thinking of England as far as I was concerned, and it was good to see her burning off the calories, for a change.

'You still with me?' growled Ziggy, testily.

'Oh, yeah! Sorry mate,' I said.

'Well?'

'Well what?'

'What bloody happened next?'

Christ, was he still on about that? 'Not a lot really. I got rotten drunk.'

Ziggy jumped to his feet, lips pursed tightly, angry and obviously disappointed. 'Oh! Bollocks to you, chum,' he snapped. 'Don't tell me then,' and stormed out.

Typical of the man, he was back within the hour and it was as if nothing had happened. 'Not long to go now, Lofty,' he said cheerily, referring to what was left of my Service time.

'No. Only a few weeks.'

'About six, innit?'

I didn't need to think. I knew exactly how many days, if not hours. I had been counting them off for weeks. 'Near enough.'

He sat opposite me in his usual pose; elbows on knees, chin cupped in hands. 'Know what you're going to do?'

'Yeah. I'm putting in for the civvy police.'

A frown creased his face, and for several minutes neither of us spoke. He was thinking, his ticking brain almost audible. Then, he lifted his chin and looked at me with sorrowful eyes. 'Can't help you there, old mate,' he said, 'Don't know anyone in that line.'

I couldn't stop myself from laughing, it was cruel of me I know, he only wanted to help, but he had a one-track mind. All he thought about was wheeling-and-dealing.

'What's up?' he asked innocently. 'What have I said?'

My last week in the RAF was a happy turmoil. Every hour full of health checks, dental checks, eyesight tests. Was I leaving the Service with lice, V.D, T.B, ear wax, piles or athlete's foot? Every item of kit and clothing had to be accounted for, and returned, no matter what condition it was in. Everyone wanted a signature. I even had to sign as witness to my own signature. How stupidly bureaucratic can one get. You can't die until you've filled in an application form.

There were people to say goodbye to. Advisory talks to attend, on how to survive in Civvy Street. The Adjutant interviewed me with the aim of getting me to sign-on as a regular. 'You've been an excellent airman,' he told me. 'First-class. Just the sort we need.' How did he know? He'd only seen me twice during my time at Grassmere. If I was so good, why didn't he tell me before? Not that it would have made any difference. I couldn't get out of that gate quick enough.

The worst part was saying cheerio to Ziggy. He was a likeable rogue and he'd been a good mate who had made the world of difference to my time at Grassmere. I think I had a tear misting my eye as we shook hands but maybe that was because I had to hand back my trusty Bantam bike. His last words to me were, 'Keep the cheeks of your arse together Lofty, and don't let the bastards grind you down.' Typical!

I didn't look back as I marched out of the main-gate for the last time, wearing civvies and carrying my attache case. I even ignored the cheery voice of the duty snowdrop standing in the guardroom doorway, who called out 'Good luck, Lofty.' Well, I didn't totally ignore him, just lifted my free hand in a wave over my shoulder. No longer was I an erk, to be shouted at by NCO's, or insulted by so called officers and gentlemen. I was me, Lofty Highman. Call me Mr, or Esquire. My two years service to Country and Sovereign lay behind me. I was going home to my beloved and the whole world was our oyster.

I think the answer I gave to a boozing pal, some weeks later, sums it all up. We were sat, hunched contentedly over the glowing wood embers of the pub's open fire-place, cuddling our near empty glasses; heedless of the cold winter night howling beyond the heavy oak wood door and the drowsy-eyed landlord leaning tiredly on his highly polished bar as he listened to our conversation and the tock-tocking of the huge grand-father clock standing wearily against the granite wall. He was waiting for us, his only customers, to re-order, or go home.

'It must have been a wonderful experience for you Jim', my pal said wistfully, a faraway look in his eyes. 'Wish I hadn't failed the medical. I would have loved to have done it. I always wanted to go in the Services and hopefully see a bit of the world. Now that you are out, what is it that you miss most about life in the Air Force?'

My answer was brief and concise. 'My kit-bag.'

THE END

ISBN 1412023920

9 781412 023924